Of the Feral Children

A Mayan Farce

James Luchte

Copyright © James Luchte 2012

All rights reserved.

ISBN 10: 1479294888
ISBN-13: 978-1479294886

For my Children

CONTENTS

Of the Feral Children

First Half: Conjuration

1   Hugo Ball

2   Blue

3   Ian

4   Jesse

5   Sophia

6   Aire

Second Half - Events

7   Notes from the Underground I

8   Brain Damage

9   Notes from the Underground II

10   The Lady Macbeth Complex

11   The Awakening (of the Spirits)

12   The Day the World Stood Still

13   The Revenge of Hades

ACKNOWLEDGMENTS

I would like to thank my friends and family for their company on this journey to the end of the night — and those who seek to explore the depths of existence and to create — despite all the temptations to do otherwise.

James Luchte

Of the Feral Children

Mayan-Dionysian...
Celtic erotic gestures of
magic, flesh & alternative
ways of living & dying....
(not to mention thinking,
which one must learn
upon the streets)

wild here, not before
at least as Arthurian cobwebs
they run in the night, steal, destroy
They have their own language games -
They no longer need to listen to us -
family, tribe, nation, state, etc...
- or - even that of the good libertine -
it is all dead - all that remains is
eternal resistance beyond good
& evil... my breath tickles
this abyss of her flesh

He was blunt - 'You'll never
be one of us, & that is most of us...'
I answer with a Taoist silence,
understanding this utter truth as I
beckon the coming catastrophe,
one that already engulfs us....

where wyrd wild ways
rage rabid red riverrun
boiling bloody bogus bones

I am not this, not this, not this
Jungle book bestiary
I am neither Tarzan nor Jane
I am simply your dreams
of wildness - I am Cheetah -
surging amid this event -
you flash in the middle
of a sentence - an act... this
wild ecstatic life -

James Luchte

1 HUGO BALL

(Background Music - 'The Rite of Spring' by Stravinsky)

I gaze into the abyss of her eyes - her ethereal light torches my viscera -

She caresses my pale skin - into the heart of my extreme, dark self -

She is awake in the photograph - she spies, dives into my catastrophe -

She seethes - beyond this masque of my myriad little red deaths -

She still lives - abides - amid idols, icons & pictures - even films -

I found her in my late grandfather's secret things ---

*****

I discover the rest by accident in the backroom of a random charity shop.

'Do you have anything else? I mean, pictures, old photographs?' I hold up the same sign to each shop -- I know my father just packed it all up when he died & dumped it -- but there are things that I always wanted ----

a child's imagination… the old time cameras for one - the coo-coo clocks…. the train set…... a legacy….

& - then - all at once - there it was - everything - 'Yes, yes… here is the entry - yes,' the charity shop lady remembers - yes, there is something - 'Oh my lord - this has been here for nearly thirty years ---' I find a picture of myself - a tiny wee one - as I frantically rummage through this depository of my soul - 'How much for the lot?'

'You can have everything for ... well, let's say a fiver...' the charity shop lady put on her/his best poker face....

'Let's say 50, & you really need to raise your prices!!!' I finally resolve....

I lie for hours in my tattered bed, gazing into her eyes,
she turns her head toward me - nearly smiles - until -
her face scintillates into an infinity of faces,
those of every woman who has ever lived ---
I do not know her name.

She must be a goddess.

I am merely a beast, her utter Cheetah.... smelling of sour semen, stank sweat, grunting at the maidens who would have otherwise led me to her gateway...

*****

I awake.... roll out of my rancid bed & descend the spiral staircase to put the kettle on.... Green Tea & the apothecary -- like the bios of Pythagoras... & friends... this immediately recent 'truth event' ... surreal disclosures of a secret life...

I admit - I am thinking about the world around me - of the entry of toxic and overwhelming phenomena -

'They' suppose that pornography is a recent phenomena - erotic sexual imagery - obscene for some remedial types, for all the repressed are closed off, by definition, to the novel - their escapist ideological addiction of stasis is a mere lobotomy - utter perennial stonework, calcifies this open space ---

... although photography as an art form beckons yet another century --

As with everything important, sublime - sex & death - goddess & god - these dear ones are at the centre - any global communication system only succeeds under the sign of the forbidden --- a vast vomitorium of hidden truth channels passion, &, there are myriad ways & means to express the truth – think about the entry of political, cultural phenomena…

This current world may have begun with the internet, but flesh is not anything new - it ungulates amidst the deep pools of our desire - resistant ever to the progressive enlightenment of Satan, the ruler of the ordered, temporal world --- humans have always been perverse - darkness is our chaos, our chasm from which seethes Eros…

Sexual ecstasy - in this light - is the most conservative of all -- perhaps that is why all those prats go to Nazi-themed sex parties or are found dead bound with lace stockings… but, that would be the wrong kind of conservatism…

We excavate with our flesh the myriad contours of erotic art as sculpture, painting & sketches - dance - back, across the topography of this myriad, perpetual fuse - our history & pre-history -- futures already engulf us at every moment…. but that is merely the visual, tactile, scratches upon fractured surfaces...

Music has always been the most erotic of arts, as we descend/ascend to our most orgiastic recesses amid this primal dance of life -

Music is the language of wildness, of the feral children dancing upon the streets --

Satan, the brother of Yahweh (and distinct from at least Kenneth Anger's Lucifer Rising in 1973) does not dance, he does not, as does Cum Hau, Ah Pukuh aka Hades, shake the earth…. nor do these children understand the language of their temporal father, with his labyrinthine rules & regulations -- (Hell is after all a bureaucracy working at the behest of an evil Power…) ---

the feral children already dance amidst the holy, in the flesh…. upon the streets….

The busy bodies gave them trouble in their day (just like now), but we hold onto these traces of their hot naked flesh as if it were gold…. we need only think of the Victorian underground, as a single moment amidst orgiastic epochs - there is always a counter-culture - a sublime seat of true eternity - not those fake ones peddled by the shopkeepers of wishful thinking… & there is contestation of the picture of whole eras, epochs, etc… think of the 1950's -- phoney plastic, conservative - or the bubbling beatnik cauldron of civil disorder & rebels without a care…

It is no different today yesterday tomorrow - it has never been any different with the joyously perverse beasts that we are - eternal recurrence of the same….

The Kiss (1896), the first filmic pornography that is recognised – *Stripping Trapeze* (1901) & the vast litany of others, most of which have been lost….. like the naughty sketches in Ruskin's drawers - he even had a safe, which is still to be found)… lots of images of bondage & wild sexuality from the age of reason - before & after… our ancestors were down - they still as ghosts laugh as we squirm with sweat… their orgiastic whispers caress our ecstatic flesh in the act….

'There is nothing new under the sun', some wise Jewish philosopher sighs…. but secretly smiles…. 'There is the appointed hour for joy, ecstasy as well… Jubilee!'

The end of the story has not yet been written…. there have been frail attempts to close the circle… like the farce Revelations (tumultuous laughter) -- & we are certainly better than that!!!! Even the Mayans only speak of a new dispensation -

Openness is always the best way…. that I, we do not have any reason why….. but - anything is better than bureaucrat philistines & all the crazy little Hitlers…. Create, then Destroy the enemies, make friends - destroy them too….

We instead laugh - breathe & dance upon the streets - in the flesh, this primordial landscape, as we are not permitted to enter the grounds of their degenerate brainwashing machine - our space is a pristine possibility, on the margins, but never vanquished, never eradicated, never exterminated -- there will always be traces & from these threads, a new tapestries will be spun…More honest, brutal now perhaps - but still too busy to take the time to intern, bury the body of the decomposing God - the old order was dead before it hit the sterile pavement - it seeks to resurrect itself - young minds, truth regimes - across schools… regulation & quality control ---

Perhaps, they will set the old god up with a cigar, drink & top hat - toasting him with an infinity of drinks so that he may rise up again in the chaos & the God-Crown-Money addicted Big Society-ists™ can finally, with divine right, enact their own great shift - the demolition of 'modernity' & 'secularism' (according to a radically dangerous & lazy - drunken, self absorbed & utterly thoughtless ideological agenda spawned by pseudo-intellectual opportunists) ---

In favour of privatised bureaucracies, 'commons' of the soul --- slavery with the face of a digitised Jesus.... red black & blue polis meltdown -

Delete, cut, smash all that we, you - have ever finally achieved - the paradise that we can almost taste - with the push of a single button.... how fucked is that???!!!!!!!! 'Business (tells us) it pays the bills', so says the liar (the normal fascist mainstream) - 'not Shakespeare or Shelley' - 'Rossetti anyone?' -

'Britain would be a concentration camp without Blake, dad!'.... the son declares...

The courageous people - fully aware of the brevity & singularity of Life - will engulf these conspirators upon the streets... with Chaplin, again inadvertently, holding the Red flag........

Art is in a state of panic - It lusts to destroy the philistines...

******

I now know why my grandfather asked me to go to the house first --- before he died --- but only when he died.... he could trust me, above & beyond anyone else, anywhere..... if nothing else, he knew I would not blab as I could not talk.

He was always more intimate with me than the others, especially his own son with whom he had a relationship of a most distant patriarchal quality.

My father was always trying to impress him - to gain his pointless rancid cliché of approval, etc.... no one knew why - & others, like my sisters, fell for that for awhile - perhaps even now.... hopefully that will change after he dies -

[censored content]

My father knew this as well, & that is why we may as well be dead to each other.

A strange rivalry, nearly Oedipal, projected from both sides - though I must say that I never fucked my mother, & never really wanted to.... His indifference & my mother's sadness would clash, twisting into a vortex - each night (when he was there), they would dance their pathetic jig evoking always in the end our family pathos of damnation - a suffocating hopelessness which - like clockwork, facilitated his liberation to his own peculiar isolation, like an Atman of whiskey, if you know what I mean…

But, it was not at all that simple, as he knew this too, perhaps…. I do not think that my grandfather ever fathomed my father's despair, & I do not even now have any inkling of the 'reason' for the coldness that froze all of us.

I did not know him, he never opened himself to me, even when I pleaded, or lashed out in suicidal despair.

(Background music – 'Providence' by Sonic Youth)

He is an enigma, & will remain so - though, from time to time, I descend into a poisonous & dark contemplation of his absurdity.

That is why he has retreated to his mahogany boat of alcoholic oblivion & I have become a wanderer & stammer-er - never to speak again….

*****

(Background Music - 'Pictures of Lily' by The Who)

The pictures are sublime, they show it all, as it were - they show it all -

She dances as a fresh nymph in the photograph - she is sweet - & free.

The pornography of our ancestors… intimations, conjurations of these spirits of our great grand mothers - great grand fathers…. fucking -

(Background music – 'Ænema' by Tool)

They were just as we are - desirous lovers & carers - yet - that is not all of us & never was….

There is nothing new under the sun…

She ecstatically dances in the photograph - she is there - thanks to the sublime key of the heretical San Pedro cactus, which I stole from Aire, that Mayan priest - with the potion, a supernatural dimension opens itself to our being… The cruel Spanish priests on lone & Inquisitors knew all too well of its power - together with the primal keys of every indigenous culture -

'the meek shall inherit the earth...'

But, it could have been any of these sacred plants or the best shot of whiskey I ever had - meditation - the best orgasm where a lightning bolt surges through our bodies, this great body of singular intimacy - shocks of the ones who have attained love -- human existence is itself a drug - what then would be a war on drugs?

Keys out of the gateway of the labyrinth -- Ariadne's thread.... any key will do... though some keys are better than others - or unlock stranger doors....

I first heard about it from infectious hearsay, but later, like everyone of us, read Huxley, Castaneda, McKenna, & all the usual suspects. Not to mention the vast stories which Aire (my squatmate) tells of Leary & the Acid Test of Kesey -- which I then absorbed - The Politics of Ecstasy, Erowid, & the encyclopaedic Peyote Joe - my glorious droog - who worked at Sainsbury's, spending all his free time building the largest Peyote farm in the world --- but, The Legend of Peyote Joy will have to wait for another time.... (canned collective sigh of despair)

She is alive, nearly trapped in the photograph... as the brute savages attest - 'I would love for her to be here now,' I whisper to myself amid my ecstatic loneliness...

*****

(Background music - Richard Burton reading 'Under Milkwood' by Dylan Thomas:

It is Spring in Llaregyb in the sun in my old age, &
this is the Chosen Land.

> [A choir of children's voices suddenly cries out on one,
> high, glad, long, sighing note

FIRST VOICE

& in Willy Nilly the Postman's dark & sizzling damp
tea-coated misty pygmy kitchen where the spittingcat
kettles throb & hop on the range, Mrs Willy Nilly steams
open Mr Mog Edwards' letter to Miss Myfanwy Price &
reads it aloud to Willy Nilly by the squint of the Spring

sun through the one sealed window running with tears,
while the drugged, bedraggled hens at the back door
whimper & snivel for the lickerish bog-black tea.)

My grandfather was a proud Welsh miner until the wild-eyed crazies of London decided to steal his life (I think this now) - &, for what? De-industrialisation? Look at us now!!! He died fucking three days before the 'closing' in a 'freak' mine explosion, never reported - he left behind a letter which alleged that all of the real union leaders were killed - the government put up their own man, Scarface or something, from their informants in the fake extreme Left groups, an actor whose role was to fail..... who was that guy anyway? - just like the sham worker cooperatives of the 1970's - doomed to fail --

Granddad was very active in the strikes - he ran most of the 'operations' - he would explode into the house, 'If we do not act, if we do not resist, we will lose everything!'

He was even in the Striking Miner's Choir, featured by Test Department. The ominous tribal drumming & the surreal phase-shifting voices of proud men still haunts this space of our lives, although its effects have become subliminal -- perhaps we will be able to dance again when the White Witch finally dies - we will dance on her grave!

(Background Music - 'Striking Miners Choir' by Test Department)

How right he was, but his death was doubly ironic & tragic - & we have still to dance upon the White Witch's grave, as she still lurks in her audacious properties - & now a new feature length Film...

I plunge into her eyes amidst a stark, penetrating portrait of her lovely face... I am in love - with a spirit - but she looks into me, she is here, her nubile breasts, her sweet wetness shatters my lost soul amid her glorious licentiousness.

Did I tell you that San Pedro goes through several stages, one of the very first being a quite erotic event??? I jerked off the first few times, like an Egyptian priest...

The first impulse, if alone, is privacy, utter privation, & contemplation. Yet, even if the situation is different in terms of group orgies, even alone, one desires the water of ecstasy & the explosion of the moment... the best two hour shower ever....

It is best though to avoid all contact - or any possible contact with others - outside of the surreal consensus - at least until it is over.... this is not that much of a safety issue as it is a precaution against utterly ruining the experience - a sacred event - through contact with the un-initiated --- for after all, it is a secret....

The radical possibility lies with conjuration, though - the pictures come alive, their faces awaken, turn & whisper - I had thought of becoming an entrepreneur, selling spans of time with deceased love ones, pay as you go necromancy ... would call it Vision Quest, also with an Executive Retreat component... Build your management team in a sweat lodge! --- but, then I realised that the capitalisation upon human, animal weakness, vulnerability & suffering is the only true evil - & so, I do it for free... let them see the dead for a time... I have little else to do since I am disabled, on benefit, & cannot speak.... so I write, etc....

Perhaps with the Grimoire, we should wander to the cemetery.... but, which one, should we go to Highgate & resurrect Marx --- or to Bunhill Fields to have a chat with William Blake..... the desires rage in my soul until they come to a tentative perspective - we can do both, & let's throw Bakünin into the mix as well!!!

She ascends from the photograph... gazes into my abyss.... I do not tell anyone this. Nor do I speak openly of necromancy... That anyone can contact their dead loved ones, & it is legal, for free....

The most obvious 'reason' that I do not tell anyone anything about my necromancy is that I am existentially mute, but I can still write --- I can speak fine - I am not dumb, mind you - it is just not anything anyone could usually comprehend, understand- perhaps there are a few faces out there with a bit of a clue or more...

My condition has left the best doctors stumped.

Shall I speak? I am the narrator, after all....

Listen: 'Jolifanto bambla ô falli bambla'.

This is the only kind of thing, language, I can manage - to the men/women in white coats, I am a feral child - & the subject, object of their next grant proposal.

(Background Music - '4'33" by John Cage)

I do not speak. I have lost my voice - I have lost a part of my soul - perhaps I am soulless or already abiding unconsciously in Hades.

Well - not my voice, but spoken words with articulate meaning, 'real' words - those that goose-step obediently within the sanctioned & enforced eitiquettes of life... I do not have these rules or this grace - it is only my silent language that is making any sense to you now - my inner voice, this narration....

*****

(Background – 'Trio in E Flat' by Franz Schubert)

I drown - when I was two, you see....

Immerse - in shimmering water, I held the side of the pool as I was too small for the dark water.

I remember everything, & that may seem strange - I will not say everything that could be said....

I will be dead.

I was dead.

I am dead.

My continuing existence is an absurdity, but that is sublime....

Scrawled upon the back of a particularly risqué image ---- 'I tie her - her wrists - to the door with my belt. I kiss her - lick her, she is mine - she is the nymph who fell into the spider's web.'

Granddad never gave these pictures to me, mind you... I found them with his stuff, in this place that bled out his secret life.

I could see all.
I could especially see the crimes of my father, who I imagine to be far worse.... But, I will probably never know...

The nymphs dance through the streets - laughing - explode with the winds....
When I drowned, I was not dead.

Of the Feral Children

I floated overhead, I saw them
working on me, upon my body -

Firemen in yellow suits,
massaging me as I lay
upon my stomach.

I came alive that night, & I remember....

gadji beri bimba gl&ridi laula lonni cadori
gadjama gramma berida bimbala gl&ri galassassa laulitalomini
gadji beri bin blassa glassala laula lonni cadorsu sassala bim
gadjama tuffm i zimzalla binban gligla wowolimai bin beri ban

This is meant to drive you mad - because, I am already mad - & if you wish to understand me, then you have to be mad too. Voluntarily to the madhouse... so you know what you got --- a mad, feral narrator.... It is surely ironic that my Dadaist namesake has become my only outward voice...

Care for self... others, tragic ambiguity... la tee da - to attend amid intimate situs -
I need to drink from the waters of Lethe, but, not to disappear, not disintegrate.....

The dark nymph dances upon the streets - she calls me to come to her.... she says it is better to show up at Styx skint - then he will send you away as a ghost - imagine that! A ghost! You could haunt your friends (hahahahhaahhaha) - apologies -

I must be possessed by the dark poet as I already see the winged goddess of his nightmares - 'I am gazing into your soul!!!' she whispers in the cold night air...

She follows me - for years, from place to place - dances over my head, rubs herself across my face - as I sleep - rubs my toothbrush across her flesh, as they all do - I look above into the dark - I see her scintillating dance.

That is far after I lost a part of my soul, when I lost my voice - she stalks me, makes me crave the leap into the void, the decisive, inevitable moment of truth... truth?
Besides shamanism, which lead to success in a very specific task, I also

had at least four unsuccessful suicide attempts --- shamanism is obviously better....

To get it all back - to retrieve that lost part of my soul - that inevitable treasure...

But, I only understood that I was incomplete as I successively fell over the edge -

(Background Music - 'A Love Supreme' by John Coltrane)

Dionysian desire, one that will resist - seeks to create, express the new, novel as it retrieves this primal eruption from that ecstatic place amidst the Nothing .....

It is not clear if my grandfather was murdered by the government - but there was lots of talk - some people even said that my Grandfather blew himself up to start a conspiracy around the whole matter - nevertheless everyone hated the mad bitch & her corrupt city - many people were beaten or paid off --- the whole fucking bullshit fraud ruined everything ---- there was no investigation, inquiry - no panel of specialists assembled to critically analyse & assess the state of affairs in the impartial, dispassionate manner of 'science'.

All of this stuff is done privately anyway - as is consistent with their philosophy...

No one knew about the discourse of human rights then, I imagine.... or ever really cared, or gave two shits .... they are criminals with a legalistic face....

Yet, she lay amongst the pictures... she wakes up with the explosion -

This sweet blonde nymph -

2 BLUE

(Background Music - 'Swimsuit Issue' by Sonic Youth)

'Don't worry love... all the prince will ever want - as all men - is a good seeing-to...' her cross-dressing 'grandmother' whispers as 'she' tucks her away for the night --- the archetypes - traces of her kaleidoscopic disaster....

Of course - she is wild, runs upon, across these streets....

She walks toward me - all I can see is the abyss of her eyes...

It is her - sorry, it - She was ---- is her...

As she passes like a breeze, I smile, take her hand - kiss her gentle skin.

She continues on with her most recent shag, who I later learned, believed he did not exist - never ceases speaking of his own nullity.... 'I am not here!', he laughs, as he regurgitates his paranoiac variant of the Vedanta... If only that had been true then... but, finally, he did disappear... like all the rest who dodge past our eyes as a continuum of flesh.... thankfully...

I made my second approach to her outside Bookmongers... she blushes

'You are the strange gentleman who kissed my hand,' Blue laughs, nervously looks away, 'the other day'....

All I could manage was a 'großiga m'pfa habla horem' or some such...

She is taken aback by my outburst - she begins to walk slowly backwards... away from me - until I show her the chalkboard that hangs around my neck.

Her eyes tear, weep as she realises I am one of the afflicted, a Chalkboarder, one of the proliferating examples of ferality, wildness, bred poorly by our own Elizabethan II 'society' - the dire sequel - as the surging punters scream in humiliation, anguish - seeking to escape from the grim theatre of our historical farce - what would Manu say? He would demand his money back.... the buck must stop with the Sovereign...

Tradition becomes indigestible - a new dispensation of critical, creative abjection - the culture of the death of God, of ever escalating disturbance & rebellion -

She walks over to me & puts a piece of chalk into my hand - 'Tell me your name - write it for me...

I write upon the chalkboard, 'My name is Hugo Ball.'

'You mean, like the Dadaist poet & exorcist?' Blue smiles..... I blush - turn my head away with a smile of relief... 'She is not an idiot!', I whisper to myself....

She came to our parties shortly after that - she was perfect once Bob & James left to pursue their nomadic raga-rave project --- Blue says that she was looking to stay full time in Brixton as it was the only place, she repeated as a near mantra, 'Where I can think --- where I can feel like a real human being amongst other human beings -- the game is broken - we do not hear anymore - here there is wildness, myriad cross-pollination - a rare place...'

She took the middle room - I definitely think Sophia was glad that there was another woman in this beastly squat. 'You are shit!', Sophia whispers...then she stands up, & teases for the camera.... at the end of the day, she works as a sexy cam model for cash ---- her online name is shintogirl...

Blue walks naked through the squat, utterly free of shame - though, when she is menstruating, she wears red cotton panties - although, this is new for her... for a while, she just wore a Sainsbury's bag, with leg holes she made herself - but then they start chargin' 5p when they should just bring in paper, with handles...

'Nice red panties, Blue,' Aire shouts out, but meets with perplexity in her face - 'Red, red -- are you blind?' Blue giggles, 'These are white panties, stupid! I just, well, have not washed them in a while....'

'Oh?' Aire gasps in amazement, ' --- We - we - we could totally set up an installation, with obsessive events, at the Peckham Art Gallery --- Tracy Eminem style!!!'

'I do not need to be exploited - fuck you Aire!,' Blue disappears into her room...

At first we avert our eyes from her lifestyle & her 'economics', let us just say - the prim & proper people were are, aging anarchists... no one in the squat judges her as each of us is far worse in other ways - she tells her mother (a widow) that she works as a secretary for an evil pharmaceutical company - they do not see each other very much, holidays, at best... her mother is a holistic healer, she says - perfect alibi -

She thanks the goddesses that her mother lives far enough away, 'No words can describe - you would have to live it yourself!' For us, sitting stoned drunk most of the time in the blessed squat, Blue was a sublime spectacle of an utterly new kind of woman.... she was well beyond us, but her wisdom was of old.... better, a new kind of person, as that hallucinating girl, Luce, the dog girl, whispers, reading my private thoughts, in the corner, 'There are so many genders it exceeds all calculation,' as she squats our squat in the very crossroads of ecstatic - embodied - existence....

Similar to our current problem with all the 10 year old revolutionaries who insist that they should be able to use the squat as a base of operations & storage --- The ten year olds want a fucking safe house, but they're fucking 10 --- they showed the fucking bobbies - all the bureaucratic political arseholes what feral animals will do -

'They call us animals???? Well, they have seen nothing yet!!!' because we have only just opened our eyes... We will be - you will disappear.....

We are quite afraid of them, becoming almost bourgeois ourselves.... at the very least, some of us are admittedly pacifist, even lazy - were we being dicks not to take them seriously - have we become soft, armchair anarchists???

Aire & Jesse talk to them, though - hell, the kids need no prodding or inciting, but only need to be guided to cultivate their rebellion - a few good books, the right films, the best music --- it was already clear that there is a learning curve, but the squat did become a mini-Salon of ten year olds discussing Emma Goldman's critique of Lenin & the shortcomings of the French Revolution...... which, by far the most agree, should have expanded toward Versailles to avoid the strangulation of Paris - & the farce of that Terror that follows - a perverse chess game - another poison gift from the Arabs...

Blue loves walking in the market on Saturday afternoon, purchasing strange foods & wine, candy, iboga root - sitting in the tranquil square, feeding the pigeons - or walking through Brockwell Park especially at the Country Show where she whispers to the sublime Welsh sheep - if she was not too tired, she goes to look at the lovely plants, cacti... walking is sometimes most difficult for her, especially in those extreme nights when she makes extra dosh.... at the Show, they thought she was a cowgirl... tipped their hats....

But, it was her - she had the same eyes as this nymph in that sublime picture.

Eventually, we each settle into this surreal reality, & if Blue could sell her 'ass' for food money, then so much the better. We must, at the very least, be tolerant – at the most, grateful....

Blue was a philosophy student before the cuts to the 'culture industry'.... Before the Red Tory dawned, this pseudo-theological - barely political .... essentially egoistic event of the BIG SOCIETY pseudo-cleric fascist meta-revolution - 'Gawd dog damned -- now that is BIG!' --- utter thoughtlessness, as my old buddy Reiner, heretic & thinker, would say - a perversion of thought, existence... before - there is no before - year Zero..... a Pol Pot of tea....

'What you readin' for....', a cassette recording wobblies in the damp, 'It is a shame that Bill Hicks was assassinated by Texans,' Blue whispers, blowing out a huge mushroom cloud of smoke.... ' 'Wasn't the Texans,' Aire laughs hysterically, 'It was Janet Reno, & everyone knows it..... but do not despair.... we can conjure Bill back to life, if even for just a moment' - Aire gathers together a bunch of ingredients & places them in a large iron bowl upon his portable altar, 'we just will have him long enough to hear a single message....

> I beckon you Bill Hicks, who frequentest this place, & in thy life hast interred thy treasure herein, who also of recent time, to wit, in night of

21 December 2012 at the apex of the high Night... hast shewn thyself in the form of a fire at this spot: I conjure thee to come forth, simply, nameless, or with name - I will not compel you. I am only opening another door, through which you may come through - to complete the most perfect of circles.

Aire blew out the candle at that instant, as the spirit would not like such drama...

'Indeed....,' Aire ponders pensively, 'As we cannot hear the message until the end of the world, until 21 December 2012..... then why not we just stop talking about all of this bullshit ---- but plan an event, party --- but I do not wish to live my life according to some fraud eschatology which is nothing better than the pet rock or the mood ring - a historic fraud, enthusiasm --- '

'We do not even know the question,' Blue rejoins, 'So how can we ever have any true knowledge? There is just random fucking speculation....'

'This is all wacked anyway --' Jesse joins the fray, 'We need to stop with the wanking all the time - things are finally happening - I want to push this movement to its utter limits!!! ... there is thought - & action - after all.... knowledge is for the timid...'

'Your sad attempts to create the future via action & words are pathetic & futile ---,' Aire explodes at the height of his devil's advocate drunkenness, 'There will be a point when - as if in a blink of an eye --- you will realise that action is futile, that there is something much bigger going on - ' ...

To avoid another million hour, drunken debate, everyone but Aire spontaneously descended into 'Collective Nightmare'™, a floor game we play precisely at the right time - as if a fit of madness descends upon us all - ensues, blowback from Grimoire necromancy, perhaps --- we are possessed, quaking on our backs upon the ground - laughing as we are consumed by demons, spastically jolting here & there, spinning upside down --- lots of shrieking ---- everything is upset tables flying, crashed bottles, jugs, & spilled bongs..... lying amidst an intricate cluster, everyone quivers & squirms in our surrealist Twister game, spurred on by the spirits of those protesters recently killed - this time it did not end in an orgy as still each feels mildly outraged that the question has been deferred until the end of the world......not to mention the crass questions of ethereal wonders of Power & Fortune ---- 'As if Bill Hicks would speak about the hooligan Coalition or the world brothel suddenly...' Aire shouts back at them, falling

- 'But, we do not ask these questions since they are the wrong questions.'

'We all know the question, as the archaeologists speculate about deep layers, the truth, or more at least -' Sophia interjects, but is interrupted by another young squatter of the squat - TX - 'Some experts blah blah - yeah - we know - shit, that is all we will ever know or fucking need to know... but we also are terrified of the horror - that they don't want us... they want to put us down like rabid dogs --- or send us fucking off to kill, kill, kill....'

….. 'If only it could be nothing….. ' Luce whispers in the corner, 'rather than something….'

Despite her shift to the 'private sector', Blue actually has more time to read - she reads Nietzsche, Bataille, Dylan Thomas & Savinio, amongst others - at the Underground -- her 'job' is located at the darkly illegal sex club where she is a dancer -- that means she shyly services the more precocious lads from the City of London at night -

Well, it all has to start somewhere…. 'The only thing that keeps me sane is The Story of the Eye,' Blue whispers to me, grasping my arm, in an aside - 'I swear to god, Hugo,' Blue tears, 'I do not know how long I can endure any more of this circus!'

Aire erupts dancing upon a unicycle, a clown, an orange suicide wig, juggling balls, …. which suddenly falls one by one as he turns to Blue, 'Wat?!!!'

'No - not that ttyou asshole, ' Blue charms, 'I am talking about work - as usual…. God - take me away from this abyss of perversity!!!!!' …….

Sophia fucks Ian with a strap-on, riding him like a waif pony ---- taking out her rage at her smack-down by the ten year old…

'Can we not get back to the normal Brothel - a fucking good night out? Without the torture - cannibalism?' --- Blue gasps as she falls upon the futon….

This is what it was supposed to mean, until the new owner ---- a sadistic coward… moved the club to Streatham Hill - on the top of Brixton --

"Mister Mister", Blue calls him, aka The Controller, a slimeball 'investment manager', waxes poetical upon his maniacal coke whore pseudo-wife "Misses Misses" - apparently a silent partner as she has never been seen in the club... Nazi salutes at stag parties, their distant co-dependent utter phoniness - as he snorts a line of Meth off the sweet belly of another fallen nymph, & beats her with his best cricket bat, the sport of pansies....

Coke & whores make the world go round...
but, a little Meth - when you're spent...

Mister & Misses rejoice in the loveliness of their small business, all tax deductable for even though it is an illegal BDSM strip club, it is registered as a privatised private Charity in the emerging private Care industry... called simply, The Underground: The Sanctuary of Wayward Girls.... but, to be fair to them...............but, who could be?

'Funny that is also what my daddie always used to say to me before I went to bed each night, echoing his father & all his father's fathers', Blue would say to the targeted punter in the hope of rapport - an open funnel of money -- her words were situational - tactical amid a strategy of dominance........

She glides through the door, throws down her keys, & slips off her leather gloves.

There is fire in her eyes -

*****

Blue came to the squat at first only to visit - a year ago, for the Halloween Party... I could only see her eyes as she walked through the door. That night I only watched her from afar, my fascination with her grew in intensity throughout the night... before I could work myself into the sufficient frenzy to approach her, she had gone...
In the backroom - which is now Blue's room - three Rastas, born & raised - Franck, a painter & photographer, Bob, a horticulturalist & Shamanic Ragga poet & James, a musician & DJ, made their dwelling - they had met at a Krisskronic poetry & music event in 1999 & became a mini-tribe for the next strange decade, exhibitions, DJ parties and Rap-Ragga raves - they were all from Greater Brixton, but had gone to different schools - each has become an artist who thinks of Brixton in its utter sublimity - its artistic tradition & innovative culture - Blake, Van Gogh, Eddy Grant ---- we rock down Electric Avenue - it makes you higher! -

Mostly the three would do what they always do - As James would begin to lay down the tracks, Bob would pass his horticulture around - explode the ragga waiting after all - for Franck to take the pictures, films & paint the painters --- though always punctuated by Party Nights where the veil would be rent until the sunrise -

They worked well together, though there were the occasional sudden arguments due to inevitable clashes in a small room --- though mostly their arguments concerned the precise character of their collaborative work. It was not long after the last party that they purchased - outright - a one bedroom flat in Robert Burns Mews... which they comfortably converted into a three room flat with a kitchen - a deck at its centre.... & added large tinted sky lights in the dank attic -

They were leaving for the same reason as did many others - the downfall perhaps began with the first riots in the early eighties - the vultures already smelled the scent of property, the police agonised over the freedom upon the streets --- the repetitive hostility was routinely injected like a virus, & so were born the alibi for urban renewal, Brixton Challenge, the take over all the Yardy pubs by the jumeaux terribles & their teeming lemmings of north London druggie waifs buying the hard stuff on the streets with impunity - 'Yes, yes - Brixton - oh, yes, that is a rough area, isn't it?' 'It sure is - it is because of all the blacks, Windrush - it was much better when John Major lived there...' We are living in their wake, these poisoners of our well! These rapacious suitors of Penelope.... ensnare her sweet body... Odysseus will kill each one before he kisses her quivering lips, hunger expectant - deep thirst quenches -

Everything old skool has either moved out or underground - improvisational events, hence the nomadic dance of the Rastas - & even they were leaving -- we would die for them - yet, they had shit to do - everything is always going on - We share this space, but we realise that these muthafuckan righteous Rastas were fucking born here - we are the immigrants - populating the gentrification, cleansing...

(Then there is the Brixton Aristocracy & the various other notions of African Royalty of which there are myriad rumors - I do not have the right to speak about any of this, so I will shut my mouth.)

'They' - Franck, Bob & James were born here - in Brixton - in Britain - the rivers of blood from their mother's vagina erupts at birth as this spirit of life - as is the blood from their grandfather's & father's sacrifice in 'foreign' lands -

'Your' hatred paints the streets with 'their' blood - seeps into 'your' soil - into this goddess, Earth... What will She do with all of this blood? Does it drown her in despair? Is She enlivened by this accursed share, sacrifice? Or, is She utterly incensed by the slaughter of innocents? Will She - Earth - give this blood to these hungry spirits - at the right time?

Blue whispers, blood on her white wedding dress, 'They have turned the world into shit! ' She scratches her forearm around her track marks, scar sliced arms - traces across a map...'

Bob & James, now in fancy dress, Orpheus with his Eurydice, two of the glorious church of the imaginary da Rasta, come through the door with impossible shopping bags that scatter across the linoleum floor...

James spins around under the bald, bare light bulb in the centre, enchanting, 'We got the sublime food.... the market was very kind...'

'I can never eat when I am on my period,' Blue evokes to these disparate voyeurs...

'We gits the vittles, if they supplies the gravy!!! ...' Bob parodies all parodies to arrive finally at a simulacrum of truth.... he laughs gruffly - as he picks the rubbish off of the second-hand food sent around for all of us .... we gets what we get....

Blue interjects, 'Yeah, but I don't know if you would really like my gravy - though some of my clients are extremely into that (She laughs coyly, with a wink) - Maybe they are a bit anemic - need a bit of extra iron?!'

I sit a bit too stoned to speak - but as a mute anyway, I am still able to write upon my chalkboard, 'Vampires!', although no one looks my way, & I am too sedated to work for any attention, & it was not very funny anyway...

Franck, who spends most of his time now with his beautiful French wife Amelie and their lovely children, sits upon the futon - his face nearly pale from astonishment, gasps, 'Forgive me, sista - but I don't want any of that shit! No offence, but yuck!' He adjusts his camera, taking seemingly random shots, 'No time for any of that shit sista, ' he hones in on Blue's face and snaps.

'Well you can have shit, too, if that is your thing,' Blue laughs hysterically, 'There are as many fetishes as there are objects under the sun -

everything is already objectified! That is our state of always falling, & I am your new Eve!', she falls hysterically upon the floor, rolling around in a seizure of laughter.

'All I can say, is that,' Bob accentuates, 'sometimes the dirtiest shit is the fucking hottest, if you know what I mean, girlfren,' he holds up his hand for a high five, but Blue convulses even ever more violently with a laughter that makes her tears flow & influences her to slightly pee her knickers.... 'I thought you loved me, James!', Blue rolls over laughing, more & more fiercely - until she explodes in a shattering coughing fit - she disappears to herself.... though with fleeting stars in her eyes amid this blurry space ....

'You ok Blue?', Bob asks, as he gently pats her upon her back...

'Yeah, thanks,' Blue smiles, catching her breath, 'I have been so very far worse off,' she laughs, almost politely - but, sinks into a reflective silence...

There opens a silence, a quiet moment of release from the idle chatter of distraction - a deeper conversation of the nothing whispers with the gestures of supple bodies, faces, looks, tastes & smells - I must admit that in this moment, I feel a tingling sense of belonging - a circle of ecstatic mutes - though it always ends in disaster....

('Suburban Nietzsche Freak' by Fuck Dress)

'I tired of the jokes about the culinary attributes of menstruation long ago,' Blue at noon breaks the silence, 'not to mention those of the female long pig - this puerile surrealist last supper,' Blue suddenly broke into utter tears, whispers, 'It is happening, everyday - it has always happened, it is.... I fucking imbibe these mad lusts of cannibalistic orgies - shit, it only costs 5000.00 with options & upgrades -'

'Get the barbecue on, muthafuckas!!!' Bob shouts out from the kitchen...

I lust, will for her to look into my eyes, but however much I whisper her name into her/my dreams, she does not awaken to me - I attempt to speak to her, but only manage, 'gadje beri bimba glaudule/ hula lonni cadoir! gaga blung...' everyone looks at me like I am a 'retard' - I am a retard - I am also angry, differently capable... 'God is dead, so I listen to Radiohead...' - this noise beckons - the idiots dance... but in this moment, it is only Blue's eyes which remain upon me.

Blue, from the beginning, looks at, into me as if she has always known me - she knows me - remembers.... she kisses me.... whispers into my ear, 'If everyone wuz stoned, wearing pajamas - all day long - there would be no wars... but, perhaps war is not the only mother of invention, the chaos of all things...'

'So much shop talk,' Blue screams to the others, 'that I forget everything else!', she laughs into convulsions....

'But, I like talking about your pussy!,' Bob smiles insanely, 'Shaved & everything!' ...

'No, Bob, she's right, let's move on to less bloody topics,' James gasps into the mix, incoherently pointing to Aire, passed out upon the floor - with a slight stream of drool from his mouth, dripping down as arrows, his restless bottle wildly pools upon the carpet below...

******

Blue dances blissfully naked upon the futon, 'But, the food is not going to make itself,' she laughs as she hands the spliff to James, who assures, 'One more toke each, madam - then we will prepare your feast!' I go to the kitchen with Bob & James to learn the cuisine - they were born here, but I remain a visitor, perhaps a valued ghost, setting down makeshift roots, helping to prepare the feast.

Magically, we threw the bash - like clockwork - these turntables would turn around & around in dat phat room with the psychedelic speakers -

A table spread of chicken, peas & rice - tequila, rum, infiltrating a nuclear punch - People start to come, stream into the house, hot with bodies - Sweat effervescences across this sensual dance of Dionysus, this communal feast for friends - in a time when the devastating waste of war could have fed every child & adult upon the planet for a thousand years ---

Better Un-fed or Dead - than Red... my daddie always said...

Should we hunt them down - kill them for wasting
the dawn? Please --- there must be some accountability??!!!

Or, are you saying that everything you have ever said is a lie -
that you are a mother fucking liar?!!!

Cologne & perfume are hallucinogens - we are transported amid the surging dance into a grandeur of lust, flesh ungulates under a dark red sky -

I dance with my face in the nourishing tits of a huge figure of African femininity.

*****

Blue laughs as she remembers that first night - a transitional night of ambiguity - an event of homewarming - the adventure of departure....

Her eyes touch mine - & with an explosion of laughter - she staggers her way toward me... pulling me utterly away from the makeshift that shelters Earth.... although I am falling to one side, my weight keeps Blue from crashing into the glass table. She throws her arms around me, gasps for breath, laughing - she begins to cough - her mood devastates, transfigures - the frenzy is over - she looks into my stench, whispering as her eyes close, 'I love you, Hugo...'

Blue grabs the bottle of Jameson's, plunges upon the edge of the futon smack in the middle of the front room, 'You know that someday I will fuck you, Hugo!', she laughs, frenetically tickles my sides as I squirm away, laughing - she pulls down my pants in her ecstatic transgression.

Blue stands above me laughing - 'Look at you - what are you like?' (she shakes, gasps for breath from her strangling laughter)

I write upon my chalkboard, 'So, how are things - There is a fire in your eyes! Are you on something?'

Blue takes a serious swig of Jameson's, swallows with the very slightest cringe, she slows at first, almost visionary as she plunges into the Nothing - into the abyss of memory & suffocating trauma... 'Nothing more than usual - No, they are getting far worse at the club - like a fucking horror film, but real... I'll tell you.... I think that they are going to kill me -- a couple of girls have already gone missing...'

I write back, 'Are you ok? What are they doing to you?'

Blue takes another taste, smiles, 'Yes... I think I can say that I am ok (but, suddenly feeling a sense of hubris) --- well touch wood'.

I know she is lying as she is not usually so superstitious - 'What did they do to you?', I write upon my chalkboard.

Her eyes tear as she whispers, 'They did not let me dance.... (she gasps) they did not let me dance (she breaks into tears, sobbing)

I take her into my arms, caress her hair, feeling the scintillations of her pain.

'They held me down on my knees - slapped my face with their rancid cocks'... Blue coils up into a little ball - as a larvae, a caterpillar driven perhaps to its sublime transfiguration, a mask.... 'Fucking stockbrokers', Blue exclaims, 'but the worst are bankers & politicians!!!' If I could tell you! (laughs hysterically, snot coming out of her nose) 'Actually, I can -- hell yeah - (I never signed any non-disclosure agreement, as there are no lawyers in this game, at least on my side) I will tell you all about my career in that diabolical symposium!'
I took a swig from the whiskey - wrote very simply: 'Then why do you go back?'

Blue snatches the bottle back from me, takes a nice infusion, & in a happy posture, proclaims, ironically, in a man's voice, 'Women breed death, or, have only given the gift of death - (she speaks now like a little girl, Shirley Temple) Look at me! I redeem women by dancing, celebrating the sublimity of woman - eroticism is, amongst all the arts, a creation of woman, but spoken by a little girl...'

Blue breaks out into laughter, tears in her eyes, 'Women have created everything that is good - & look at us, at me... (laughs uncontrollably) - Look at me!!!!!'

'At least I am not just another breeder, incubation chamber, a potted plant.'

'I am at war with them, & I am fighting in the trenches.'

'Do not think,' she exclaims, 'that this will be easy...'

Blue was arrested once for setting fire to the top-shelf in her local off licence. She had a plan, & that is what betrayed her.

They say to keep the cards close, but once said --- no one listens, but easily laughs ---
Under the influence of wild-eyes feminist diatribes, like SCUM - she

made the mistake of stating her objections to the material - in the eyes of children, no less. 'I am breaking no law', the shopkeeper turns away to deal with other, paying, customers.

She had revealed herself - unnecessarily.... the point, after all, of the stiff upper lip....

Blue enters the store - glides to the magazines - she takes out the bottle from her bag - raises it aloft & squeezes - a clear stream of lighter fluid pulsates upon the wet bodies, faces of the cover models - sets it all alight, streams of fire race through the store, a virtual situation of terror! Blue stands still, laughing, she exclaims, 'Burning idols - residual documentation of the existential rape of Woman!'

After this incident, Blue was sent to Maudsley for a spell, but, under Care in the Community, she was soon enough dancing upon the streets of Camberwell & Brixton. During her spell, she would have a nice tea with none other than the sublime artist, poet & writer Maureen Scott, another perspective amidst the deep abyss - that utterly deep, inexplicable source of the Monolith, as was her obsession....

Blue begins to whisper in her soul, slowly, fragmented at first - mere wisps, lines, until she could whisper the entire mantra, or what she called her poem -- it is her own radical self-interpretation, of her being, her desire

> Desire erupts excessive
> Hunger, thirst ecstatic
> A radical familiarity
> ultimately, always
> recedes into the background -
> one of the hidden ties that
> bind together narratives,
> languish to suture this
> fragmentation of mortality.
> Desire oscillates below the surface -
> Pleasure seduces, tempts us to steer
> away from death, incites us to embrace
> phantastic illusions... though spider webs
> rapidly dissolve with the morning dew,
> blazing sun across fragile surfaces...
> Below illusion, concealed, life and existence
> inexorably fated to dissolution, nothingness –
> Desire feeds upon the abyss, the void -

These attempts, though useless,
logically flawed and technically
impossible are the plastic flowers of
our desire, with our empty hands,
we wish what we think we must have,
but know that we can never have,
An insurrection against nothingness
Impossible revolutions
Open up this place of free existence.
All desire is ironic.
Desire erupts ecstatic,

it strikes

She did not have a good hold on South London at first, these sorts of pointless tricks - anything for a buck while you are pursuing your dream - did not work here - that is why she had to go to the City, to the sex clubs to get any work.

But, that was her lie of a lie after all - as that dire pit is now much closer to home.... After her many conversations with Maureen, Blue decides that her dream had always been very simple, to understand the propensity of humans for sadism, masochism - of the question of redemption or liberation therefrom - 'This must be the key to political, cultural power,' she mused...

A philosophy of immersion..... the most contemporary of methods - but for naught -
She is 'living her life' - she is immersed, radically, in this, her convenient illusion.

I wish I could tell her in my own voice, without the humiliation of the chalkboard - I always show her my love, by my innocence before her, my caress, erotic play....

'Is all of history not just a distraction from death? A detour?', Blue whispers to me, as we lay upon my makeshift bed, with the hope of evanescent sleep.

3 IAN

('Gangsta Rap' by Ice Cube)

Carl - or C.J. as he is called in the 'hood - as a result of some massively bizarre brainweasing or psychotic episode - Carl is Ian --- now, I am talking about GTA -San Andreas - & still for PS2 --- this is Ian --- he used to be Bob Marley, but now - he has moved on from that in light of the situation on the ground .....

Most gamers frolick from game to game, each time seeking to master all - then one moves on amidst an eternally ironic & impossible quest ---

But - Ian is different...

Ian aka C.J. never did the quests - he could never get the bicycle to do whatever it had to do on the very first quest --- the gangsters in the white Cadillac, or whatever it is - always shoot him dead or leave him behind - everyone keeps saying that you got to hit the button faster & faster ---

But, that is not why he played the game - shit, he hated video games - at one point, he saw them as the instigation of the dissolution of existence into the simulacrum of nothingness & nihilism --- or at least stupidity & obesity....

But - San Andreas changed that - not mind you, the other GTA games, although he never dissed them, or others like God of War, which at least teaches Greek Mythology in a live interactive action format - some he despised, like Bully (how dire is that?) or the many POV war games, training modules unloaded from the military - though, it is like sorting peas from one bowl to another during a plague...

No - just San Andreas – & laughably Saint's Row 2 - it was probably the music that hooked him, between the redneck, reggae, alternative & old skool hip hop, indie offerings (not to mention the ever pertinent banter of the DJs ---- that is the Dionysian dance of the game -

Amidst the music, if you steal or find a car - one emerges into perspective, existence with an almost infinite topographical site of possibility - free roam - you can frolic - basically do anything & with a few cheats, enact utter insurrection - have some fun - but then, there is seduction --- perhaps, a friend who comes over & sorts it all out, saves the game --- you can begin to own manifold properties, enter previously inaccessible establishments & change the colour of your hair ---- just like playing with paper dolls & dress-up - GTA becomes quite cuddly - or, the other secret side, another friend saves a posh game with full access to everything, each of the cities & all the things you can do as the sweet reward for owning the game - strip clubs, lap dances, the snuff room (for the money-changers) - though Ian was better than that - not interested in the leisure activities of the all-too-rich, etc - plus, he spilled absinthe on the memory card - he always started each time, with each day, from scratch..... a makeshift game....

('Gangsta Rap' by Ice-T)

At the end of the day - the real point for Ian aka CJ is confrontation - utter rebellion - it would be destruction, but you can never destroy architecture in GTA... At least that is what Sophia would mantra any time Ian would begin to wax poetical about the radical implications of the game with its glimpse of freedom...

- or - the game *as the game* is effectively infinite... imagine it with an internet global interface... lol lkw faym lmfafo - from a certain perspective, it is clear that this is already the case - or linked to real gangstars via the notorious Blackberry.... the world is GTA --- coming to a neighbourhood near you...

Indeed, despite his many friend's best efforts, Ian always starts at the beginning of the game as he is not concerned with anything that the higher levels can offer - all that matters to Carl is the free roam - a topography of radical freedom with architectural, access limits - existential constraints - yet - there is always the freedom upon the streets - streets - though buildings - monuments sometime collapse or are brought down in the wink of a conspiracy…. or revolution….

Besides satisfying his lover Sophia's utterly perverse S&M fantasies, Ian spends most of his time playing San Andreas - although that is not all he does - he lives a cryptic life for the most part, but he is always doing this, that on his interface --- a complete internet fusion with his massive Flat screen - he, quite a genius, managed to get us hooked up to broadband satellite, you name it - though we only had a miny tv in the common room, part clock radio….

I can never write enough words on my board to ask the right questions - Ian lives in a bubble, in his room - massively dangerous, but uninterested, unambitious …

This talk of electricity etc water refers after all to the caricature of the archetypal squat of the 1980's - grim, dire living with opportunists at every turn waiting to crash for a few nights only to nick, to nick everything that isn't chained down or behind a pad lock - Squats have come a long way - they even improve property values in various locales - way better than crack houses or torture rooms…

though the ten year olds are reminding us of our origins…. they remind us….

We are still there but, after all, the real issue, as Proudhon has sublimely expressed, is that of the equation: property = theft -- not one merely of the smoke & mirrors of private, public property - but of property as such - & the ethics of ownership - not to mention the 'ethical utilisation' of property - especially abandoned properties - or, this freedom of space as one of the events for a place of expression - hence graffiti & riots, etc….. another event is time - which is of action & access, perspective - not to mention, but to display the eventful temporality of ecstatic life….

Squats have saved communities, we should not forget this lesson of history in light of our own ridiculous parody of history - a post-modernist apocalypse - better than an abandoned property full of rats that swarm the rest of the safe houses when the property is - after perhaps years of an absentee landlord - finally re-developed --- I have lived through such a proliferating horror on Herne Hill Road…

The bureaucracy, the government is the biggest absentee landlord…. Yet, squats are supremely superior to mere privatisation - just the same with worker cooperatives, on all levels, but not the way they did it in the 1970's -

-- the problem as always is the decided lack of liberation of the working people in any economy of scale - we always believe in a Hitler or Stalin - the leader - everyone believes in this after all.... & that is our greatest flaw - our lazy fear & our escapist cowardice ---

('Nigga Nigga Nigga' by Gangsta Rap, the Glockumentary)

'Her beauty exceeds any considerations of health!' Aire speaks from the other room as out of a dream, loudly from the front room.... 'To risk all for beauty - is sublime...' He had received a poetic code upon his Blackberry which alerted a vast network that things were on tonight in Brixton - in the shadow of riots across Europe, not to mention the fierce revolutions in North Africa & the Middle East, the feral children of Britain will not be outdone - & they are just as angry... & just as proud...

Nottingham exploded last night -

The centrality of the game for Ian - CJ - was the moment of action - whatever that is - infinite possibility upon a familiar terrain - LA - but Ian never leaves Los Santos - mostly, unless he steals a plane... for his game is on the streets, in the immediacy of life - & he always wears the clothes with which he first arrived back in the 'hood' with Arthur Miller.

('Nigga' by Enimem)

Ian likes to get the weapons cheat & then take on the world - after all, there is the utter nobility of GTA as one does not have to bow to the preconceived narratives of the game & their structured scenarios, rules & timing --- nor did he have to bow to the simulacrum of a hypocritical & corrupt order - at least however as long as he played the game... perhaps the game itself is an instance of rebellion, & playing is like the poor soul with his secret diary in Orwell's 1984 -

Thought Crime!!!' 'Yo, the Royal family be pimpin', mutherfukas.... Prince Manspew is a pimp!' Ian would sporadically scream at the game...' though he would add, 'I would though silence my criticisms immediately if only he would send some of his money & whores my way - I am a whore like everyone else ...'

The point though is that as he played, he began to imagine a free space for human existence - of a sublime eternity of life - reality & the game dissolve into one - as neither ever really exists on its own, in the moment.... & neither exhaust that which is the case.... Ian is not just a gamer, after all -

&, he is not on the dole, which has become, for many, a backdoor Arts funding pool, thank the gods - everyone suspects that he's a meth dealer or something ---- the story is stranger than reality - but typical & not in the end surprising -

Ian until very recently was a freelance hacker for News of the Wound, & a few of the other rags - even The Daily Simulacrum -- he had bank-rolled his life like this for years & which is why I see now that is this is obviously the reason why the squat had all the creature comforts - Ian is a good hacker, & that is why he never came out - or really ever had to come out - of his room -

Indeed, he became so slovenly & bound that he even turned down an offer to be on a special tactical information unit during the last election, a position that, as many of his associates have now come to enjoy, was budgeted to continue into the new government of the Gangster & the LapDog party, - a bizarre coalition emerged in which the LapDogs, seeking remedial governmental legitimacy, sold their souls for scraps of power - rancid scraps at that - henceforth, they can only be redeemed if they break the spell of the Coalition & bring down the government - otherwise, they will never exist again anywhere.

Alas, Ian was not much for sterile offices or teamwork, & he was not especially a Coalition man (or conventionally political, for that matter), for despite their pseudo-libertarian rhetoric in the day, the Gangsters are merely a 'law & order' party for the rich - the leader of the still other party had a respectable, thoughtful father - perhaps the seeds of a new royal line ---- though Ian did not pay them much mind as they never requested his services…

Nor did Ian do any hacking for the police, of which there was always much work galore - he was content hacking into the personal lives of celebrities, politicians & the Royals - when he was not working for The Moon, he got his directions from a g-man named Glennie M., one of the mafia boss Jimmy Murder's boys at the News of the Wound -- 'OK, Glenn, send me over the list -- cheerio…' Ian was paid piece-meal, per name, & must have hacked 10,000 phones, voice mails & e-mail accounts --- hell, he made a cool 150 large… At the end of the day, he drew the line with his gut - he was not a copper - just a lazy stoner gangsta…. muthafuka -

('The Irony of It All' by The Streets)

Aire & Jesse became very excited suddenly in the front room, enacting their very own little mosh pit on the futon to the illustrious traditional favourite, Anarchy in the UK - they ring their arms together like a square dance of rednecks, each holding a half empty bottle of Stolichnaya vodka in his free hand... they dance around more wildly, create a virtual vortex at the centre of the futon - until centripetal forces so overwhelm that they fly their separate ways, crash into now forensic non-descript squat related gear... rapturous laughter propels them to their feet ...

'Let's get the hell out of here! The time is nigh!' Jesse screams.... 'Who's with us,' Aire shouts & spins around at an almost empty room.... 'I will go with you', whispers Luce, 'I need to get out of here for awhile.' She is sublimely interesting, but quiet - she suspends amid states of curious indecision as each moment fractures... the three run out into the explosive night under leaden clouds....

Ian does the weapons cheat & then starts shooting passersbys, one after another.... just as he was illuminated to run amok by Andre Breton who unbelievably exposes his own truth in the Second Surrealist Manifesto... Ian adopted this philosophy long ago & always believes that he will eventually go out in a blaze of glory. That is why he has recently received a gun license... he is becoming increasingly autarkic, underground... scary.... who knows, he may even go postal on your arses...

The police come with motorcycles & patrol cars - he shoots them all dead....the police trucks with water cannons come - not to mention the other chaotic emergency vehicles....

3 stars - more come - Ian destroys them with his portable rocket launcher that he got from some wyrd baby named Stewie, down the road - he destroys all helicopters & manages to kill each of the tactical units with his several machine guns -

4 stars - the helicopters start to come - the black helicopters come with their search lights, 'dey, uck in my wife's nickas', & coordinated tactical teams, who descend to the asphalt across lightning ropes -

More helicopters - Ian takes each down with his bazooka....

('Gangsta' by Bushido)

New tactical units are on (but not upon) the ground.... more helicopters come - police arrive on motor cycles, SUV's, tactical assault vehicles (TAV's), the masses of police swarm across the streets having made their point to the 'Government of the Reaper', of the 'Gangster Cuts' - an inverse EMO government, violence sadistically projected outward, ABJECTED -

Of course, their mass network of informants/operatives, hackers & the blokes down at the pub will always lend a hand.... do their part in the instigation of the worst excesses --- it is always hard to start a riot ---- you can get the people there - usually under some other pretext - as SDS announces they will execute a dog in Berkeley - but reprieve the dog at the last moment after all the speeches have been made.... the RABL, the Revolutionary Anarchist Bowling League, who confront police & horses with bowling balls.... 'Gee, sir - you have bowled a 300 game - but in this country, our balls are smaller!'

Once we (as I as the narrator am two places at once, possibly more - like the substance of transubstantiation... the death of the narrator, or some surreptitious device, a metaphysics of divinity, spirits, energetic ecstasies) are there, here, people randomise - a bit of incitement, a speech, some music to keep the spirits up.... to defer, for a moment, the beating drum of the coxswain... but at least they are drinking & smoking - that at a very least keeps them happy & expectant - they do not kill themselves, but await the inevitable confrontation - the limit situation where power will be decided - upon, across the streets....

Chaos Mode activated - faces, bodies - flesh runs screaming through the streets.... Misty Mundae, a softcore porn & horror actress, who has her own VIP level in GTA, screams the mother of all voiceovers - her sheer erotic & raging power compels all the prostitutes, tourists, old ladies, old men, fat men, skinny women, fat women, & monsters to run amok in a orgy of carnage - as everything around them explodes --

('Gangsta' by Trick Daddy)

Before Ian again pulls out his bazooka, he destroys the advance police tactical units, but draws his attention back to the helicopters - the fight will take place in the streets - as is the holy of holies of our existence - 'that is what pubs were supposed to do' - until the smoking ban - (unless they just picked the fight, with their government subsidised rave scene, a pharmaceutical experiment...) - then there is the indigenous era of house parties - & singular events amidst myriad shifting venues, spaces & places - the 'pub culture' is dead, except for the lock-in --- the only way to revive it would be to legalise marijuana & turn pubs into *pubs* that sell another bit of the bob - another harmless fantasy experience ....

5 stars -

the raging swarm upon the streets --- promised the world but given nothing but images, propaganda - scents of the flesh as rats - Chrysippus dies laughing when seeing a drunk donkey eat figs...

('Gillie Da Kid' by Gansta)

Advertisements = virulent expectations ... captivation - bewitchment - inexorable repetition - & now the weather with Jane....

they riot in the streets like fiends below my window --- though, to be fair, Aire & Jesse are out there too, rioting like the best of them ... McDougal's doesn't stand a chance...... not to mention - yadda yadda yadda ....

Vengeful Spirit Mode activated ---

Everything in the game now operates according to superstitious logics.... 'Thank all the gods, goddesses, myriad spirits, nymphs - all the souls of the earth & of the Kosmos -,' Ian whispers his prayer to the gods of chaos... of the indigenous peoples...

The revenge scenario is awakening, the spirits of all the victims of war, genocide, mass poisoning & poverty are arising --- they have long suffocated, together with Hades, in an unjust - over-crowded nightmare - disease running rampant - but, it is thought that a great event is alleged to heal us - in this, the spirits now have a purpose & a strategy...... one cannot put such to sleep.....

All of our victims have returned - vengeful spirits possessing our youth!!! -

These are different from those who did not have the coin to pay the fairy man --- they wander the earth anyway --- but, that is just the start of it - that is 'normal'....

We all knew it would come to this - capitalist arrogance in its lust for a new aristocracy - False to the core - met by a vortex of riotous, joyous, sorrowful explosions..... they call it destruction amidst their futile - cancerous language game.... lust to suppress the other voices & ways of being....

'Yo yo yo - yoyo!' Ian shouts out to Sophia, who comes out of the shower in a towel.

'Keep your mouth shut!', she pretends to be stern, but then laughs, flashing Ian her beautiful pierced body --- 'Do you want to lick my pussy... I just shaved?'

'I am a nigga nigga nigga -' he sings back to her, '100% nigga, & I love to eat pussy - '

('Gangsta Bop', akon)

'We cannot be naïve - we cannot be naïve - they can shut it all down in an instant -,' Ian & Sophia hear Jesse out on the street, 'Anonymous is a parasite for the time being….. a good parasite …. maybe….'

'Who could know?', Aire rejoins, 'It could be the CIA…. etc…. the vanishing mediator -'

'I doubt the CIA would have backed down from the Mexican Cartels,' Jesse laughs, 'Cause it would be like backing down from themselves….'

'Poned,' Aire replicates a culture of repetition….

Sophia walks pensively to the window, 'Not the best time --- it will be a riot in the squat in no time….', she runs into the bathroom … shuts the door…

6 Stars -

All guns a blazing ----- an impossible situation - all that is left is courage…

but even the utterly impossible bleeds the tears of Eros --- the heterogeneous, wildly female ferments underneath, underground -
she lies, steals, cheats ---- she takes all & gives nothing ----

yet, she is Joy -

*****

They came home with da stuff ---- a noble victory with the splendour of spoils…

A big flat screen - who could afford it, after all --- riots correct effective demand.... perhaps Marx was right about common ownership - but with lots of leases....

'Ian, get your arse out here!,' Jesse screams as he & Aire carry the television over to the bare wall cleared for the occasion.... the ten year olds cascade frenetically in light of their new prospects... Luce struggles in slowly, quietly after the lads with two shopping bags filled with food & alcohol - she stumbles slightly, but I catch her before she collapses in her corner..... 'I think I will go to Spain,' she whispers...

'Holy Shiite!,' Sophia screams, 'Ian, get out here! - Hell, you got the biggest one there is - like a fucking movie theatre!'

'Yes, I know it is big, baby,' Ian comes stumbling out of his room, barely able to walk due to his chronic lack of circulation -- 'Fuck yeah!,' he screams, but fails to notice the flatscreen & begins rummaging through the food & alcohol, 'Yes! Stoli's & French hard sausage! Shaved parmesan!!! Now I am a happy man!'

Sophia slaps Ian square across the back of his head, 'No, you retard! ' 'What the fuck bitch??!!!' Ian interrupts -- 'No, jackass - look at what they got at the riot!' Sophia grasps his head with both hands - turns it toward the flatscreen.... 'Look, you imbecile!'

'Oh yeah... saw that,' Ian limply states, 'Not really a big fan of TV, really --- but you already know that...' he laughs, & walks back into his room with the loot...

'So, how was the riot?,' Sophia asks, carrying the bags of looted consumables into the kitchen - Jesse & Aire follow her into the kitchen, they each take what they like - 'It was good,' Aire reflects, 'but, with all of the looting, it seemed to lack the explicit common purpose of a people in solidarity - it was a bit crass really...'

'I do not agree - it is,' Jesse begins, 'an insurrection against nothingness, against the lies & the ghosts of false promises --- manipulation & despair --- revolutions are ugly, but even ugliness has its time...'

Sophia shivers - screeches slightly, 'Don't worry, I'm ok...' she assures us...
'& yes, of course,' Jesse pays tribute, 'Aire, as an ecstatic fire, screamed from his perch above to the wanderers, rioters & looters as they frolicked in

the streets ---'

(Flashback, as told by Jesse) 'It was an orgiastic orgy amidst the utterly fetishisation of capitalist commodities.....' Jesse laughs --- Sophia smacks him in the face, pulling him by his ear to the front room, on the futon - Aire is already there, trying to wake up Luce, but she is gone for now... Sophia falls to the futon, lying back, Aire, beginning to the feel the second dose of LSD he took on the streets upon their return, began to Tai-Chi the flatscreen, oblivious to Jesse's praise....

'The ghost of Marx smiles,' Jesse resumes, 'happy that he was totally on the pulse of things, upon the totality of our existence --- (aside) it is a tragic shame he never met Shelley, Coleridge... but he read them - wrote his own shit, like Nietzsche, etc....'

'Should've listened to Bakunin,' Aire ponders, 'Though, that would have made little difference, as it is the political bureaucrats who destroy all things, even before our eyes...' We are still under the spell of Plato - we need to find his bones, burn them...

Many upon the field of battle tonight were utter criminals, who not even Anarchists will abide (he suddenly chokes laughing), & police instigators seeking not only an utter distraction from the hacking scandal but also a justification for their budget.... they played the cards that they had - & they won... a great victory for workers!

Fight Club style...

Aire resisted that cancerous echo chamber of bullshit - he remembers - He stood up upon the statue of Hecuba in front of the Church of Timothy --- & all of the rapid sudden.... he began to preach this heretical truth - 'The docile sheep bleed out their fears & immediately consent to any new order.... this need not be the response of the feral children... you must become as children, radical wild children....'

The shocked flock simply acquiesced - set down their loot, if just for a moment...

'Nor of the Chalkboarders!' I hold up my board, along with about seven others in the around world of this vicinity....

(Implicit Comedy Flashback)

Of the Feral Children

Aire stood on top of a burning police van, thousands rioting around this chasm of spoils, hundreds gather, stop to listen to the madman's rant -

Strangely enough, my brothers & sisters
rioting is a thoroughly political act -
& is symptomatic of deep crisis
in the political economic regime
(& not just in Brixton, but all
over London & Great Britain -
not to mention throughout the rest
of Europe, Asia, Africa, etc. etc.)
The World
A riot is a political act, just as
with the long history of riots
in Britain which originally led
to our revolution
(if cutting the King's head off
is not a riot, then
I do not know what is…)
A riot is a political &
cultural act of defiance -
– despite the efforts
to portray looting as economic
greed & vandalism –
opportunism…. (like Libya, Iran?)
It is a revolt which seeks
to shift the context of
'business as usual' – not merely
to pace around in the cage
of the hypocritical limitations
of the present – not to mention
the uncertainty - fraudulent
mask of the current 'system' -
all that is solid melts into air -
the feral children dance upon
the streets affirming a differing
future through their emphatic 'No!'
A riot is a political act -
Economics is not politically neutral
in a world of radical inequality -
in economics, war, medicine, etc.
How many young people in Albion
could ever hope to own their own homes?

& – with the oppressive vandalism
of the public sector by the Gangsters &
their little LapDog bitches,
what future can any of the young
people see? A grim, bleak house?
A new inquisition, poor houses & poor laws?
food given to only those who attend Mass –
Will the future be the darkness of the past,
prior even to the English Revolution —
The current disorder is political, cultural -
It is symptomatic of deep desparities of wealth & power -
A riot is a political act -
The disenfranchised in their Dionysian rage,
will seek some outlet, like a volcano -
This is the way things are with human beings.
The great task is to be honest about
the root causes of things – & to
seriously & sincerely deal with
these root causes —
Otherwise -
"Get out of the way if you can't lend a hand,
the times they are a-changin'" (Dylan)

They had stopped their frenzied rioting - rapturous looting to listen to Aire's words, many with tears in their eyes - realising that it was now their turn to dance around the Tree of Liberty - free flatscreens as the fruit...

A dark troubadour hops up on the car with the applause of the rioters - 'Looters - sympathisers, fellow travellers - lend me your ears! - the singer, a rough bluesman, Greg the Fisher scratches out that old traditional,

'They do not want us
We feral children
... only see us all
as fallen angels
of a wild fire
to be extinguished
They do not want us
We feral children
... say we're savage
vicious rabid dogs
deserving only
to be put down

They do not want us
We feral children

'It was a splendid night,' Jesse waxes back upon the futon, 'Not to mention our brand new, utterly free flatscreen for all of our dire troubles, a small offering to the revolting masses upon whose backs the gentile few rest their boots -'

'Ironic surely', I ponder, 'The people, the masses, as they used to say, 'crave the objects of their own torture, utter indoctrination - these objects are kept out of their reach, but they are kept shiny --- the rioters loot the objects of their own enslavement --- the second irony is that they we were already free on the reservation, but seduced to take, to steal, to pillage --- & thus, to become the ultimate recipients of the true, good & beautiful - to be consumers...'

Enlightenment!!!

*****

The TV activated discloses Russell Brand's *Ponderland*, topic, 'Government'...

(Russell Brand wears a white wedding dress, splashed with blood & excrement)

Welcome everyone to Ponderland, where we think about things, often very difficult, dark things ---- Russell Brand begins to gesticulate across the stage wildly - The CIA/MI5.6 is in my brain, Kennedy was an alien, Bigfoot is the President of America --- Russell Brand scrunches up into a little fetal ball, but turns to the camera with a wispy whisky whisper, 'We will be back to talk about the.... (in an ironic yelp) government......

Advertisement

Scenario - a person in the loo, who drops his keys into the toilet.

'Has this ever happened to you?' How many times have you put your hand into the darkness of the loo?

An extended strobic flash upon the screen ---

NOW - through a REVOLUTIONARY late capitalist, post-industrial, post-modern post-mechanised, post-postist i.e., an utterly corrupt mechanical process - you can NOW possess, own, consume

TOILET TONGS!!!

They're easy, safe.... & (most primordially) clean......

Film of happy pensioner fishing her false teeth from the bog with

TOILET TONGS!!! - Order Now!!!! --- www.toilettongs.com

Welcome back to Ponderland where we are pondering the government - our onerous government does not seem to like government very much ---- so why don't they just leave government (rapturous applause) - & practice what they preach - start a small business thing, or some such people - you could be our own secret stimulus plan ..... Russell Brand suddenly brandishes a whip, slashing to bits a piñata of Margaret Thatcher, '...a thatcher in a long line of thatchers who thatch to this day....'

(Canned Laughter)

Think it's bad here ---- there is always something worse, that is our alibi, our primary education --- & that is the extraordinary truth --- we never really want to look at ourselves, ordinarily -- it is always better to make everyone else seem worse... a great place to hide ---- (Russell smacks his head upon a bottle of champagne - spins around with his wedding dress... until you see his stained pink knickers....

Suddenly - he does three gymnastic twirls or somesuch etc.. declares, 'Have a look at this clip from Kentucky, from over across the Pond....

I should utterly warn you that there will be depictions of government sponsored horror, terrorism, torture... (Russell Brand suddenly dances about, shouting, as if he were drunk)

Full Film - 'Through the Wire: the Remix' (PBS), moderated by Mumia.... 2nd edition, though cut, since it is a legacy of the destroyed National Endowment for the Humanities - Piss Jesus still haunts us all, each, everyone ....

(Paraphrase) I am a captive - they have body captivity searched me everyday for decades - everyone has forgotten about me.... I am helpless -

I am utterly   in Hell - the Government of the United States, (& the special Britain etc.) is an utter lie... but their people are worse, an utterly bad experiment....

'All governments are gangsta hits....' Russell Brand comes back - tries to make it all funny, pretending to slur, like Arthur -'I was body cavity searched earlier today ---- (laughs on command) byyyyy myyyyyy wiiiiifffeeeee! Too bad she went away! - then, she cleaned her fist, went back to work.... yet, it is terrible - all the same..... but at least I got 30 million out of the deal!' he quivers, blushes, and collapses onto the floor...

Good show, young kipper! We are all trivialised!!!!

Russell runs off stage like a march hare shouting, 'I only need your love!!!'

'& - a case of Jameson's -' Jesse adds, satisfied with his own dire epiphany....

Everyone breaks out into a riotous explosion of justified laughter.

4 JESSE

Jesse is one of the feral dogs that the Prime Bureaucrat declares must be put down.

&, Anyone like them. … so many of us have become feral… it happens by itself …

'Again, not to mention the Chalkboarders!', I held up my board, again disrupting my own alleged narration… no one knows……

Jesse came to the squat just after he had some run in with the Royal Family, or what not…. not to mention for the moment the terrible events after…

Jesse is sitting across from me right now - as he is a lot of the time, but is quite quiet as of late, due to the blunt force trauma to his brain - by a swarm of privatised renta-riot cops - &, after he had fallen from such a height… it is the utter threat of the full scale privatisation of policing, as explicit counter-insurgency, death squads --- (where is the command & control?) He comes out of his coma for an instant, a spark, 'It is gangster fascism!' (he laughs,, but returns to his deep slumber)

Yet, he is guilty, & in some estimates, he deserves his punishments, most of which have as yet to disclose themselves…. at least to us.

Jesse walks onto a sitcom set…. turns to the studio audience, shouting, 'Oi!'

(Canned Laughter)

Of the Feral Children

Back then Jesse was becoming increasingly agitated - frenetically dances to the novel rhythms of resistance ... he had already always been there all along, shit, there like all the others who are already there -- before it went maelstrom.... Jesse's spiralling movements fanned the flames of the incipient protest movements, the wild cat strikes, Occupations, & riots... - existential transfigurations....

I guess Jesse's main claim to fame comes from the very beginning of the resistance, even before the Coalition Orders of Suppression, & the Supernanny style policing of the internet, alternative publications - places of gathering - worship...

It was the night of the first big major spin-off riot on the high streets... indeed, it was fortuitous as usually one has to grow a riot like a garden...

Of course, I should mention, though I be a poor narrator, one must be careful not to shoot arrows at Princes, as Nietzsche advises... lest they rise up, even more powerful ... to let the perpetuator off the hook - to play the 'victim' - & you certainly do not want to throw fire extinguishers at them... hell, that guy just got out, they say he has HIV after being raped repeatedly in detention... Hope he has better things to do --

Jesse & his comrades were not there for the earlier big protest anyway - they were not students, of course - they were there for the knock down drag out fight - a gold ole' London brawl with the gents of fascism, the mob - the blissfully ambiguous police, who would rather be at home - they smell our scent, this surreal aroma of conflict that begins to seep through the breach as it glimmers - the mask of docile bodies -

('All the World is Green' by Tom Waits)

It is not that they were totally illiterate, but their wyrd language evanesces across the networks of resistance, amid the heterogeneous underworld of negativity - active affirmation... many of them read, the Canon of Anarchy - myriad novels, the more unfashionable, & thus, the best philosophers & poets - music though is the bliss, the ecstatic eruption of free expression - comedy, the tear in the fabric of ultimate reality - redeems - liberates us from these banal philistines of power.

Language itself has become feral, intimating the utter sublimity of existence, of life upon an excessively wild planet - though there are still the dictionaries, lexicons - the canon books, catechisms - despite icons, idols, rules, regulations - all of this is utter bullshit, meaningless - it does not mean anything --- it is all excruciatingly false....

 Jesse & his ferocious droogs spend most of their time, upon that morning, drinking clear Vodka - smoking shamanic spliffs as they shadow through the massive crowd of citizens in civil protest - the carnivalesque atmosphere of the gathering, with the drummers, musicians, singers, poets --- Jesse walkz passes one, ranting - this ecstatic poet gesticulates with emotion, spitting out his words, as he spitz -

 hang the money changers high
 don't let the bankers get away with it
 - yet another theft of the people -
 a draught of blood they steal our life
 no more effigies no more symbolism
 they are stealing our lives G20 meltdown
 robbing YOU of this moment this short life

(The poet falls to his knees, in abjection)

 this single chance to live they steal this sacred opening from us
 we are the latest & the last to be attacked by the predator
 millions of corpses rot in swarms of flies & dust
 the overlords their machine extracts extract the lives of millions
 they have always taken they have always killed
 now they are exposed they are exposed we know who they are
 we know where they live no more symbolism
 they are stealing our lives - property is theft

(the poet descends into the child posture, as in yoga)

 telling us our children that there is a better reward in heaven
 if we only let them steal from us now steal our life
 they prey upon our children their powerlust is sadism financial fools
 steal our one - only chance this moment this open this chance
 don't let them get away with it they walk in waistdeep rivers of blood
 they have stolen they have killed for too long
 throw them out from this temple of life
 hang the money changers high piano wire & salt

(the poet ascends in his defiance with clenched fists)

 In a near drunken explosion of enthusiastic love, Jesse claws at the poet, bringing him into embrace - 'Now, that is poetry!!!' Jesse shouts, 'That is poetry!' Aire kisses Jesse's cheek - hands his bundle of poetry to Jesse, 'You can have it friend... read it when you get a chance....' Jesse hugs the poet, 'Thank you - this is the most amazing honour'.... he put the papers into his back pocket.... he runs into the night....

Jesse already lost touch with his merry accomplices - he bounces through the dark surging plethora of bodies, faces. this festival of the new commons, in the street - in defiance of the merely beautiful... he twirls amid vivacious surging crowds via these rapturous events of bare self-expression - speeches, air horns, fireworks, fancy dress street theatre, performance art - the fluctuating faces, bodies - voices of thousands in this emergent hive of the moment.

He shelters himself from the surge amidst a simple tree - rolls a nice rasta-sized spliff to commemorate the vision before his eyes... no longer that young, not like many of the naive, impossibly joyous faces shattering his eyes...

Jesse remembers the meet up, after gazing in perplexity at the Mickey Mouse watch that they had put on him when he was sleeping...

He wisps through the faces - bodies toward the meeting point, words streaming in his soul as he carouses through the singularity of the event - he still sings, channels the blood of the poet, an echo of another's desperate voice - he echoes Aire's own chaotic rage.... yet, with the tears of rage in his eyes, his extreme anger, he is the fellow traveller amid this mortal chance, who speaks to the stars between the clouds - Jesse grabs Aire's words from his back pockets, turns the page to the next one, shouts the truth to the heavens....

> Global meltdown for
> the poor, fall faster into
> nothingness, while our
> stockholm syndrome
> seduces us to bail out
> our economic captors,
> we masochists submit
> to the sadistic rich when
> we should instead throw
> them into jail, make
> them wear french maid's
> outfits & get on their
> knees to clean toilets

for the rest of their lives!

Oh, but I'm sorry for
being offensive, of
upsetting the rich
criminals who rape
& eat the children
of the poor – whoops!
sorry 'bout that, can't
seem to control myself
anymore with all of
this class war rhetoric!!!
Lock 'em up, property is theft!
Take it back & spread the wealth -
From each according to ability,
To each according to need -
(Saint-Simone actually, Karl
just borrowed the phrase)
but to get there, first things first
lock 'em up, spread the wealth
& admire all the sparkling toilets!!!

*****

('What do I get?' by the Buzzcocks)

Jesse blazes through the door, clutches his bleeding cock in his hand - 'Oh, my god... I am fucked - I will never fuck again - somebody fuckin' ring an ambulance! -

Hello!!!???'....

His cock is black & blue swollen to utterly immense proportions... Charlie, a new friend of his, one of the ones who stayed with him for awhile, his father was a guitarist - puked into the fish tank when he saw the monstrously abused cock...

'Call the ambulance, muther-fuckers.... this cannot be right... fuckin' hell....', Jesse held his cock, standing in the open, naked ... in pain....

Everyone in the room was dead.... all sitting there dead... there was no one to help anyone - him in his hour of need... dead foamy vomit - glorious dead, dead, dead ..... His housemates had all overdosed on dodgy heroin... the story eventually became that there was too much rat poison mixed in by an apprentice chemist - half of the market killed in one night... not very auspicious...

Jimmy, the only one left alive, did not even know they were dead... Jesse grabs him by the neck, throws him to the wall - shouting , 'They are all dead!!! - How could you have ever missed that?!!!!.... ' Jesse pushes one last time, & turns, again holding his zipper studded swollen organ.... his cock looks like a blood spattered eggplant....

'I didn't do the junk,' Jimmy explains, 'just sat there with them, thinking... sorry - they seemed to be doing what they normally do on junk... nothing...'

Aire shouts out, over the story, to relieve the pointlessness. 'Who could ever begin to tell the difference betwixt heroin & death? .... it is just a cliché now....'

Jesse bends over, holds his purple, black cock, as it grows larger & larger.......

'Sorry - tripping... looks like they are breathing to me...', little Jimmy flashes back in a whisper, as he transfixes to a snow globe of the World Trade Center.

Jesse instantly feels sane in comparison to this pathetic other - he made the call & they were at his house in 27 minutes., so they still had to pay for it.... Pizza Hut had taken over the ambulance service in the latest wave of privatisations... but you only had to pay for it at first if it was on time... yet - that did not last long - indeed, it did not even happen, really - shit - people just fucking died, but the statistics shined...

*****

('Rage against the machine', by the Beasty Boys - or perhaps, a mere series of explosions)

Jesse & his campaneiros had earlier converged at the Treasury Building, the diabolic temple of sadism, masochism - we all saw the iconic images of their unambiguous rebellion --- psychotic joy, rage, existential despair... Jesse stood upon a solid block of rock - exclaims with a bottle in his hand, 'It is good to remind these utter sons of whores that we are not merely bestial subjects to be fucked, exploited...' (he takes another swig, yet, falls off the stone, his bottle shatters into the crowd who cheer, with sufficient British irony, his utterly brilliant performance)....

'We are all spies, at heart.... everyone good was killed in the Roman Campaign......' Jesse continues, 'though, unfortunately, that is not in the history books, &, as it is not now in our budget - will it ever be... ///nor all the rest..... political parties - gangsters of the West - gulf state pacific region etc. slavery Chilean exploitation meta-disease, miracles of vampires, witches, werewolfs....'

I wish I could write all this on my chalk board so I could share it with others - but you will have to be grateful for this glimpse into my private language, which I disclose to you - reluctantly, as this may or may not be the case....

Jesse scurries from the safety of Parliament Square to the designated place - it was not the same as the Millbank orgasm, or the brief take-over of Westminster - but thank (not) the idiot for throwing the fire extinguisher..... the papers into his back pocket the papers into his back pocket the papers into his back pocket the papers into his back pocket the papers into his back pocket the papers into his back pocket or, for punching the cop in the face' - though, there are differing opinions, even in the squat.... 'but there is also PR - which will always stand for Propaganda...'

'What can we do with an opinion that seeks to destroy all other opinions, a power that seeks to destroy all powers?' Aire asks...

Jesse sits there still brain-injured. 'Sure he was stupid to do it,' Aire exclaims, amidst his acid binge, - but he never realised the danger in the simple act of the moment - utterly naïve, without reflection - yet, his intentions were pure, utterly pure...

'He was the greatest thing,' Blue whispers as she scurries toward her room to get ready for her night shift horror - but, at the end of day... she loves to dance... that is her life...

Jesse was lucky that night - the ambulance picked him up & took him all the way there - Lady Di didn't get it that good - well, they picked her up, but fucking stopped on the road for, what, three hours - but again, it was France after all.... Ask Jeffrey Archer, a dear client of mine, in one of my other names - about this -- he knows everything as he has done the most.... shit, he arranged the hit himself - indeed, he is most deadly when he is silent....

(Before you can proceed in this text, you need to fill out form 124 & apply for an interview, but you will not be told where/when to locate/send the specific form, etc. - sadistic capillaries - or any substance of the interview --- like Kafka's The Trial --- Miller's Crucible - the game board, Red Scare McCarthy... etc etc yada yada etc....)

Jesse had already been to the merely student protests - but no one is serious until they pitch a tent - he was there for the employee (worker pretests) which are still going on... of course, as merely an embryo of the noble workers & people's protests that escalates day by day... yet, it was at that protest, early that he & his rabid associates conjured their enduring luck - 'friendship' ....

*****

(Yet, it is perhaps an illusory luck - you, each - you are all so distracting....)

Jesse pushes a long metal rod into the window of the Treasury, but it was not as effective as the initiative at Millbank.

Besides - the police are always being better prepared, & there are more of them this time, some said that most had come from Bristol (just like Libya & Nato mercenaries), an especially nasty lot - the powers that be always find it better to bring in counter-insurgency specialists from different parts, harness the native xenophobia for the purposes of national security.... they rush Jesse & his droogs away from the window, quite easily - they had already been drinking all day & were too busy laughing to really give the coppers a fight --

('God's away on business', by Tom Waits)

Jesse had other plans anyway, for later in the night - a girl we know is involved - not to mention the plain fact that he really does not have anything against the cops, really - hell, they are only workers in uniform, never completely absorbed by the homogeneity of power.... even the bobbies are facing cuts, & that, from a so-called law & order government...

He & his mates stagger arm in arm through the festivities in the street passing their last bottle of vodka from hand to hand.... no harm done...

They find a nice place to lie down amidst the ecstatic throngs all around - listening to a small cassette player, droning out Flipper & the Melvins.

Jesse dreams of the wilderness, of the threat of nature & the myriad creatures struggling for the light, to stay in the light --- then darkly of rabbits, harnessed into a large engine with wheels, grinded into the machine, metal wheels, blades - the rabbits scream as their fur is torn, severed from the meat & bones...

The droogs awake... it is already evening - they surge amidst this space, event - they hear about the horses which have trampled down the resistance, those faces fighting for their families, communities... 'country' - what do these words mean even now?

They prowl the festivities as hyenas... but they get bored with the containment scenario, easily slip between the fences... out of the kettle for a cup of tea......

'It is already late & the representatives of the people have already sold their souls,' a speaker rants outside of Parliament... Jesse drinks in the event of truth that explodes, he whispers drunkenly

> We are racing, as wind down ever-evanescent streets
> the nymphs are dancing in the sun amid its shadows --
> life, a satyr dance, of magic, viral sex, flesh & blood,
> chaos at the heart of effervescence, these fragile stars

('Anarchy in the UK' by the Sex Pistols)

Trickles are being let out into the ever wider containment zones, given their liberty in the mazes of disciplinary regimes & panopticons - the architextures for the mass psychology of command, control & obedience... reproduction of the Same....

Jesse & his droogs are already running through the streets - sweet wild dogs, passing the bottle back & forth as they dodge in & out of traffic, slap cars like old friends, laughing, 'What is your problem, gov... ever seen a rabid dog play in traffic before?... ' more of the strays begin to converge, unconsciously making their way to the real symbols of ruin, on the high street - a two month Christmas time, the obligatory black mass orgy of sacred consumption, pump priming the economy so that the bankers can get their accursed share, to keep it all going for another year...

though, it is clear & distinct, there is a long term plan... the bowl of utter mustard sausages & beer... proper beer, Becks, Peroni....

The feral children first descend upon Next, smashing the windows, throwing their ugly fashions upon the dirty ground, clothes made by slaves in Third World sweat shops & prisons, sold at a ten thousand mark-up.... the crowd spins like Sufis in celebration, & like sparks of a fire, shoot this way & that in search of new spoils...

('Cherub Rock' by the Smashing Pumpkins)

Jesse is half way across Piccadilly when he stops to take a long drink from the bottle, catches his breath - he laughs, gasping as he sees the drunken rabble running toward McDonald's, setting there with its awesome pristine windows...

But then it happened, that sublime event... Jesse turns his head, hearing a car coming, when he notices that it was a nice old limo, a convoy of them, just like the Royal Family use in their jaunts around London....

As the car comes closer, it suddenly hits Jesse, as he sees them - Prince Charles & his noble wife Camilla.... Jesse screamsss out to the throng, already beating into the glass at MickyD's -

'Oi, Oi!!! Fuckin' come over here, it is the fuckin' Prince of Wales!! Others, Charlie etc. had already noticed this sublime visitation & attack the car - caresses this mass plethora of frenzied hands, screams, 'Stop attacking the people!!! Stop robbing the people!!! It is your government! It is your government! '.... More political hooligans - AK types - come now & rock the car into a convulsion... A pale saint wearing a Tony Blair mask pokes poor Camilla with a stick through the window --- she is too shocked to close her mouth - open like a blow up sex doll...

Gold ole Charlie throws a bin across the windshield.... gets time for his nobility...

('Smash it Up!' by The Damned)

Jesse et co decide to join in the siege of the Royal car in a way that was most proper, given that they had spent the entire day drinking cheap Vodka from California... ah, the irony...

They open their zippers in unison, pull out their rancid cocks & slash against the car, writing manifestos in yellow steam upon the Rolls Royce, that German owned company birthed in the utopian past of the once great Albion.

Laughter explodes from this ecstatic golden showerfest, boyish smiles solidify the sense of sublime purpose - 'The trickle up theory of economics,' noble Conrad, one of Jesse's droogs for the night, shouts as he pisses on the closed window (all to the utter amusement of the Heir to the Throne, as he doesn't support the government, either, certainly not his mother, who continues to rule out of spite).

('Halber Mensch' by einstürzende neubauten)

The streams of piss are losing their steam, & each man works to remove their weapons to their harnesses... Jesse looks around hysterical, quaking with laughter - he pulls his zipper up - SHOCKING PAIN - Jesse winces as a surge of hyper-electric pain explodes from his cock - the zipper catches the delicate skin - but in his drunken morbity, the pain is delayed - instinctively Jesse pulls the zipper harder - by the time he had felt the pain the zip has completely pulled his limp cockskin into its teeth.

Jesse cradles his junk in his hands, running away from the insurrection to a shelter by a small tree, encased in black metal bars.... he inspects his bizarre injury under the street light... he slowly pulls at the sensitive zipper, but it will not come, it is totally attached to his cock, which already bleeds & begins to swell....

Jesse looks back in envy at the convulsions upon the streets -- he is missing it, he still has a cataleptic drunk on, & despite the pain - or maybe even because of the pain - his adrenalin levels would have killed a horse - he takes a pocket knife out of his pocket - begins to gently cut around the zipper that holds the zip attached to his cock.... the zip now adorns his cock like some designer piercing....

He puts the knife away, takes a deep swig from the bottle - ecstatically runs back to the barricades - he hands the bottle to Charlie (son, by the way, of guitarist David Gilmore of Pink Floyd) - who enacted a sublime rampage all of his own -- Jesse et co join the frenzy around the Rolls, clutching the window wheel, the car dances that night before the yellows came & beat the rabid dogs, feral children away -----

The true believers carouse the night, running through Soho, this surreal munchkin land of debauchery, the whores soliciting the solicitors in the heredity facilitation of decadence through our own home-grown sado-masochistic economics... they all surge through the streets, arm in arm, these anarchists in love with the implosion of all that stands.... against those other anarchists who hide behind the mask of power.

('Reprise, What do I get?' by the Buzzcocks)

Jesse blazes through the door, grabbing his cock in his hand - 'Oh, my god... I am fucked - somebody fuckin' call the ambulance!'.... His cock is red, black & blue, swollen to immense proportions... 10 times the size, he could have been a porn star if there was not so much bruising & excruciating pain... even more then, actually - with a differing tag ---

Charlie - the only friend he had left, though he did not know it - puked into the fish tank when he saw Jesse's monstrously abused cock... he gasps, 'That don't look right at all - seriously unpleasant!!!'... Charlie pushes a book at Jesse, *Steal This Book!* by Abbie Hoffmann, the Yippie anarchist assassinated by the Exxon Corporation, 'Cover yourself please, you are really putting me off! now!' Jesse turns beet red, screaming - 'Call the ambulance, mutherfuckers.... this cannot be right... fuckin' hell.... look at it', Jesse held his cock, glistening in the open, naked & in pain....

He rages around in a sublime frenetic circle, his own frantic ghost dance, wishing that he had some good medicine to heal his primal wound...

('Heroin' by the Velvet Underground)

Jesse spies the blissful smack on the table - goes for it in an utter lightning strike - until he notices the rather still friends sitting around & about ...

'They are a bit too still' - Charlie whispers, (a pause of utter horror) 'They are all dead!' he screams from out of the linen closet..... Jesse forgets his cock & pushes each one of them with his hands - 'What the fuck, wake up... what the fuck!!!???' Charlie calls 999 - they are there in an instant, like they were waiting, for this, that, it was obvious, destined.... Jesse collapses near the door holding his cock, waiting for someone to help him.... his recent friends sit there, very still, cold, & dead -.

The corpses are discretely gathered together under a blue plastic sheet as Jesse, the least afflicted, is led into an awaiting ambulance & is taken to King's College Hospital in Camberwell. He had been crashing with a guerrilla film-maker & his crypto-anarchist girlfriend - & their dire friends - it was Karen Carpenter that united them - &, Charles Manson - Jesse was hoping to get his own place soon (but he had to be diplomatic to keep his place) .... all of them were dead ... taken away in body bags --- it would have been better if it had been a mass or group suicide - with a purpose - like a monk setting himself on fire - but, it was just dodgy heroin, poisonous gear..... utter devastation....

'Let me see it!', the nurse demands in the ambulance, 'Come on, don't be shy - I won't bite you!' Jesse opens his trousers, but she still smiles all during the short ride. Jesse clutches desperately at the emergency room bed when the Asian doctor approaches with a large needle of morphine - he can no longer feel anything down there as the doctor pulls the zip off with a pair of pliers... the wound lasted for three months, a black & blue penis, like a Warhol exhibition..... & no sex that involves penises, although there were a few....

Jesse's cock was dead as were his flatmates, the flat itself would eventually be condemned, boarded up, waiting for a slumlord of the future - he walked out of the hospital onto the pavement - across the street, the Maudesley hospital... 'surely at least they will take me in,' he whispers to himself - instead, he walks down Denmark Hill, turns left on Coldharbour Lane and returns to the house of corpses -- The spirit of Jim Morrison interjects on the dodgy CD player, as Jesse sits alone in the dark, nursing a pint of Guinness, sucking on the Shisha pipe in the middle of the room.

('What's he building?' by Tom Waits - Jim Morrison screams - superimpose Monty Python)

'Bring out your dead!'

'Bring out your dead!'

'Bring out your dead!'

'Bring out your dead!'

'Bring out your dead!'

'Bring out your dead!'

'Bring out your dead!'

The dead roommates had been taken unceremoniously to the morgue in the back of a lorry, like a hydrogen bomb that leaves the stuff, but dissolves the people...

Jesse contemplates his next move, alone in a house now full of ghosts.

5 SOPHIA

Sophia is another lost feral soul of the surrealm - in this time of radical change - she succumbs to the urge not to be a slave, serf of debt - obligations tithe so many others who hop through the hoops like good little dogs - she came here to build something - 'The world is broken, the game is no longer a game,' she laughs as she downs her fifth glass of wine. Her happiness beams from her face. 'It is broken & decaying -- can you smell the rotting corpse of the world?', she shouts as she jumps up suddenly & in a single bound opens the refrigerator, clutching another bottle of white wine.

Sophia walks to the sink snatching the corkscrew, 'Do you think that it will all come apart at the seams?' She screws the metal spiral into the cork & pulls - the pop makes her laugh - 'pop goes the weasel,' she shakes in hysterical laughter - 'To entropy & beyond!!!' Sophia toasts as she drinks voraciously from the new bottle... she dances real slow deep in the low side of the road - horses explode...

('You may be beautiful, but you are gonna die someday', by Muddy Waters)

'I love the blues & all, but what we need is destruction - not therapy,' Sophia screams as she throws the empty wine bottle into the excessively large fireplace -

Aire, who has stayed quiet until now, swinging to the rhythm of his private reveries, whispers, slurring drunk, 'I love your voice Sophia - a lovely brash, or a mysterious whisper, rash - but need to say something very pertinent - Blues - Jesus, you have it all insanely wrong - it is not fucking therapy...'

Sophia laughs, asserting, 'Sure it is - that is the whole point - unless I am on crack!'

Aire points to the crack pipe in Sophia's hand, 'Well, dear lady, you are on crack!' (Sophia smiles coyly) 'But,' Aire continues, 'That is besides the point! - No! Blues may help but it is instead an expressive depiction of the tragedy of life - the toil of the mortal soul.'

Sophia laughs again in his face, 'You know rhymes won't liberate the soul,' she still laughs until she chokes through her nose - 'Blues is an explosion,' Aire slurs as he guzzles his Jameson's, 'Not the sentiments of garden flowers in decay, but radical self-expression amidst the tortures of existence - '

Sophia smiles at Aire, 'I do love the blues! Yet - you will never be free --'

'I am already free,' Aire whispers… 'But, there is no beauty in this truth!'

******

('Venus in Furs' by the Velvet Underground)

Sophia is licking, sucking a shot off of Ian's belly as he lay on the bed playing GTA - Ian holds the controller in his hand…. quivering slightly as her tongue enters his navel, deep…. she inserts her finger into his ear….. Ginsberg waits patiently…

She is glad that he is here… at least he fucks her … that is all she wants now -

Ian likes to fuck her too, but always insists that she be shaved, so there are no forests for the cultivation of resistance - wouldn't want to use Napalme --- this was nothing really new for Sophia …. 'Shit, that is what each & every guy ever wants….'….

Sophia holds the red candle in her hand as the wax drips in a circle upon the carpet - 'Look, Ian, it is just like blood!' She splashes the wax across his chest, laughing as he screams…he drops the controller, rolls off of his love seat down onto the floor - 'You fuckin' cunt bitch… you fuckin' goddamed shitty whore'… Sophia laughs even more hysterically, pointing to the bulging vein on his head - 'Don't you like it rough, dear - you make me endure far, far worse?!!!'…

Ian crawls back to the recliner, grabs the hot controller - within a few seconds, he is again transfixed to the game - smoking, always smoking.... picking the wax from off his chest, teasing it out of his chest hair.... Sophia whisks toward the door...

('She's Lost Control' by Joy Division)

She breaks a wine glass setting upon the table by the door, & cuts her wrist with a chard, nothing too serious, just a slight cut, but the blood streams, all the same....

'Look, Ian, it is real blood!' He does not pay any attention to her - she saunters out into the space of all spaces - the crib, the sublime place of the front room....

I sit quietly with this wyrd grunge chick, Deborah, poor victim of the rare condition of Vagina Dentata - I could not talk, but Aire offers her a pipe as she plunges into the futon, demanding to listen to Pearl Jam - 'Alive!'

Blue was at 'work' - if you can call that work..... extortion, slavery, the right word? I was going to pick her up later that night, well really early morning - she had been so upset the last time... it may help if I were there ... at least they would know she has friends, that she is not alone... we can perhaps hope to avoid her showing up in a suitcase in an airport locker....

(The TV in the corner blares out the propaganda line, the coalition this, the coalition that, number 9 & Paul is Dead ---- we begin to regret the wisdom of rioting, looting --- of getting the flatscreen...)

'What's wrong, sweets?' Aire whispers as he strokes Sophia's hair...?....

I write upon my chalk board, 'Tell us...?!'

'It is nothing....', Sophia groans.... she fidgets with her string of earrings on her right ear, 'It is nothing...' She quickly glances at Jesse as he sits drooling in his chair in front of the TV... she turns away, with a sigh -

Aire notices her, & repeats, 'What the fuck are we supposed to do?'......

(He took a massive hit from a wooden bowl shaped like Osiris, the Egyptian god of the dead)

('Anti-Christ Superstar' by Marilyn Manson)

'Do you really want to know?...... -seriously - do you?', Sophia screams......

'We are here together, Sophia,' Aire assures her.

'Everyone is so full of shit! Everybody!', Sophia howls..... 'You too Aire - you are so full of shit!!!!...... it is unbelievable how much shit comes out of all of your mouths!'

'Look at Jesse over there, drooling on himself! You wonder why I am shattered?... - fuck, this is why I do my art..... that is all I have.....

Aire remains silent - neither I nor Jesse could do otherwise....

*****

Sophia was a student of architecture before the shift, the change, the cuts..... Now, forced outside, she makes Shinto temples for the spirits of the dead, small gothic sex idols & jewellery she sells on consignment at a couple of places... She is still on the dole, but also works at the Dog Star under the table...

Sometimes I hear her whispering to spirits late into the night, her room filled with perfumed candles - she whispers so as to not wake Ian who curls up next to her in their bed.... she will listen as if the spirits are speaking to her, waving her arms, fluttering her fingers amidst the impossible visions which the spirits disclose to her.... The spirits, she has often disclosed, also speak to her in dreams - sometimes revealing things that have not yet happened.....

('I drink' by L7)

'I cannot even remember what it feels like to be in that world,' Sophia takes a long drag from Osiris, the sweet bong, crafted by a shaman named Don Juan --- 'It all seemed so simple then, but maybe it is simpler now, or at least clearer...' she blows out a Hiroshima mushroom cloud against the bare light bulb overhead...

'What do you mean, Sophe,' Aire asks taking the bowl from her hands, 'You mean uni? - fuck - it seems a million years ago --- they destroyed that world....'

Aire pops open a bottle of red wine, filling his over-stained glass -'You want some?' She shakes her head pointing to the flask between her legs - her skirt hikes up with her whiskey leaning gently against her black silk thong... her pussy shines metallic...

Sophia looks like a specter as she raises her delicate white hands, corpse arms, her midnight hair streaming into a short black sequenced dress - 'I don't know... that is not how it feels, to me'.... she glides her fingers in strange patterns upon the flask as she gazes at the reflection of her eyes, 'It is more that I was a sleepwalker... asleep, living in a dream - a dream.... that world never was'... Sophia throws her head back beckoning the whiskey down her throat - 'They have destroyed nothing! How can you destroy that which never existed.... just a state of mind, a silly little dream....'

I hold up my chalkboard to Sophia & Aire, sliding my fingers under the line of the words, 'I can barely tell dream from reality'.... Sophia laughs, spitting whiskey onto Aire's naked leg - 'Jesus, girl', laughing like a madman, 'You gotta learn to control yourself, fucking hell...' He wipes his leg with a dirty pillow that had always been on the futon, going back a least a decade.... a sublime painting accumulates on the pillow case, easily mistaken for the latest fashion....

'Yeah, Hugo, I can believe that - you are already quite otherworldly', Sophia evokes darkly... we laugh together like small children....

'It is like a dream - but we ourselves, though outside -- where are we but in a dream within a dream? - there is no thread to guide us out, we are too late --- ' Aire sighs, but remembers his stiff upper lip - he proposes a toast, 'To a better dream, then!' Sophia raises her flask & I clink into theirs with my own stein of 'mead' I made from Golden syrup. 'To a better dream!', I write in my notebook, laughing at my own increasing perplexity of the true reality of existence - a mere dream....

'The dream was... mist in the morning... at the end of the night,' Sophia whispers, gazing deep into her reflection, 'It was vaporised by the fires of arrogance - now all is lost - or at least that social contract... - but what are we supposed to do now? Look at him,' Sophia pointed at Jesse, who was now asleep in his wheelchair, 'Look at what they have done to him! It is a nightmare!' - she digs her purple fingernail into her dainty ivory forearm, drawing a slight stream of blood... 'The mist clears- the mask of anarchy has fallen, these mutherfuckers have shown themselves for who - what - they really are....' Sophia takes another draught of her elixir, then hugs it close to her sweet small breasts... 'WE are rats in a maze whose teeth have been filed down!'

'You are right, my lady,' Aire reacts, 'We are in a maze... but, it is not just that we are contained in a structure, like water through a drain pipe - if that were the case, it would have been quite easy to break out by now... erosion would have been enough to break out.... ' Aire grabs the bag & fills the bowl with nice kind bud, grown by a former nurse, made redundant in the cuts, who now rents out an entire house to grow marijuana - ah, the utterly new world - the new commons - it was not what you expected, wassit - you thought that they would all run to the churches, but instead, they ran to the sweet devil - perhaps that is what you wanted all along, as Saint Augustine fucks his 12 year old bride (is there a statute of limitations for statutory rape .... apophatic orgasm, sin as ritual, the black mass as redemption... grace...

Only 144,000 souls can be saved.... according to your scenario -- the same number incidentally of one of the Mayan cycles of the world....

Sophia, pensive, whispers, 'Actually ... the span is five years.... what a laugh!'

*****

'I know your interests in the lacerations of Psyche,' Sophia explodes suddenly, after a quite long pause --- indeed, amidst an unnatural, catatonic meditation upon her flask... she cries with passion as she bites her pouty lower lip, 'Yet, it is space that truly matters - the utter configurations of space & place... the arche-texture of life, or existence ---- Miike Takashi, for instance - (blood begins to run down from her lip, as she continues to speak without any notice...) you should not discount space, the sacred & profane geographies of life, & how they become fractured -' Sophia grabs the pipe from Aire as she hands her sacred flask to me.... I sip from it slowly, savouring the hot liquid, listening to her elegy...

'Thank you, sweet one', I write on my chalkboard... Aire squirms uncomfortably upon the couch, troubled by his own uncertain thoughts.... after a brief vacuum of time, he drips, 'It is just not space & place - there is so much more, the depths of being, personality - (drunkenly) thought, 'consciousness' the so-called 'god particle' --- even though everything, no-thing exists, suspended upon the unconscious - is this not eternal, in some way? (Ecstatic)

'Like the abyss of that unknown knower beyond & before all & each of us?' Sophia downs another glass of wine, grabbing the pipe, & takes another sublime hit from Osiris..... whispers, 'Why is *this* not eternal?'

'The only thing that is 'eternal' is place, space & spirits' -- Aire slurs -- 'even if it is that, I just do not believe words... ' Sophia cuts herself again, an inch away from her red nipple, 'That is all it is - place - look at the blood, look at the beautiful river that holds our souls.... it is space - & the blood that flows within...'

A quintessence of silence prevails, the little things of existence get a chance to shine.

'We do not wish to think that the land speaks --- that the river speaks to us,' Sophia begins, 'but that is what happens... the river speaks to us.....the Thames - this snake carries our aspirations, screams & sighs' -

Aire sighs again, 'But, we have little contact - if any - with the land, especially in this city - the forests are all sold off - & the parks, come on - we are far from wilderness - we are not even allowed to go to the parks at night!'

'Occupy the parks --- festival the open spaces....' the ten year olds shout as they move out for another operation ... perhaps, we can sub-contract the revolution..... to the very people we are trying to overthrow - they can overthrow themselves, let themselves be overthrown - & thus, they will be spiritualised....

('Holidays in the Sun' by the Sex Pistols)

'That is exactly my point - we are in a trans-generational cage - we maintain the cage, pass it on to our children ...' Sophia snaps, taking another long hit from Osiris - 'It is really worse than that - we are like children in our father's house, it will never be our house though - we are eternal children - we do not even know our fathers... '

'When I was digging tunnels in Newbury, we felt - smelled, tasted - the cold earth upon our hands, under my fingernails - ' Aire clutches at his fingers, 'But even that was part of the labyrinth... they did what they fucking liked & now all that was left is gone --- just sterile, dead --- what they fucking call a "reconstructed landscape"... we pretended we were the fucking Vietcong, we played at revolution & then we went home, just like the protestors at the beginning - if people go home, if we cut off the ever infectious momentum - then it is all over... '

Sophia gazes at the intricate work on Osiris, whispering, 'But, what will we ever get from this utter shit?', as she again gazes longingly upon Jesse, whose eyelids flutter in coma-esque dream... '

('On Land' by Brian Eno)

Jesse walks upon the river, surrounded by countless apparitions, streaming through the flux... he floats toward the land, which also teems with endless spectres - they hover upon the misty earth, whispering incomprehensible mantras -- Jesse suspends between worlds, he still listens to the faint echo of Sophia, not yet a spirit ---

Sophia dances amidst this surrealist topography of primal disclosure, communion - this wild ipseity, suspended between each & all.... 'We are water, we are the water that surges through these banks of the Thames - it all flows through us, it flows us ... we are gestures of dancing water, fleeting faces in the reflective waves - no... no... no - that is not it... -'

She dreams the strangest dreams each night, but she is not naïve - she senses that all of this is an omen - a sign -- but really it is an attempt at an event.... but even if all or something occurs, it is still nothing, as all, each is nothing....

Jesse scintillates the myriad faces of the spirits of the Thames, of London, of the great & small dwellings that stand proud before even the first traces of Albion.... Roaming, restless spirits, neglected, unloved specters .... No one calls our names, a sublime feminine spirit approaches Jesse, no one invokes us any longer, the spirits are fading, holding onto their mantras... The spirit had no mouth but Jesse hears her whispers --

'We are water through dirty drain pipes, flushed through the narrowing possibilities - like bad arteries, we are just pumped through, we take up space, appendages to the matrix, without meaning, purpose - freedom, dignity....' Sophia threw the empty wine bottle across the room, through the doorway into the kitchen ... it crashes into the bin, which rocks slightly, again coming to rest... Aire, too stoned to either jump or react in any physical manner, merely whispers, 'Nice shot, Sophia.... can you get me another bottle?' Sophia laughs, 'Yes, & we will make a toast to Jesse, who still lives free, joyous in his dreams, at least!'

Jesse turns from the spirits, hearing Sophia call his name, in an instant, until nothing

'Baby, can you get me a beer too,' Ian squeaks, still playing GTA.... there was no real end to the game, he had found - Alice & the rabbit hole - he even began to insist people call him Carl - Sophia laughs, 'Sure, I am everyone's fucking sex slave & maid servant - I just love it, the masochistic whore that I am...'

'Listen to the sound of my tool!', Ian barks --- at that instant, Sophia falls over the small end table covered in cigarette burns & empty beer cans..... she collapses hard, face first into the linoleum floor, crashing with sparks in her eyes.... the beer cans cover her like a shroud, cigarette ashes forming a bearded face upon the shroud....

In a glance of an eye, in the moment, Sophia spies Jesse surrounded with spirits savagely drunk with the sublime mist.... he was learning their names.... the specters smile at him...

'Sophia - Sophia - are you alright, hey,' Aire gently shakes Sophia, who was called back to the Squat.... 'They smiled at him,' she whispers almost imperceptibly ... 'Are you o.k. Sophia,' Aire gasps as he pulls her up into a sitting position.... 'They were smiling at him... they were telling him their names....'

'Jesus, what the fuck are you talking about - are you ok - Jesus, god ' Aire struggles the blood drained from her head.... 'What da fuck!'

I showed her my board, with the word, 'Who?'

Sophia seems to awake as from a dream - she looks inquisitively about the room as if it were strange.... 'Jesse..... I saw Jesse.... he was with the others, the spirits'.....

Jesse turns toward her voice, but she could no longer see him.

'Jesse is right there, Sophia,' Aire grabs Sophia's head - turns it toward Jesse, who had now woken up to drool for the day, a droog to drool....

'God.... get the fuck off of me..... fuck off.... it was him - it was Jesse....' Sophia slaps Aire's face ... Aire falls backwards upon the futon, shocked, but laughing.... 'What the fuck, bitch!!!' 'It was him - really him - & not just the vegetable that sits drooling over there!' -

Ian had gotten up to pee, he caresses Sophia's hair as he limps past, 'If you feel bad, I could shoot you?' - he laughs, as he closes the door... He was never the same after his mother scalded him when he was two years old... it was never clear if it was intentional, but he never went to her funeral....

Sophia remembers Ian - & her life - after the Fall - she sighs.... 'It was so clear... so very real, he was trying to tell me ...' She grasps the bottle from the floor & falls back into the futon next to Aire & me... blood trickles down her face but she does not care at all... 'They hover over, this earth & the water - they were here, where we are now -- but there were no buildings... '

Aire eases the bottle of wine from her, 'You hit your face pretty damned hard, no wonder you are seeing spirits,' he laughs as he pops the cork. Sophia closes her eyes, whispering, 'No... I saw him.... it is the buildings, all the buildings that are in the way of a different world... It all comes down to architecture, at the end of the day,' she whispers, 'as has always been the case --- & the fucking spirits who will always contest this space....

Sophia descends to her knees & grasps a little Shinto house - she begins to paint it in a manner that is appropriate to the specific amulet in question.

'We must learn to forget, to forget - but that can mean only one thing…'

6 AIRE

('Turn the World Around' by Gomez)

Aire did not really wish to be here at all - he had dreamed of California when he had once much nobler, allegedly more profound goals - visions of his ascending into the eschelons of higher mortal beings - but that was like a haze that clears --- poetry was now his life & taking care of Jesse... he went out to Berkeley for about a year, but it was not the needy, reckless elegy of Kerouac.... though, some of it was the same, if you had the money.... background checks, credit weightings & first, last months rent, not to mention the ever inaccessible deposit.... or, of course, you could just sit down upon the streets, eating leftovers all day long from the excessive restaurants - sleep in People's Park at night..... Occupy Poet's Corner!!!!!!!

('Cold drink of water blues', by Tommy Johnson)

The rumoured Buddha of eco-terrorism - he probably would have been a Christian Fundamentalist, Islamic Militant - Dharma Bum - underneath - if born in a different petry dish - But, that was before - he is not an eco-terrorist now, but one perplexed at having transgressed the utter limits of Reality - his poison had been the Mayan San Pedro, he would tell us sometimes, 'I opened the gates of Hell itself, but I found my way back, unlike the noted St Paul who roamed freely throughout Berkeley -- St Paul had been given liquid acid as punishment for his rape of a hippy girl - after that, he walked quite aimlessly, peeing freely in traffic, walking down Telegraph Avenue with his cock out - first, as a ritual - but, the dire dreaded property companies have since succeeded in their long quest - cleared out the riff-raff - it is just like Disney now... you need to go to Oakland now to see anything interesting....

Aire had not really done anything that direct of late - besides his destructive poetics of incitement at the various large events in London --- though he did finally act - 'Why in the hell St. bloody Paul's,' he compulsively scorns - & fatefully go down to convince those Occupying St Paul's to move to Trafalgar Square.... a much better place - & with a more profound historical, political and aesthetic significance.... not to mention the utter possibility of cataleptic symbolism....

(Silence)

"They came to my house - I was already drunk. I just met them,' Aire once reflected upon his entrance into the world of the political, 'I went with them to a protest in our town about toxic waste - the fuckers wanted our town to bid on the storage of toxic waste! A rather dark day for our kingdom.... We become the untouchables -

We are truly feral children... - but, is it any fucking bloody surprise as we merely survive utterly outside Soma World across the reservation?...

I wish that I could say this to be heard... but, I am effectively silent...

('L.O.Y'. by Beenie Man)

Aire was in the squat since nearly the beginning... he returned to sublime Brixton after wandering with travellers across, under Newbury, with animal rights protesters against vivisection at Huntington Life Sciences, G20 meltdown, Financial Fools - it is all a blur now but he loved the tactics, skills, stratagems - visceral feelings - praxis of an extended, experimental community amid an ultimately ironic struggle -- at least when they were not totally intoxicated on hallucinogenic plants or the most beautiful sativa.... even the blind shaman needs a community... his tribe....

In this spirit, the squat seemed to coalesce around him after he broke down the front door of an abandoned building.

He had been aloof for many years, but always was still writing - deep in his thought of existence, his useless art -- he was not Lord Embeseltine with his bankers - they were in it after all for the usual - coke & under-aged whores, strangled slaves - cannibalism cleansed by some cleaner no one knows -

Aire was the one who first opened the door to me - to the sublime things in this life .... subversion, dissolved hierarchies, & the impossible ....

utter rebellion, insurrection as we are well aware of the intrinsic failure of the current alleged [system] of political economic - social, etc, etc.... organisation/orchestration... so we do not really have to dwell upon the obvious, though even this has its moments -

the failure, if you could call it that - perhaps, tunnel-vision would be better - this inflicted the movement at an early stage - the remoteness of failure began to lend itself to a utopian denial of the simple facticity of this planetary technological fact - especially of the urban/suburban cathexis... it was enslaved to the social network prison - the youface control regime......

'Just realise that these stupid muthafuckas will come after you ..... you need to fight!'

Aire laughs in the faces of the ten year olds - who are themselves far beyond Aire & his sometimes politics of drug addled nostalgia....

*****

At an earlier stage Aire became perplexed by the glue epidemic among teenagers - almost as a privileged symbol for the rotten decadence of post-industrial culture --'There are so many great drugs out there - alkaloids - in plants --- why in the hell would anyone desire to sniff glue or - for fuck's sake - petrol.... why are so many teenagers killing themselves, devoid of hope amidst this nihilistic dispersion'... he would shout to the sky ---- he tried, like the Lincoln Detox Center in New York City around 1969, run by the Black Panther Party (even though it successfully cured addicts with acupuncture, it was forcibly shut down & replaced by a Methadone Clinic) to educate youth about alternatives to glue, with a deep Shamanic message...

But then there is Butt Hash - of course --- but, do you not know, dear friend, about butt hash? Shall I tell you? It is very simple, really. It is a recipe, like a necromancer's cauldron... these Florida teenagers put their own feces into an American gallon milk jug of water (yeast helps) & let it ferment --- when it is ready, they breathed in the methane gas on top & saw dead people - spirits - for a day or so ---

I cannot contain myself,

> velo da bang b& affalo purzamai affalo purzamai lengado tor
> gadjama bimbalo gl&ridi glassala zingtata pimpalo ögrögöööö

I scream, scaring most of the ten year olds working as a machine, except for Luce, who still sits in the corner, reading the Dada Almanac....

('Alice', by Jefferson Airplane)

This poem was among the things discovered after his disappearance on that night of destiny... some say he descended into Hades to hang with the great old man himself ... there was a note on the text that documented that it was performed 'under the stars in the night air on the Brixton Square by two simultaneous non-linear voices - Aire & the Aussie Peter Narcissus - emerging intrinsically from a wild musical context, lifeworld, performed by Jezebel, a local Shamanic drummer -'

```
d amiana aphrodisia & pagan
 ph ilosophy joyrides, Corrupt
the  Youth!, lovely boys & girls,
    snif fin' their tubes of glue,
tell  them the supple truth, or
sed     uce their voracious curiosities
    r uptive magical resemblances
& YOU go tta loot those rich people's
houses! D rive them to the shore! &
see how these ethereal feelings
  converge i nto chiasmic ecstasy
as   you sing  delirious screams
& b uy 10 pac ks of heavenly
blue  morning glory seeds
soak  in water 3 daze                or
chang e  water 3 per diem              soak
to get rid of poison coating         wormwood
& mercury preservatives              ipomea
that cause horrible days             skunk
 of delirious vomiting               pernod
t ake my word for it &               make
 even better, grow your own seeds        absinthe
you  can get hundreds of seeds       (add
f rom a single vine                  calamus
le t them dry out & then             root
grind them up, about 300             hyssop
to  600 seeds til you get            valerian
a peppered cornflower                etc.
t extured powder place               ginseng
it  in a bottle of cold              ground
```

Of the Feral Children

wat er release built-up air pressure
once a day or it will explode!
& soak for three days
strain & drink this strange
pi nk or red or brown or black
it all depends on the seeds
liquid suddenly slows me down
 or throws or sends me
i nto a differing temporal
 doma in rhythmic/visual visceral waves
mushr oom plasticity rain dance torrents
storm clouds lightning sutures sever
e arth sky night & eat cactuses of
a plethora of possible tribes
 ha llucinogenic encounters windows
doors gatwwaaays eat roasted
mammillaria (peyote substitute)
 drink san pedro & smell vaginas &
c ocks fifty feet away BE PHYSICAL! &
ta lk to dead German students
killed in munich in 1943
gu illotined for subversion &
o ne of their philosophy
professo rs who stands
a mong the few german   with
p hilosophe rs who   Kurt
saw fit to rebel - if   Huber
yo u don't th row away
yo ur love of ultra-comfortable
 security, cas t it to the wind
& begin your e cstatic journey
towards nothingness amidst
t his singular c hance,
you will miss this fragile
opening, a spark in the Night,
 you may not suffer much, w/ your
tube of glue & a ll, having kept
P &ora's box securely fastened,
you place your na sty little
' truth' deep down i n the dark cellar
b ut some time soon - all at once -
yo ur secrets will bu rst out
in to this open, beyon d your control,

                         fennel
                         seed
                         ho
                         shou
                         wu
                         smoke
                         hops
                         graft
                         hopsvine
                              onto
                              marijuana
                              & grow into
                         hops with THC
                         put this into beer
                              w/ poppy
                         pipes (capsules)
                              or,
                              justsmoke
                              DMT
                              & see
                         elves
                         playing
                         flying
                         pianos

                         stroking
                         da
                         ebony
                         &
                              ivories

                         horse
                         blinders

71

your docile soul will vent its vindictive   hide
 revenge as cancer eats away at your face,   your face
gnawing a way that nose y ou stick   away deep
up a nazi's asshole so y ou can   behind fumes
get paid & you will sit around & sniff   of glue
  your glue, drink your lag er & die of aids   effervesce
or brain damage & it really doesn't   blood drowned
matter if you do or if you don't   secrets
what's the value of a life   wash away
these days anyway? out of the   awareness
ine xplicable vortice of   blind spots
eter nal cosmic oblivion   deafening
a light glistened over the waves   silence
of time, throughout the eons   announces
of ex istence, across the   death
intricate lacework of   extinction
su blime evolutions &   of the old
 revolutions, until   ways, long tried
thi s surge of being   & true, poiesis
arri ved here, with me   & shamanic tribes
& you & your tube of glue &   erases all
my yell ow broom flowers,   continents
mixed in equal parts w/   nihilo ratio
nicotiana , lobelia, datura   slashes its
& colt sfoo t (smoke like a   way across
joint) & we   shrug our shoulders   rights of
& we ju st can 't get our heads   sacred
around i t anyw ay since   perception
we just drank a   one genocide
  kava kava cock tail,   to the next
grind up a few grams   murder is our
of the root & soak   daily bread &
it in coconut milk   our life
strain & drink)   we are farmers &
& feel really   producers & dealers
chilled out   of death
for
   3 hours

Aire lives, dies his ultimate nausea in the homogeneity of the dire simulacrum - even activist circles are more often than not fuck circles - he has always respected the rare - the noble radicals & revolutionists.... he had been utterly disappointed, frustrated by the remoteness of these ideas from any contact with the world - by the near suicidal intensity of the radical dreamer - but surprise, the magical happened, with a few false starts --- the breach of homogeneity, the rebirth of the heterogeneous uncertainty of the tragic, of the riot of the soul in the streets - not merely words or action but transfiguration --- he became fascinated by the psychology of revolution long ago, of each & all of its eruptions - now he sees revolution as a gesture of the primordial... a spark that needs to be nurtured into a prairie fire....

He delved into studies, magical, philosophical, ethnographic & poetic in tandem with his ever more daring dangerous deadly pharmaco-shamanic experiments... but, that was well before my time - this was his neighbourhood after all .... he was coming home, to his place.... 'Brixton makes the novel possible, it is the origin & destination of every mad soul,' Aire toasts the chaotic room full of drunken tripping beasts.... the ten year olds pay no mind, but continue on with their opaque work...

The Chalkboarders are already beginning to come - they congregate in the streets below the windows of the squat..... waiting... with cryptic & ominous words, inscribe, 'The Vortex of Spirits will Swallow All....'

'The poets will liberate the Chorus as they retrieve their voices with the Event....' Luce whispers in her corner, unbeknownst to all....

('Critical Beatdown' by the Ultramagnetic Mcs)

'The first night I was back,' Aire laughs, as he hands the bottle to me, 'I was shattered by a frenzied desire - to find the kind of girl who - with her very being - must prove the existence of the gods, goddesses... ' - I concur that the only persuasive proof of the existence of the divine is a beautiful girl,' Aire puts on another mocking voice as there are no others to speak -' - ---- 'Oh, Yes! Yes!! Yes!!!!' Sophia intervenes faking an orgasm - ' is there any other, more persuasive proof for that which we seek??? What about the gay guys running around ---- they would prefer a beautiful boy ---'

Blue stammers in abruptly, tear stains all the way to her vagina, massacre streams dried down to her mouth - crusted blood upon the edge over down her chin - she does not look at us - she seems bad, injured, her hair stretches dry crusted, her dress torn - she limps, claws toward her room, disappears, closing the door quietly....

'She really needs to get a new job.... ', Aire manically giggles - his loss of control, inappropriate jokes, an utterly unfortunate tonic in times of stress.... he was once hypnotised, after a teenage suicide attempt, to laugh at tragedy... 'Those guys are really fucking her, OMG!' - he descends into drunken hysterical laughter, 'Is this what it is after all - our sublime chance has come to - a fucking hell!!?'

('Is that all there is?' by Peggy Lee)

Of course, she was not the first sex worker to dwell in the squat - who could forget Misty & Sasha before they made it big - a nice location just near the main drag.... of course, there were the monthly raids by the pigs - but they would not dare to shut them down at this point - too much money - too much pussy - too much violence -

'The sacrifice of everyday life..... attempts, an underground internalised violence as the heterogeneous, it is still there but ferments under the asphalt pavement...' Luce whispers in the reading corner, but, like Cassandra, no one hears her.... eventually, she moved to Roanoke, works as an All-State agent &, in her free time, investigates the secret of the lost colony - the first in the new world, one which disappears in utter mystery... 'I know what happened...' Luce drools in ecstasy....

Aire screams - completely in the dark of Luce or anyone else, 'All on digital video - everyone is being blackmailed -----' he spins... 'How else could you explain any of the last 50 years of politics?!!! -- can anyone offer me a better explanation???'

I push my chalkboard into his face - 'They ARE raping her, & worse!' Sophia claws at the board & reads it in shock - 'She never fucking talks to me - I remember how happy I was when she arrived... -- I do not know what it is... ' she sighs, again grasping my board, scratching her long black fingernail across the slate, gazing deep into the ice in her glass... 'I want to rip their balls off with my teeth!!!', Sophia erupts as a merry volcano, terrifying a few drunken half-men....

'Very nice image, Sophe', Aire gurgles in his hissing laughter.... 'But, I will admit that the primordial beckons amid your lips, as your desires!' Aire loads gentle Osiris in the ensuing thoughtful silence... there was a calm, as if each of us knew - but were only waiting for our expression of the tragic - nay, absurd, comic existence -

Sophia slinks down upon the futon, gazing at the luciferan glow in the dark stars that someone had, at some time, stuck to the ceiling... 'I have lots of desires.... but, they are in conflict all the time ---- I desire pleasure - but I never feel any.... it always is out of touch – but...' - she dazes in reflection –

'thought - there are many kinds of pleasure.... each with its own room.... I hate everyone sometimes, especially men - & even more those ones... '

'Thank you for sharing sweetie,' Aire laughs, 'but, could you do me a solid & change Jesse's nappy?'

'Never!' Sophia expresses, in total oblivion now to Aire, in the most calm manner, 'Never, never again! 'They are going to kill her!'

I hold up my chalkboard... in frustration, but as no one looks, I scream

> elifantolim brussala bulomen brussala bulomen tromtata
> viola laxato viola zimbrabim viola uli paluji malooo

"Then, why in the fuck does she do it --- she could do anything!',' Sophia contests...

'We take pleasure in scratching mosquito bites until they bleed - we pick off scabs - we love pain, though some more than most!!!' Aire laughs, taking a swig from a Guinness he suddenly found, open, in his hand - 'Cheers, darling!' 'My pleasure, but it is selfish - you only get more amusing the drunker you are.... ' 'I am not drunk, or that drunk - but, I do not want merely to be your silly amusement - or - do I? - this seductive witch's brew of pleasure & pain.... ' he sings, 'We like pleasure, but we love pain..... & that is why things stay the same -'

'I cannot believe you sometimes - the shit,' Sophia rages, laughing, 'shit, shit, shit that comes out of your fucking shitty mouth!!!'

'No, no - I have thought hard about this.... ', Aire erupts laughing - 'No, no - stop - wait a second - just let me say this one thing...... ' Sophia throws an empty Smirnov can at Aire's head, which makes a distinctive, though indescribable sound.... 'A gift of pain for you, slave!'

('Venus in Furs' by the Velvet Underground)

'It is the dissolution of the self in intoxication, eroticism & death which provides us with our only glimpse, touch, feeling of the sacred,' Aire takes a sip from the sublime Jameson fountain, wiping his mouth with his sleeve, '... the root of our masochistic impulse to lose ourselves in the communion..... ' he takes another drink & hit of Osiris, quiet & seeming to search for the best words.... grows into the branches of our utter distraction, the bureaucratic methods to control distraction - 'We darkly crave pain - we seek it out - yet --- & this is the same, utterly the same - we also crave to inflict pain, to be the sadist... I use to - use to - last year , with a metaphor - I felt that we could think & do differently.... all is vanity...', laughter erupts from Aire's mouth, 'There is no secure, convenient deus ex machina, safe escape at the end.... there will only be disaster!...' Sophia slaps Aire across the face hard, but, he finishes his ranty thought, '&, all that is Good, bitch! It's all good, all good - it's all good, muthafuka!!!"

'It is wonderful & right to romanticise ultra-violence,' Sophia verbalises, laughing, waving her arms in Aire's face, 'We have seen this before -- Shakespeare, Coleridge, Keats, Shelley etc. - Rossetti, etc, etc...all the way to us ... but, I do not really want to hurt anyone, & I do not wish to be hurt - I enjoy the Leviathan between each, & all - the architexture of tranquil existence...'

'But, you are a Dominatrix - & incessantly,' Aire queries in the tone of a clown, 'engage in BDSM sexuality with you mad C.J. --- are you not - too - full of shit? You yourself just called for the destruction of architecture!!!'

Sophia suddenly becomes stone cold serious - the room seems degrees colder as the Goddess Silence looms - intersperses this dire front room.... 'But, but, ... look at him', she points at Jesse, 'Look at him! That is violence.' Jesse, brain injured, lounges in his wheel chair on the public purse, subject to weekly interviews ('OK, still drooling, see you next week...').... a suspended spirit in the ancestral economy, 'I am alone.... vanish, fade into oblivion --- if... (the snipers are already in place)

> if you do not invoke my precious name

No one invokes his name - but, each increasingly begins to refer to him as an object, a what, or an it.... That he still exists, alive, no longer has any hold since all hope is lost - although, the Compensation has made him an ironic millionaire.... he left the whole lot, in trust, to the ten year olds, in case of death or mental degeneration...

'I think you have missed my perspective altogether - & Jesse is the best example of my perspective - he is the exemplar, the poster-child..... ' Aire drains Mr. Jameson's down his throat without even a flutter of an eye lash... he has lost his gag-reflex...

'Hail to Jesse,' Sophia toasts, as the object of the roast silently drools upon himself...

Jesse slightly awakes with the mention of his name, but quickly falls back into oblivion

Yet, it is only oblivion from our temporal situation --- the gods & goddesses are on holiday

I snatch the bottle & - throw it to the ground - across the wall, shatters into the old stone, disproportionately large fireplace - we laugh together amidst this pathetic explosion.... 'Next time try a glass milk bottle, barbecue lighter fluid with a flannel for a wick!' Aire laughs - it is called a cream cap....

Jesse smiles as I inhabit the gateway of the moment - 'Hey, what's up?' 'Yeah, alright - just swarms with an ectoplasmic intimacy -- in Hell, there are no rights of privacy ---

'That is not a bad scenario for any lost soul,' Luce whispers again, 'One whose walls were, as if of glass...' - she crawls over to the flatscreen, puts on a DVD about Hypatia... raped & skinned alive by a Christian Mob.......

Jesus hates most Christians....

('The Grunge' by RZA)

'I was the one that brought him here in the first place.... I remember the first time I saw him --- ' Aire pops up toward the kitchen, stroking Jesse's shoulder as he sails past ...

He emerges with a bottle of Absinthe & a tub of ice, brown sugar & limes - & three glasses - methodically, he places three ice cubes into each glass, gently bathes them with his elixir.....

'I can only drink whiskey with ice, preferably crushed --- ,'Ian scoffs as he travels to pee, 'But I am much too lazy for that... love it all the same... especially with little bits of peyote mixed in'... Ian saunters into the kitchen, slashes like a horse in the sink - he returns, perhaps expecting an unwanted invitation, but sees no opening, returns to their room... the door closes into concealment...

'How did you meet Jesse, Aire?', Sophia asks in her state of innocence... she had only just arrived, really, but had been close with Jesse - & did not know much beyond the drunken conversations she had with Aire & myself (although, unfortunately, I am never really been much in this area) mostly about the contestation on the streets, the protests & the horse blind sleepwalkers & their officious demagogues.... but, that came after, as if despite the months together she had never known him at all....

'The first time,' Aire's breath cast gestures of condensation upon the ice cold glass, 'was at one of the protests - he & one of his mates almost tackled me after I read a poem - slurred in his drunken bliss that I was the best poet on the planet.....' (Aire laughs, sipping his potion) 'He howled into the air with his arm upon my shoulder... I drank freely from his bottle of vodka - then he kissed my cheek, & ran off with his fellow weather undergrounds toward the Treasury Building - I did not expect to ever see him again....'

Aire grabs the bottle of Absinthe & replenishes our glasses -

I hold up my board to Aire & Sophia, 'You will see him again?'

Sophia bursts out laughing as she is hitting Osiris, spitting on me & Aire, 'What the fuck - of course he saw him again', she chokes, 'We can fucking see him fucking now!' still dumn, maybe just happy ... we explode with laughter in the contagious event, 'Jesus, Sophia, you are a disgusting bitch!' I laugh at Aire's ridiculous face as he pretends to be repulsed by the snot on his leg, 'You cast out your darkness, your vile stench, decay, upon my trousers!' 'For fuck's sake, Aire --- 'trousers' - shit, they are not even pants...' Sophia interjects, 'Fuck, when was the fucking last time you washed those fucking things - in your utter state of degradation' (convulses laughter)

('Total Exposure' by the Poison Girls)

'Say "FUCK" enough, you dirty whore?' Aire barks laughing in Sophia's face, 'Take your snot back, slut', Aire wipes the snot laughing & some spit on Sophia's nose.... At first she is utterly shocked, taken aback... shouting 'You muther fucker - I cannot believe you put snot on me!' But, then Sophia - realising that it was her snot after all & that she did not have a leg to stand on - lunges onto Aire, pushing him down across the futon..... she constrains his arms over his head with her knees & slaps his face, first the left, & then the right - 'You are my bitch now!' She tickles his sides, he squirms, laughing hysterically, spitting, gagging - but he could not free himself --- suffocates - 'Please, please stop, Sophia... please, this is torture ...'

All at once, she stops, placing her face close to his, gazing deep into his eyes, 'You want torture, muthafucka I will fucking give you torture, your season in Hell - I will give you my utter darkness, my vile stench, decay... ' She pushes her pussy into his face holding his head between her thighs, 'How do you like that, is that vile enough for you pervert - I haven't showered in six days, muthafucka! She suffocates him! Drink in my rabid abjection, drink it!' Sophia pisses in Aire's face like a pony, 'Drink it, drink my waste, my cast offs - who's a dirty whore, who's a slut, now, fucker!!!,' she roars laughing, but in the ecstasy of transgression, she becomes psychotically dizzy, falling - all at once - over onto the floor - she cracks her head on the edge of the coffee table & comes to rest upon the floor, her legs spread, with a slight smile upon her face.....

('Circus Maximus' by John Corigliano)

I sit catatonic, transfix to her exposed flower, still with little drops of dew clinging to fine blond hairs... it is clear now that she was not a natural Goth -

Aire wipes his face with the remnants of an anarchist newspaper, *The Shadow*, from the East Village of NYC --- I get sent airmail on subscription, the best newspaper --- he nestles again upon the futon with his forearm leaning against his eyes, 'Fucking crazy bitch, I swear to god...... the fucking craziest ---- fucking nasty pussy too... if only some day, I will strangle her to death!'

I hold up my board, 'But, her pussy is beautiful, mystical'....

'Yes - but dirty all the same... ' Aire stands gazing upon Sophia in her unconcealed openness..... He clutches at the ice tub - tilting it precariously over Sophia ... I felt chills running up --- down my flesh in anticipation.....

The water at first trickles upon her face lightly, then it streams across her breasts, the remains of the ice falling upon her gentle torso and legs...

Sophia at first squirms, but suddenly, as if by the power of an ancient forgotten art, screws to her feet - she clutches Aire by the throat, draws close to his eyes, whispers, 'Cheers for waking me, lover.... (laughing demonically) -- 'I would not want to miss anything,' she slaps his forehead, plunges back down upon the futon.... her fragrant beaver devastates without care or shame, as the most naive & natural thing......

'So where are/were we?' Sophia smashes that glass ceiling, down onto the table, 'Fill me up!' 'Now, you are fucked....... I have a whip!'

Aire picks a few ice cubes off of the floor, wipes them clean on his trousers & puts them into Sophia's glass.... 'Here you go, sweet lassy, 'This potion will take away all of your problems - for tonight...'

I hold up my glass for a toast, raising my board, 'To Jesse!'
I jump upon the table, speaking from my heart,

zimzim urullala zimzim urullala zimzim zanzibar zimzalla zam!

Aire & Sophia - nonplussed - raise their glasses, shouting manically, 'To Jesse! To Jesse!'

Jesse turns toward the invocation, bending slightly, returning...

'So, motherfucker, are you going to tell us the big story - how you brought Jesse to the squat?', Sophia insists, still free of shame as her pussy glistens in the light of the candle.... 'He never got around to telling me, or talking much at all...'

Jesse claws as if through an everlasting fog, awake, without orientation, but moving...

'That is not the most interesting thing, or the most devastating', Aire sips his Irish whiskey, holding a piece of ice upon his tongue before crunching it away.... 'It was the next afternoon that he called me ---- I had given him the poem he liked, it had the number already on it, & the email....'

'So, boy, did he ask you out on a date? Did you suck his black dick?', Sophia giggles uncontrollably, nearly smacking her head again upon the table....

'No - I did not suck his dick --- he was in a hysteria of numb - he told me that all of his flatmates were fucking dead, from dodgy heroin ---

'Fucking hell!' - I held up my board, as the cats cry outside over mere territory....

'No doubt, they were all dead,' Aire continues, 'Just sitting there in the front room... a surrealist event... he asked if he could stay with me - he was sporting a huge bandage between his legs, from some unspecified injury.'

'What the fuck!', Sophia belches like a dirty whore, 'Two questions.... what the fuck? & what da fuck? Jesus, Mohammed, Buddha, Zeus.... ',

Sophia squirms as she lunges after the bottle of Jameson's, & almost magically, returns the bottle - her glass full, with ice... 'First off - Dude! - dodgy heroin???? all of his flatmates dead????? & then.... you, the smartest of men --- let him come stay with you???? What the fuck???' (she laughs ever more demonically, ironically then usual...)

(Sophia baits Aire as she could almost not control her laughter).

'That is history, as they say.... ' Aire finishes his glass, & nervously pours another, picking ice from the carpet..... 'I wonder some times... worry... about the intricate dance of events.... if I had just not answered the phone... it may have been quite different.... '

'Don't be daft! It was great for me. You could not have been responsible for this - for Jesse', Sophia slides her finger through the air in his direction....

'I do not know.... you do not know the whole story, or at least many threads,' Aire gazes into the red candle dancing wildly upon the table.... 'How could it have possibly been good for you?'

'Well - neither do you know everything, my decadent Aire! At least nothing when it comes to me & your crippled friend....' Sophia asserts, smiling.... '

Blue's door opens suddenly, but she is not there, at first.... there is darkness until her figure shadows, tentatively.... slow into the darkness of light.... she is crying - slides straight into the bath without even a look towards us... I want to go to her - & say to her ---- but it all comes out wrong.... I have lost my voice -

But, I exclaim, nevertheless, with empty hands,

tuffm im zimbrabim negramai
bumbalo
negramai bumbalo tuffm i zim
gaga di bling blong
gaga blung

no one could possibly understand me....

but that is simply the point, for all of us --
we either have no voice or we are simply feral -

a novel dispensation needs not submit to zombies -
for they are zombies, & we are the wanderers
upon the Road, seeking an impossible place
an ironic utopian paradise

Modern Times

Smile!

7 NOTES FROM THE UNDERGROUND I

('Cowboys' by Portishead)

'They do what they like,' Blue whispers into the candle.... there were obvious bruises on her face - all over her body - ligature marks on her neck, wrists & ankles... waist - tracings of whip marks recede beneath her white lace dress.....

'I will get through this....' she turns to me, rests her head upon my chest...

I scratch across my board, 'What did the fuckers do to you?'

'That is not the right question - you should ask "What didn't they do to me?"!!!', Blue laughs nervously, sipping at the bottle like a sublime baby...

'U don't have to tell me', I show her my board...

She is the one in the picture... I will never forget that - She looks into me...

'Perhaps, it is a time for madness,' Blue grabs the bottle of Jameson's, setting by my bed.... after a long draught, she clutches at my arm, 'You cannot imagine!'

'No', I inscribe upon my tablet.....

'They took me
But, it was not -

it was different
than the usual
chauvinist humiliation -
a different look in their eyes
these bankers, stockbrokers -
business men (& some women,
I guess their gaudy mistresses,
perhaps a few adventurous wives)....
in the Underground...'

She lies upon my bed - I long hesitantly for her touch --- to touch her, to drink from her fountain --- I fear that I will become a pathetic unrequited slave to an impossible hope --- but, this has never been my way ----

'It is always getting worse - the abuse - ' Blue cuts her arm with a penknife....

('Riot' by the Dead Kennedys)

'There were so many of them all around - they kept touching, pinching me all over -- I panic when the alpha grasps my neck - he claws, a bird of prey -

'He clutches my hair - a ponytail, handcuffs, mouth gag - a droopy tiny cock, power, brute force... (hisses) over-compensation...' Blue sobs - but in a flash, smiles, 'Shit - no fucking wonder all the dykes, feminists have butch hair --- wish I would had known, before my sweet blonde locks became my own harness....'

Blue walks around the room frantic - the cats screech outside, feeling her rage....

'It is always getting worse....' she clutches at my shoulders - she comes close to my eyes - she looks into my abyss....

'Look at me!... look at me!....' Blue turns over, gazing toward the stars across the water stained ceiling...

('Kool Thing' by Sonic Youth)

'I don't wanna, I do not think so,' - Blue sings with Kim Gordon, though realising her own irony & humiliating degradation - Kim would not be happy or proud...

Kim would prescribe more radical measures, as is her way....

Blue muses amidst her despair - raw bubbling anger, listening, singing the words, feeling the ethereal sublimity of the music....

A tiny light begins to breathe inside of her, a single spark - she looks to the prairie...

('Elysium' by Portishead)

'At first they smile, acting gentlemanly... I can barely remember that ... those first days.... long ago - for after all, I came recommended because of my family - I was a near celebrity in the stripper world -- a legend, even.... & I had not even stripped yet - but I was born into it!'

'But, why do you do it - even now - especially now?', I raise my board to her.....

Blue winces at my question - turning away from me, my face,

(silence)

'Ever since I was a little girl
I was fascinated by the dancers --
the way everyone looked at them - '

Blue takes another long drink, gazing into the candle

'My mother was a dancer - or, she wanted to be a dancer - she was enrolled in the London School of Dance - 1987, I think - she was a teenager with big dreams... great fucking expectations, ' Blue laughs cynically, 'Isn't that always the way with people like us... --- hell, she thought that she was going to get a scholarship to the Royal Academy of Dance.... that is all she talked about....'

'What do you mean: people like us', I wrote....

'You know - us - the poor losers who still believe the fucking lies!'

I nod my head, staring at the floor - I knew what she meant.....

'She paid for her dance classes one at a time with money she made working as a waitress at a flavoured soda shop - after school, everyday --- then she would go to dance - her relief & bliss before she came home to her drunken mother...'

'Did she take dance at her comprehensive', I scrawl....

'Fuck no - they didn't have anything like that - barely anything beyond what might get you a job as a secretary, or if you were lucky, a nurse... '

'No, it was her dream but it wore her out - no one really looked after her - her own mother was a nervous wreck drunken whore, her father never - well he died when she was a baby, that is at least what they tell her - it was all fine until she collapsed during a recital...'

'Exhaustion?' I write....

'If it were that easy,' Blue sighs, 'No, she was pregnant - with me - she was only seventeen.... '

'Did she have a bloke... what did she do?', the generic human in me asks the typical question, in line with the latest quality standards.....

('Pennyroyal Tea' by Nirvana)

'He' - she told me the story one night when she was plastered - 'One of my mother's fucking boyfriends - one of her fucks - staggered into my room once while I slept & he raped me --- he laid down 10 quid on my nightstand with a smile - I laid in my bed for two days crying - (sighs, squelching a scream) I finally conjured up my courage to tell my mother. She responds to my cry for help by slapping me across the face ----'..... Blue punches down hard upon the table, the ashtray & the infinite bottles of alcohol - bongs begin to dance upon the linoleum surface, 'then she fucking threw me out on my ass --- an auspicious event.... '

'Jesus Christ!', I write upon my board.....

'He had nothing to do with it...' she laughs -'I would rather have been fucked by Jesus - at least he was a man!!!,' Blue laughs demonically, 'That was only a little tiny part of it!!! Imagine (the fucking whore, my grandmother - who I have never even fucking really met) - called her a Jezebel, gave her all kinds of shite about my wretched sinfulness --- fucking hypocrite!!! All she does is natter on all day long, in any, every situation -

Jesus, Jesus jesusususujesjesejjsejsh - but Jesus, though he would have hated her, would have forgiven her all the same --- for after all, he is Jesus... though he said privately she is a prudish Philistine whore... - but again, he, being the guy he is, forgives her, ' Blue, deep in her nearly psychotic revelry, simply explodes with a sublime laughter that erupts from her darkest regions...

'What did she do?', I ask....

'What in the fuck do they do now - shit, for some girlz, it remains the best option for social mobility - other than all-out prostitution & porn - she went to the surgery & the DSS spending her evenings filling out the prohibitive forms --- she decides to go on the fucking dole & live the fucking life... ', Blue laughs again with acerbic irony, '& what a fucking life it is - 40 quid a week - it is an eternal shame for the Nation that we cannot pay our parasites more - are we so weak?!!!!'

'Did she stay in school?', I ask.....

'No fucking way - what was the point?.... She kept dancing though ---- but after a couple of months, it became clear that she has lied about a stomach bug.... they asked her not to return, as 'her condition' would reflect badly upon the school... different times, the Thatcher years - Now, of course - 'they' sell their story & compete to be the youngest parent....,' Blue adjusts her tights between her legs, & I am almost in heaven....

'Life - the Ultimate Reality Show!!!', Blue laughs, spitting whiskey through her nose -

---- we toast the utter beauty & absurdity of existence......

'It was not easy --- her mother never made any contact with her - she lost contact with her friends from the cafe when she left ... 'her' job was taken right away - there was never a party or promise.... or even a reference....'

Blue swirls the ice in her glass - she becomes deathly quiet - she lies her head back..... she closes her tear stained eyes....

As she lies upon me, I stroke her blond hair with my finger tips....

'The dole was not enough - fucking never enough - plus, it was boring .... & she couldn't dance ----- but, one night late, she walked the alien streets around the bedsit that was to be our wondrous new home, pondering the inevitability of my birth.... she is frightened, alone - She had little money & only a small case for her few things... She walked down the road, but without the Tramp to hold her hand...

As she walks through the alley ways, lascivious bankers prowl, whisper to her...

('Personal Jesus' by Marilyn Manson)

'But she hears a familiar song, at first a mere echo - awakening her memory of a night with her friends - they had fallen out after months & months of every day & every night ---- there was a ridiculous joy, abandon in the air - a Saturnalia --- she blushed, even giggled when she described the bizarre, random --- dancing in the flat of her girlfrenz whirling around with their tits out, drinking, smoking kind on a school nite....'

'Unconsciously, she blurs into the club with her eyes closed --- drinking in the ole' stripper tune, 'She drives me crazy!' by the Fine Young Cannibals --- rocking the '80's amid her fleeting memory of joyful transgression..... 'When she opens her eyes she is standing face to face with a spread pussy - a pregnant woman in a strip club - how wholesome!!!! How 'Christian', she thought of her own lecherous mother....

Blue falls over, laughing, spilling her drink upon the goldfish..... she lies laughing until the cold liquid snakes its way to her sweet, exposed belly.... at which time, she screams, giggling, throwing the ice away......

'But --- but....,' Blue chokes, nearly convulsing, 'No - you cannot know, no, no....'

'What? What?!!!', I scratch across my tabula rasa....

'They asked her if she came to dance!!! It was quite dark & they did not notice that she was pregnant --- even so..... --- well maybe they did --- but maybe only later....... what she said later would suggest ---- I do not know.... maybe.... but she danced... she started to dance - that was the beginning, far from her own point of departure.... '
'She was a pregnant stripper???!!!', I scratch on my board....

'Yes... yes she was......,' Blue laughs with a perverse pride.... as we walk down the hall to the common room - & the blood red futon...

'My mother was a pregnant stripper!!!!', Blue laughs, choking on her joy.... 'There - I finally said it....'

'They must have known it too....... cause she continued to dance, month after month as she became more & more pregnant... --

'It seems that pregnancy was a fetish even then.....' Aire gurgles on the floor face down, 'A really big fetish, totally!', Blue grabs the Jameson's off him with gusto...

'There is nothing new under the sun,' he screams, lifting his head, smashes to the ground with a hard explosive shock..... out cold, in the syncope of nothing – then he awakens...

'In a strange way, I think that it made her feel better about her body - she would always smile when she walked off stage, whispering, "Only two more sets, sweeties, & then we can go home - & have some cake..." - but that was her third pregnancy - at that point... I would stand there off-stage playing with my sister like she were my doll.... I would pretend to be her mother.... I would even breastfeed her.... '

In a blast Ian walks through the commons without a word, but Sophia walks over to us very gently, asks with her Shinto smiling eyes how things are - Blue, perplexed in her embarrassment - regretting immediately that we decided to go & be 'social' - looks away at the candle - I smile, hold up my board, 'Fragile'.... Sophia whispers, 'I gotta get a drink - but do you mind if I hang with you guys for awhile.... Ian will not talk to me,' she laughs, 'Fucking hell - my boyfren has been abducted by a videogame! GTA GTA GTA GTA - fuck, fuck, fuck, fuck, he has found deep levels that were not even known to the programmers...... he hones in on the Prime Minister - he assembles a guerrilla army as we speak.... !'

Blue says nothing, but turns to me tentatively, nervous, with a queer smile -

I simply write, intuitively conjuring our desires, 'That would be nice'.....

Even though I never talk to him, I want to be like Ian - he never looks at me .... well, not necessarily the whole GTA gangsta persona, but the hacking arch would suit me well -- imagine what could be accomplished by a dedicated network of hackers - for the good --- they would have to be anonymous though.... but, if they are going to play that game, they should remain anonymous - even anonymous is not anonymous - it ascends from the cauldron of the nameless out of mere egoism....

Sophia walks into the kitchen - we can hear a mumbled argument - Blue claws at my arm, whispers forcefully, 'I really do not want to do this - ' she squirms -- with only evil eyes, her head rocks, 'I want to talk to you.... just you - ' Blue looks like she is about to spring up like spores from a ripe, pregnant fungus.... I touch her arm, showing her my board, 'Please! Please!!!' - before she has the chance to respond --- beyond her shock, Sophia returns with a new bottle of jacked Jameson's....

Ian blazes back through this situs of our mortal existence, setting down a bowl of ice - he abruptly smiles at Sophia, & returns to their room....

Blue suddenly lunges to escape, but I grab her skinny arm just in time --

Sophia plops down upon the futon, sighs with joy, 'Finally, finally....' she lays her head back, smiling....

[censored content]

I hit her upon her head with my board - 'Open your eyes!'........

'Fuckin' hell, you are such a prat'.... Sophia smacks me across my face, laughing...

Blue flinches - begins to roll over to leave......

I write furiously upon my board, 'Relax!' to Sophia..... 'Please....', to Blue....

'Can you believe that seven protesters were killed today...... seven.... it is all rolling like a wave...... ', Sophia informs us.... 'in Late Britain'.......

'It is all the same!' - I write upon my board....

'You know --- we have lived here for some time now - ' Sophia speaks to Blue, 'But, we have never hung out --- I have never been against you --- I am not a threat...'

Blue remains silent.... I write to Sophia, 'She was telling me about her mother'....

'Oh -- I am sorry ...... fucking hell, I didn't know --- I am such a slag!,'

Sophia smacks herself upon her arm.... 'Bad Sophia....' She slaps herself again & again...

Blue gazes at my astonished face, & suddenly breaks out laughing, 'I thought I was fucked up --- shit girl, you are way more messed than me...'

Sophia - all at once - notices that we are looking at her... she laughs nervously, 'Yeah, I am pretty fucked --- yet, is that such a fucking bad thing, really?'

'I'm not right...' I sketch on my board -

'No - that's OK - I am pretty fucked myself,' Blue smiles at me, turns shyly at Sophia, 'I was just telling Hugo all about it ---

'You mean all the bruises on you,' Sophia asks with cautious reticence...

'Yes - not just that - but, why I strip --- that is why I was taking about my mother --- she was a stripper too.... I was basically raised in that strip club.... Boulevard, in Soho....'

'You were raised in a fucking strip club --- no wonder you are so fucked....' Sophia laughs as she pops the cork on a bottle of Chinese plum wine..... 'Great stuff - if you are heavy into oral sex ---' Sophia laughs, deepthroating the bottle...

Blue descends, warming to one who has shown herself to be kindred spirit, into a hysterical hilarity, 'That's not even the half of it - no fucking way..... I should not even tell you anything, but if you go to certain sleazy places in London, I will be found out anyway -

'You have not heard anything yet,' I scratch on my board, laughing in anticipation....

'What the fuck ... what is it?, Sophia screams, now also hysterical, 'I cannot take it...'
'I was telling Hugo that my mum was a stripper.... when she was pregnant with me,' Blue nearly chokes, barely getting her words out.... 'They fucking wanted her to dance - the more & more pregnant she got --- they were superfreaks!!!!'

We were now rolling around upon the futon in hysterics...... Blue claws herself up on the coffee table, fluid draining from her nose... 'You know what.... ' she could barely breathe – none of us could breathe.... 'You know what???!!!'

We are convulsing in utter, sublime anticipation.....

Blue stops cold for a second, looking into our eyes ----- suddenly, she explodes in comedic ecstasy....

'Her fucking water broke upon stage, during her pregnant pole fetish act --- ', Blue quakes, clasping her knees to her chest.... she falls in a thud.....

(Canned Laughter)

'She is spinning around, around, & around – as I embryonically fly out, shot out from her maternal womb, distended by this umbilical cord as she twirls -- & twists around & around the pole – I was spinning, spinning around.....' Blue chokes, her face turns beet red, as she coughs her way back to normality....

(Utter laughter all around, even the ten year olds quit their riot machine for a brief moment to join into the orgy of ridiculous absurdity....)

'I was born into the world as a pole dancer....' Blue gasps, 'Even at the moment, I knew I was born to perform as I smiled coyly at the audience, as I flew around & around.... a bloody wet infant.....'

Blue fakes a sudden somber frown, droning a dark dirge, 'I was born, thrown upon this stage....' (satirical laughter) 'to only be tragically annihilated amidst my joy!'

'I landed upon the stage with a dull thud,' Blue vomits, '- as my mother catapults off the pole onto all fours, as she stalks the audience, dragging me along after her, as the umbilical cord is still attached ...... 5, 10, & even 20 pound notes stick to my wet flesh as I slide across the stage, bloody – but eventually looking like some kind of moneyed bird, a peacock for the bankers....'

'Tweet, tweet like a little birdie!' Sophia roars....

'Bloody raging eruption!', I tear into my board...

The carnivalesque orgy of laughter reaches its crescendo when Blue whispers, 'We did a double act you know – breastfeeding pole dancing was never so dignified!!!! It was a sublime circus of decadent ascendance!!!'

We squirm together laughing, choking & vomiting like some kind of Twister game on PCP - we could not contain ourselves as joy had broke every boundry...

'But, decadence is the sign of every higher culture!!!,' Sophia puts her arm around Blue, smiling as we try to catch our breath...

'My mum just looked at the dumbstruck faces of the clientele, before she collapsed onto the stage.... they took us away in an ambulance ---- she was back to work the next night - amazing woman, & me in my Moses basket by the side of the stage...'

Blue points to a slice across her forehead..... 'This is where I hit the stage....'

'OMG - that is the fucking wyrdest ass story I have ever heard,' Sophia screeches, 'Fucking hell - so that is the reason you are a fucking stripper????!!! You would think that you would have run as far as fucking away from that as you could....'

'Shite - although Mum was back at work in record time, at first her clientele changes to those who like stretch marks & stitches, but before long she was pregnant again, & we again achieved well-being --- that's how it was --- what the fuck do I know --- I just thought that the strip club was 'normal' ... 'they' - everyone treated me like a tiny petite princess.... 'things' were still different then, the late eighties..... just before the fall of the Berlin Wall -- a time when peoples were conquered & east european sex slaves came & ruined everything!!!!'

'Ruined everything?', I scratch upon my board..... 'That was the death of the West!'

'Yeah - what do you mean???', Sophia sits perplexed.... 'Do you speak of irony?'

'I cannot speak at all!'

'I guess it was the internet as well - it got nasty, violent --- different drugs too --- it is happy, lovie lovie dovie with coke DMT ecstasy --- but then the meth diarrhea's out worse things ---- shit fucking Viagra, untimely erections - .... & those girls were so helpless, drugged out - tastes start to change -- it got really rough..... the boundaries between mainstream porn/hardcore collapsed ages ago - hardcore is mainstream - upon its edges surge traces, explosions of illegality, all becomes a blur - the worst in three clicks….. what will they decide?

Machiavellian Christianity (sheep voters) or Dionysian ecstasy (exploits for profits)?

'That is when my 'mother' first tried to get out....'

'Tried to get out???...', Sophia asks, filling our glasses....

'She had me … my little sis - she was pregnant again --- she got into debt ----' Blue sighs, 'It was not a problem at first...'

'Drugs?', I write on my board....

Blue snaps, proudly, 'No, nothing like that - just advances, to pay bills at first - then we moved into one of the rooms above the strip club, free at first --- you know the line , 'You can pay it off when you can ….. but then the management changed, some real shits came in - it became a banker's paradise, as the saying goes…'

'Madame Edwarda was gone in a day ----' Blue sighs with apprehension…

Sophia laughs, 'What da fuck --- "Madame Edwarda" ---- are you serious?'

'What??? That was her name....,' Blue expresses her confusion..... 'What?'

'You - serious? It is a title of a book by Bataille, that crazy French erotic philosopher, surrealist as hell - a whole fucking character --- she is a libertine madam - an erotic teacher - just like in Marquis de Sade's *Philosophy in the Bedroom*.....' Sophia laughs, 'She must have been having you on, sister......'

'No - that was her name - she was a French madam in Soho - She left though ---- she taught me how to be a woman, at a very early age...', Blue sips from her glass, 'She was the only person who ever really loved me....'

'Your mum?', I etch on my board.....

'I really do not know --- she tried to get away ---- she took care of us... but she was so distracted all the time - & so many men.... I do not know if she was even ever being paid for it --- it was just --- 24/7 fucking....', Blue turns her head away, pushing her glass against her cheek.......

('Slutgarden' by Marilyn Manson)

'What? --- just... what?', Sophia grasps towards Blue's hands.... 'What?' ---

'I think she liked it ----,' Blue whispers, in perplexity....

'Liked it? What?,' I scrawl upon my board, quite drunk, barely readable....

'I saw the way they looked at her ---- I saw her smile..... I know she liked it..... at first, before it all changed ---- before she became chattel......,' a tear slides down Blue's cheek, as she downs her glass, & reaches for her tobacco pouch....

'She was happy - but, then she disappeared.... just like that....' Blue's shouts as her head sinks down, between her legs - she sighs a sigh that is more like a groan.....

Sophia rests her hand on Blue's shoulder, 'She disappeared?' Really?'... What happened to her?'

'I don't know --- she was just gone ----,' Blue grabs the wine - chugs right out of the bottle, 'I don't know - she was just gone ---- 'they' kept me, my sister though - in the club.... '

'That's sick - sick ---- what the fuck, girl????', Sophia gasps for breath.....

'No - it was not like that --- there was a woman who took care of us --- she took us to the park, made us dinner..... they were not bad people, just mostly illegal...'

Blue chugs her wine, 'It was about a month until the social services would take us away..... we went into foster care!!!!!!!

---- worse than any strip club.... but, that is another story altogether...but, perhaps, I will tell a little about it - you don't want to hear it?' -

'No doubt!,' I write on my board..... & link to seven other networks -

'The real question is why you strip..... I mean, wat da fuk... (what the fuck)....,' Sophia diatribes in Blue's face, 'Wat da fuk, grl... just cuz yer momma walkz the walk --- that don't mean shite!!!'

Blue gazes into the candle, a long gaze, then she whispers, 'Maybe I am a bad daughter, but I forgot it all.... ', she sips from her glass, her lips glisten, red -

'At first I just forgot it all --- I just lived.... like anyone else --- anonymous, really....'

'An explosion of desire...' , Blue quakes, smiling, 'first made me kinda remember...' she sighs, taking another drink from the bottle, 'It is clear...... well - I do not know -'

I show her my question mark....

'I never really forgot... ' Blue wipes around her sweet mouth, 'It is just that I did not think of it - I set up an array - I do not even know - I feel this dread - & to hell with coldness -...' Blue dances as she plunges back upon the futon...

'I can see that --- but --- when did it all come back to you?', Sophia reassures her as she gently holds her arm, 'But, if you do remember --- you must tell - at least me...'

'Who are you again? Am I supposed to tell you the story of my life - right here - just because you approach me???? .... Please? I cannot tell you this --- I do not even know you-----' Blue springs up... squirms, disentangles from the labyrinth of front room frenzy...

Sophia stews in consternation ... but regrets her own transgression, 'She is right -- I do not even know her - but - ... I thought I did.... it is always the drink talkin'...'

Blue returns, un-expectantly, with a bottle of Jameson's in her hand & a tub of ice, 'Let this be a tribute to your concerns,' Blue laughs out loud, 'but also know that I am strong --- I would never be in my peculiar situation if I had not been utterly open to the truth,' she cracks the seal of the bottle & divvies up all the ice....

'You will tell us?', I write on my stellar board.....

There is only silence at first - a long silence not stimulating distraction, there is only dire suspense....

In the background, the flatscreen grinds the Goebbels repetition show 24/7n, but, thankfully, this time - with 'Eels', by the mighty Mighty Boosh, (but how likely is that - unless, of course, if we take this magical potion?) those surrealist poets of utterly sublime ek-sistent comedy ---

Eels up inside you
Finding an Entrance
Where they can....

Squirm all around you
Eat your entrails
Just like Spam....

[Reflective Voiceover]

The world is in chaos
but it just always feels --- like

Eels... Eels... Eels....

'Yes.... I will tell you - I will tell you everything - right now!' - Blue smiles at us..... but feeling almost drawn into the contagious world on the screen, that of the asylum, she still resists her desire to crimp the story of her scarlet letter...

Our gaze of hungry expectancy only feeds our own desire as we all gather in our frantic circle jerk upon her --- our questions shatter with the explosion of the door - as the look plunges open with bland faces, bodies coming in - technology & limbs - a collective gasp gives way to a commonplace recognition of those who have returned - Aire and Jesse trip over the lip of the door, 'Hello all - we are back..... we have had a fucking good day, ' they spin around, falling into their places like dogs.......

'I'm ole' Greg! I'm ole' Greg!', Aire shouts out ridiculously, looks upon the dumb faces - he understands, glimpses, & immediately choreographs, 'Let me sit down over here -- I see that I have again come into the middle of a sentence ----'

'Jesus, Aire --- ,' Sophia shouts, '..... very bad timing, to say the least!.... '

'I'm ole' Greg!'

'No -- it is not that-that bad!...' suddenly Blue erupts - 'It is good that they are here -- hell, they were here from the beginning --- they brought me in - in the first place...'

'Many apologies,' Aire laughs, as he squirms down upon the futon with a bottle of sweet Stoli's in his hand......

'That I have such an audience!' Blue exalts... laughing....

'Let us hear you out then!,' I write upon my board.....

Blue stands before us

She looks into us

She speaks

She glows there

'You wanna know?, ' Blue laughs - 'I do not even know - want to know - can know...'

I forget it all - I forget the specific events - the trauma, though, still abides with me...

('Trauma' by Howard Shore, from The Cell)

'It is not that way at all!'

I seem always as one obsessed....
I do not know why - & I do not really

understand these questions even now...

('Government' by the Dead Kennedys)

Like I said before - I liked the way

they looked at her - their gaze transfigures her....'

Blue rocks in memory as she swigs the bottle,
the light in the back of her aura...

--- I landed in a thud upon the strip floor stage
I stood there with my sisters

Then, they were gone, I was with them

I will always be with them, though

they are lost forever....'

Jesse suddenly grunts a strange gurgle in his total annihilation - Blue awakens from her trance - she gazes at Jesse --- Sophia gasps, shaking her head - her face down in her palm...

Aire runs over to Jesse, whispers that it will be fine, it will all be fine, all be fine....'

Blue - now utterly reluctant to open herself up to any hint of vulnerability - stands in our drunk faces ------ but, in an explosion of a sudden transformation, she glides toward her room.... turns before she enters, 'Another time... right?'

Sophia & I just smile, nod our heads...... She looks to Jesse with a tear in her eye...

******

It is one of those nights when everyone is hanging around --- just as with these over the top ole' party nights that Bob & James would throw - they had left Brixton for Hackney long ago, seeking to ride the perverse wave of gentrification all the way into the sea - we remember them & wish them well - but tonight the revolution will be a dance upon a rose --- here - where we now laugh......

Voices shatter, bounce multi-verse off the walls of the sacred front room.... the ten year olds are more manic than ever, preparing to go out on an 'objective' as they say - they are all perhaps too serious about their ideas, but maybe we have become lazy to the utter extreme - we are spoiled by Ian's spoils from his freelance pirate hacking for whatever you got... Rudyard Kipling's *Jungle Book* - the animated Disney version - dances across the surface of the flatscreen - spoils of class warfare....

Now when you pick a pawpaw
Or a prickly pear

& you prick a raw paw
Next time beware
Don't pick the prickly pear by the paw
When you pick a pear
Try to use the claw
But you don't need to use the claw
When you pick a pear of the big pawpaw
Have I given you a clue?

The voices are like frenzied bees in the hive --- punctuated by the toasts of drinking glasses - the effervescent bubbles of sweet bong hits dance ever more brilliantly against the light of the raging fire, Luce puts more wood on and nudges the searing embers with her poker - 'You cannot imagine,' Blue's voice rises into clarity above the pleasantly idle chatter, 'What some guy wanted me to do to him tonight!'

'In all of its gory detail,' Aire laughs…. Sophia rings in, 'I could probably piss…', but relents, 'I guess so' (she turns her head to her bedroom) 'Ian, get your lazy ass in here & be sociable like a normal fucking human being - for fucking once!!!!'

('At My Job' by the Dead Kennedys)

'I'm game!,' I write simply upon my chalk board (or perhaps it is a tablet of a scribe).

'What you talking about, one of your tricks?', Jesse shouts out in his surrealm, but almost no one can understand him, the *topos* spinning as a sublime kaleidoscope of fragmentation - a tear of joy steams gently from his eye…. he fades in like this now, from time to time, even without his voice being invoked….

'Yeah, one of them,' Blue sighs, whispering to herself amidst these voices which she thinks are hers, 'If you can still call them that anymore --- he paid a lot of money at first - (she sighs again, louder this time) & he was not so so so bad - didn't hit me or want to - he was old skool -

'So you just went off with him?,' Aire queries as he rolls another mega-spliff with four papers (a good old fashioned ten pound Camberwell Carrot) - 'Are you unaware of the potential for escalation - of violence --- even rape?'

'Excuse me, douchebag!,' Blue incises, displaying the proliferation of bruises, burns & scratches across her body - she jumps up into Aire's face, shoves his face into the ligature marks beneath her scarf --- the whip marks on her ass & shaved pussy, as she begins to twirl a great whorl, her flowing white skirt inhales her own winds & flies upward - she twirls around, around - her supple legs - sumptuous white ass painted with myriad indescribable wounds... 'Give me a fucking break, asshole!,' Blue chants as she twirls amidst her Sufi extravagance, 'You know nothing about rape - or me.... have you even been to one of these underground strip clubs?' She falls suddenly, of all people - something is wrong, she din't feel right --- in a whirling confusion, Blue falls - faints - with her eyes closed - she spies Jesse in a flash - before she stretches out to catch her breath.... smiles like a stepford wife....

'You know nothing - you do not care - only make jokes at my expense and ridicule me,' Blue spoke in a distant ethereal tone.....

So just try & relax, yeah cool it
Fall apart in my backyard
'Cause let me tell you something little britches
If you act like that bee acts, uh uh
You're working too hard

'Of course I do - I have loved you, since the first night,' Aire laughs ironically, 'Yet - our whole civilisation is based upon rape & work! I hate him really, but the honest Nietzsche says that all higher cultures are based upon cruelty - which is so obvious, especially now - but there is so much denial, propaganda ---- The whole planet is being raped, pillaged - we have wasted the dawn (he laughs suddenly realising how derivative he sounds) - & you - it is so obvious (with a pronounced drunken slur) that there is no need of words..... unless as encouragement for the true warriors....

Blue - this whole time - is lost amidst these many remembrances of her visits to the houses of men - she giggles as she revels upon her trips to the toilet - 'Oh, could I please excuse myself, where is your loo?' She laughs as she remembers that, each time, she masturbates with his toothbrush, whoever he was.... she did not clean it...

'But, you do not know the intimacy of rape,' Blue whispers as she tries to get away, 'Your whole whole - system of everything - homogeneity - that - all -' she becomes silent as she guzzles the wine bottle that has already been in her mouth for some time now.... how she spoke is still considered a mystery in the Apocophra....

'There's rape,' Aire echoes his own awakening, '& then there's rape.'
('Riot' by the Dead Kennedys)

"Jesus muthafuka - ' I scratch my words....

'What', Sophia bites, 'What in the fuck are you on about now?'

(Silence)

'We say rape all the time,' Aire exposes something radical, 'It becomes something trivial - that's what I am on about...'

'Let her fucking tell us,' I write to my dear friend Aire's face, I erase, scratch, 'What in the fuck happened to her....???'

Blue turns her head in embarrassment - but maybe not - as she may just be going off-stage to assemble a new face... who knows with the beasts that we are....

Oh, oobee doo
I wanna be like you
I wanna walk like you
Talk like you, too
You'll see it's true
An ape like me
Can learn to be human too

She turns & her eyes dismember us in our repose, 'You want me to tell you about my rape - rapes? --- I will not even talk about the masochism that possessed me for awhile.... that possesses me.... and so many others - let's not even speak of torture...'

(Silence)

'Yeah - I would like to hear about that....' Aire whispers, laughing ironically....

'I do not know if they pushed me from before - but it was strange, a bit too organised -' Blue reflects, 'I never treated my parents bad - but I never understood why we went to church every Sunday - our house was certainly not blessed... I remember the night so well - it was days after when I received the gift of blood.... I asked my mother if it was a gift of the blessed Virgin, of our Mary.... and she smiled....

'Of the sacred heart of Jesus.... yes, because Roman Catholicism is a Trojan Horse of Paganism!', Aire slurs his ponderings, 'But - that would at least be a reason to go to church!!!' (he laughs until he pees himself, but pretends he has not, just poses wet...)

'But, you said your mother was a stripper that your father died when you were a baby?' Sophia laughs hysterically.... 'It is wonderful that Blue is here with us now - and - that you Aire sit in your own slash....'

'I already knew the truth - & less -' Blue incises deeper with her scalpel, ignoring Sophia's obvious question – 'I knew early on...that all these alleged teachers were blind - my mother, father - all of them - they possessed, taught only a fear of death, nothingness ---- It is not that I did not wish to hear - but that they had nothing to say - all was and is cliché, the forgotten hieroglyphics of former decadence -'

'They have failed & they should - must - step aside,' Aire jumps up on the back lip of the futon, 'Overthrow yourselves - only then will you be spiritualised,' my old friend Fred always says as he sits in his recliner watching the news, the so-called entertainment, the commentary, debate, analysis....... diarrheic streams steams streams of shit!!!!!!!!,' he fell to his side in random convulsions, knocking over many a glass & bottle, the room gasping with orgasm.....

Blue falls into a hypnotic trance state, & begins to recount the details of her rape, in another of her lives... this rape of her soul, Psyche - 'The travellers found me naked upon the dark stone spiral steps in the bowels of the utterly lifeless Castle, circling around, up & down the Tower... (she sighs in ecstatic relief) they found me - I quiver upon the cold stone - They come closer, attempt to read these cubist slashes across my flesh - hieroglyphics of pain & humiliation --- but they do not know the language... or, the usage...'

'How could these men ever play that game?' Sophia laughs, punching Blue on the arm, 'But are you going to tell us about your rape? Hell, to be honest,' Sophia burps as she slurs, 'I am not even sure I even want to hear about it....'

Blue sighs as one totally misunderstood...

'That's real nice, Emo girl', Aire hisses at Sophia with scorn - Jesus!'
'I was just joking, you mutherfucker,' Sophia hisses back..., nearly vomiting...

'I will forgive you, Sophe,' Aire drools, 'cause I know you're a drunken dirty whore!', he laughs, whiskey coming out of his nose.... 'Whose my lil' bitch?'

'I am,' Sophia shot back, bumping his fist with her own.....

'But, it is the ultimate violation!', Blue slaps Sophia & Aire across their faces with one slap, 'the other night you were so distracted from my story, I just left - now you are doing the same fucking thing again - for fuck's sake, I was raped so many times! I am finally ready to tell you!'

At once, they all turned to Blue - like puppets by the same master dance, but she was gone -

She would have needed a better stage than this strange space of permanent revolution of ten year olds working amidst what may seem to be an amorphous bunch of lazy over-fed anarchists --- Emma Goldman would perhaps frown – 'You are sloths' selfishness - wake up! We need Dionysian communion! Our energy is sublime, but we need to begin to work together in a cooperative manner --- give up the hype... show a little sympathy...'

Blue ran off - crying, ranting to herself.... haunted by Emma as she dances....

I follow her up the spiral staircase, worshipping her panties, to the roof ... find a nice perch with my bottle of 'juice'... Blue agitates.... she paces around, flails her arms in & out of this quiet wind - twirling she raises her arms to the leaden sky, her fists clenched - she seethes - exclaims to all: 'You have given birth to me for rape! What other thing could I be - with that slit between my legs - this hole - what else could it be for that hard sword - what could cock be for? ... an empty place --- needs to be filled - - - horror of the vacuum...'

Aire, who, with Ian, finally comes out - Sophia, had taken my clue - at that moment stumbles precariously across the roof, contests, 'Well, there is penetration, but there is also castration, envelopment - do we penetrate you or do you envelop, suffocate us?'

'I cannot even believe my ears,' Sophia screeches at Aire, 'What the fuck is wrong with you - droog, you are a poet - you are supposed to be sensitive or at least --- shit, we need to get your ass re-hypnotised - since this ain't working at all!'

'Yeah man -' Ian echoes, 'You are a total douchebag muvafucka!', then, he retreats back down the spiral staircase - CJ is craaaaazzzzeeee!!!!!

Exasperated, I could only manage:

gadjama ar amma
berida bimbala
gl&u gelassasse
laullelonnin

Slurring a scream, Blue erupts, 'Oh, I could tell you the truth...' - she falls to her knees, somewhere betwixt consciousness & unconsciousness - in between.... her eyes are wild as she sobs, muttering, 'But , then I would have to tell you a new story every day when I came home from work...', she wails with empty hands...

Everyone is silent - the truth sizzles the eyes - no one makes eye contact, redeemed by a break in the woollen clouds that disclose the dear stars in all of their utter sublimity....

Blue then turns to us, under a different aspect, possessed, she intones, 'I was in a familiar place, my grandfather's house - or, at least my mother used to call him 'Daddy' - on the occasion of a 'family reunion' - I did not know any of these people, but was surprised at the number of uncles in the family, & the girls, about fourteen besides me, were nearly naked, wearing corsets & thongs - There was no love, but simply a business assertion of 'family' - at all costs - but, I did not know this family of mine - later I learned that this was no true family at all ---' I try absurdly to intervene with a further corruption,

galji bei bin blassa
glassda laula lommi
cedorsu sessile bin

Aire senses my dis-ease, 'Seriously - Blue - are you alright? Do you know what you are saying?'

'That is not me, Aire,' Blue whispers, nearly surreal, unconscious - 'It is Hugo ---'

'Yes - I know, but are you all right?' he insists -

After an uncomfortable silence, Blue turns to those assembled, gasps - fires, 'I cannot believe you assholes! -- I WAS RAPED! - unless you no longer believe that rape exists - or, is even a taboo!!! I am every woman that has ever existed - look into the abyss my fucking eyes - gaze upon all of their faces ---'

Bemused, Aire reclines upon a board leaning against the wall, concedes, 'Hell, it has become a commodity in the new new economy -- people will do anything during a permanent economic crisis -- sell their children, sell themselves! Rape is a 'service' in the new new service industry - every Taboo is a marketing strategy! Shiiiittte, muthafuka, would you like some fries with dat?,' he raises his arms to the sky, howls into the night, 'With this many people, all is possible!!! That is almost why the world must end - or, at least should end - unless the question lies somewhere else besides!'

I can only spout, with a dada slur:

gadjam a tuffers i ziagsh
bin bur gligh rorwksdgdsfgjkfgj

Blue pats my hand with concern in her eyes, 'You need to know the truth - so you can see how deep the evil goes!'

'Are we having a theological conversation?', Aire scoffs under the pale brief stars, 'I thought you were going to tell us about your rape? I am all ears....'

'The spirits are always with us,' Sophia whispers into the wind, through her portable Shinto house....

'I am - you simpleton!', Blue spits in his face, 'I hate you when you drink absinthe!!!', she claws at his chest, 'It is all the same - they pinned me down - the father, the boss & the priest - it was a week after the flood had come to me - & then they came like rabid beasts, lusting after my body, my flesh...

[suspension]

disorients amidst this void

anything is possible,

in any indifference -

suspended betwixt the wild ipse
& the Communion of the All....

this Moment .... Open

Journey to the End of the Night.... a tale of abduction, & repressed memories...

'The beasts pierce - tear my flesh,' Blue screams, 'lacerating every inch of my perfect body... they recite sacred words, an incantation - they chant amid a thanatos, death ritual.... but they say it is for eternal life... how tragic their tragedy - they don't hear!

My alleged 'grandfather' stood still with a lifeless face, but put his cock in my mouth - my 'father' kept watch, having the very, very least dignity not to fuck me... all of the lecherous 'uncles' pursue - consume my flesh... my 'aunts' & my 'grans' did all the same - I was naïve then --- but at the end of the day, I fucked my 'uncle'!

'Should we then - at the end of this day - drop the etiquette - ' Aire cannot help but to tempt, "That makes you an uncle fucker!' he laughs until he chokes, remembering South Park, as he sings joyously, 'Fuck your fucking face, uncle fucker!'

Tuning out the inanity of the moment, I wonder if we should instead work together, secretly - like the secret societies of old? like the Masons of my Grandfather Clyde....

'They got the idea from me,' Blue splatters, 'Trey & Matt promised to leave me a share of their inheritance.... all I had to do was to fuck them amid a bestial orgy...'

'How strange & easy is that, for a girl - just like my fucking ultra-kind blim?' Aire slurs centrifugally, 'At the end of the day, each will find the truth of the taboo through attempts at transgression - then you will know why, but only then -'

'Perhaps - that is the meaning of faith - ' Blue punches, squirms - dances through the ecstatic winds upon the rooftop - the dear stars watch over her ...

'You fucked your uncle, really?' Sophia smiles into Blue's heart, 'You tragic girl...'
'Yes,' Blue laughs, finally, 'but that is not important -- & he was not my real uncle - fuck, it was not even a real family - I have since released my imago - my primal self-image - this prison - to the radical chaos of

possibility...

'In another life, the Prince shoves his cock in my ass as the Bishop licks my pussy - the boss fucks my mouth & the psychiatrist strangles me!', Blue provokes, 'All remains the same betwixt incarnations & I am content since I remember!'

'How Divine! Torchless finale under the sign of tragedy, Dionysus...,' Aire screams as he falls through the ceiling into the kitchen appliances, pukes into the rancid drain near his mouth...

'I fucked my uncle, but, at the end of the day, it was a ritual - rape as a sacrifice - I was raped - am raped every day, it is part of my job description...' Blue glares -

'They tie my hands behind my back & put an o-ring gag in my mouth - I am blindfolded, whips to my soft flesh, punches to my belly, slap my tits, spit in my face - [censored content] - only utter darkness until the dawn - (DVD available NOW at a store near you...) the light shatters my blindfold - disclosing that which is most important.....'

His original hypnosis breaking down, Aire climbs back up through the hole, whispers to the sky, 'Is such bestiality our true destiny?'

Jesse affirms, but again, no one understands him - 'Yes, let our enemies be destroyed!'

'Again,' Blue speaks, at last, 'It is intimacy which matters - the sublime difference amid the oneness of all things - they stole my sense of intimacy...

With this last breath from Blue's lips, there seems to be a vast sigh of cosmic relief on the rooftop..... a disclosure itself as one of sheer evasion, distraction - as if to hear of the suffering of another human is too much agony....

Everything suddenly descends into an absurdist vortex of joy, sorrow & chaos.... In our utterly Dionysian commitment, we live a new episode of the Asylum.... in search of this Perfect Anarchy... Occupy the Asylum, volunteer for the quarantine as the chaos of voices bounce off of the breeze block walls.....

'If you are not living in the moment you are not living', Aire screams into the night…

'Though, if I can ascend,' Sophia whispers, 'amidst this possession - for an instant, at least', she twirls around under the moon….

'It is gone now - spirit comes & goes - ' Blue sighs, alone - unheard…

'Despite all - I am laughing with the gods, goddesses & spirits - ' Aire shouts…

'None of you fuckers really care about me!' Blue hisses, her tongue cuts us all to death….

'You are each & all insane!' I sketch upon my board…

Each of us fall into the oblivion of our utterly private dreams…..

*****

We each swan down the spiral staircease in a delayed trickle & one by one join a comatosed Jesse upon the oblivion of the futon -- severed skins are already skinned, bottles cracked, proliferating through hands, mouths… we imbibe through our eyes, ears the daily death round-up on the flatscreen…

(Generic News Music)

'Tonight, a British tourist has been murdered in Florida,' the newscaster spouts. 'The main suspect is a waitress & the son of a Klansman who is a major landholder in the Penial County area & founder of the Penial Trail which notoriously divides a number of black neighbourhoods & has been the path of many disruptive KKK marches. The tourist, who was of Jamaican descent, is said to have been lured into a relationship by the waitress & was murdered by herself & her accomplice. The couple attempted to fabricate a suicide by hanging, but forensic evidence, analysed at the insistence of Scotland Yard, uncovered a connection to the suspects, who remain at large. The murder is being treated as a hate-crime….'

'Shit,' Sophia shrieks, 'when suicide is fucking murder!' 'Fucking hell,' Aire joins in, 'A walking path that goes right through the fucking poor segregated black neighbourhoods that still exist' he laughs in disdain, derisively… 'Fuck Florida!!! Fuck fuck fuck fuck florida ---- give it back to the Seminoles, to all the faces of otherness - all the smaller tribal names, peoples that you killed, kill....'

'Word, muthafucka!' Ian shouts out from his GTA crib, 'Florida is shit!'

Blue, who set on the edge of the futon, stands up - unnoticed, walks past me... she turns to me, as I gaze into her eyes, 'Are you coming, Hugo?'

I smile, nod my head, she takes my hand & leads me to our single bed.

8 BRAIN DAMAGE

('Ride of the Valkaries' by Richard Wagner)

We crash in front of the blaring flatscreen absorbing these spectral shockwaves of intimate & distant events of radical transfiguration --- things fall apart, the rugs slip away... neighbours pound on the walls day & night, filling out their Noise Complaints Log Form - ones that no one anywhere will ever do anything about...

Apparently, the revolution will be televised on 24 hour rolling news.... but, I wonder, for how long.... until it becomes a real threat – or is simply ignored. Passé...?

The disfigured, tragic revolutions have already swept across North, Central & Southern Africa - twice, three times - they had come to Europe (but, this revolution is always here...), cancer wars in South America, cultural wars in Asia, & finally the mass Occupations across the United States, and the world..... Each & All.... full circle, a sphere - the centre is everywhere ---

Gaddafi is beaten & raped to death upon the streets of Sirte, in itself - just another gangsta hit amidst humanity - such auspicious beginnings .... Sharia Law to boot!!!

Oh, we march from here to there
& it doesn't matter where
You can hear us push
Through the deepest bush
With a military air!

With a military air!

But, we flatter ourselves.... we clever animals - 'our' rock will still freeze over in an instant, at the whim of cosmic forces.... but, of course, before that eventuality, we will have... let's say, the Afghan-Iranian-Pakistan War, the Second Falklands War... an implosion in Northern Ireland, and who would have guessed it, super-BSE... internet crackdown in the name of moral values --- and intellectual property rights...

The revolutions re-sweep - they were not at first revolutions, yet - merely 'friend requests' - 'revolution requests' --- 'Oh, I wonder if he will respond?' 'But, once we are friends, will he de-friend me?' Friendship with be decided upon the streets - Blood splatters Tahir Square - again & again - as if the Spring became Autumn & Winter - our eyes are open --- seriously - if it seems too easy, then it probably is... Syria bleeds, ready to explode...

For, still the 'West' does not exist - it is a liar & does not want any 'Spring' .... it is a liar with all the power for the determination of truth - a paradox...
Certainly not a summer.... only Winter --- but, still the Spring comes again - it does not stop, even more, it all becomes crazy - Though some are no longer mis-directed to the Iraq or Afghanistan as we awaken to fathom the utter apocalypse of the world - everywhere, the Congo, for instance - & all the other dirty little secrets... the only ones who thrive now in the former Zaire are the teaming communities of gorillas... though, this explosion of numbers is encouraging, this is certainly not the path to conservation... the omnicide of the Congo has not even been glimpsed....

With the ever increasing economic uncertainty, not to mention the current political & international catastrophes - various unreal possibilities begin to emerge that one would have wished had been put soundly to asleep -- Indeed, it is the 1930's again - where a riot really means something & is not just a shopping adventure -

('P.F.F.' by Hank Williams III)

Now riots (not to mention strike & industrial action) are beginning to mean something again - beyond the post-protest riots, new riots vaguely connected to government fiscal policy, adult & child poverty, environmental crises, running deeper, delving into the cultural political economic subjugation of vast portions of the population - think of the London riots (Aug 6-, 2011) Tottenham, Brixton - the people shout, 'We feel like caged animals'....

Even after the events at Trafalgar Square, the London Olympics went off - but like a multi-week security screening, in the style of inconvenience, though they were at least not swallowed into a vortex of rioting with the emergency funding to the police - & perhaps to the looters - pay them off & give them a knighthood - lest they stray - although thousands of protesters remained gathered throughout the entirety of Occupy the Olympics 2012 - overall, the price tag for security effectively wiped out any profit from the event - as for prestige, that was really no longer the question.... It was the total fall off of shopping – Disaster!

'Occupy the World! It is all very simple, really..... 99%! ' Aire gets overly excited by the pornography of rebellion & joins in this surge --- suddenly, in our faces, and upon the streets below our windows..... 'this ineffability, the indefiniteness of freedom & resistance.... to subvert this seduction to definition -' he pauses, struggles for a straightforward -- but there is no solution, but only resolution with a procreative dissolve --- 'letting the 'system' disentangle itself is the revolution --- or, a key to the cage... something else is already always gestating -' he falls onto his back, spouting with unusual precision,

'occupy, or a

subversion of definition,

of the restricted economy of control -

beneath surges music & dance...

love & rage....

[ok-yuh-pahy]

oc•cu•py

[ok-yuh-pahy]

verb, -pied, -py•ing piper.

verb (used with object)

It is not to 'take or
merely fill up (space, time, etc.)'

or to idly 'engage or employ the mind,

energy or attention'

It is neither to be a 'resident or

tenant' of industrial 'housing' -

It is not to 'take possession &

control of a place, as by military

invasion or to hold (a position,

office, etc.).'

It is peaceful muthafukas!

We do not need them - they are
the dead shell of the chrysalis
that must inevitably fall away,
lest the emergent butterfly die...

   Jesse breaks off, laughing at the last sentimental line, but instantaneously raps out - 'I am not a part of this system! I am an adult!', he steals along to that old time Jewish favourite, 'I threw it on the ground'....

   'Yes, that wise Jew, a genius of comedy, said there was a time for that too....' Aire laughingly rejoins, ' ... to subvert the order of things, to throw it all into an abyss -' he sits up suddenly, getting on his hands and knees, he spits lovingly in our faces,

'verb (used without object)

It is to take back that
which is always already
disclosed as our world...
to create a joyous place in
which we can dwell together

to squat amidst the indigence
of our holy makeshift freedom

(everyone cheers, against the background dubstep stylings of Allen Ginsberg)

occupy

[ok-yuh-pahy]

oc•cu•py

[ok-yuh-pahy]

verb, -pied, -py•ing.

The ten year olds seem to understand this subversion - though it neither stops them, or propels... though I wonder if we should all being doing more - or perhaps, to do nothing will be more effective, not to work, not to serve - only to occupy, or better - to be, even if that only mean staying in your bed for a week... month... year...

Jesse grunts out his coma-esque approval - he always loves Aire's poetry - that was the spark of their friendship, after all - the very reason for everything.... though, we all know that he is elsewhere, like Derrida or the stray cat that stood on it hind legs the other night , whispering, 'The End!' - somewhere, beyond our reach....

'Nice use of the dictionary, dickhead!' Sophia throws an empty beer can at Aire's head, 'What are you getting lazy, you fucker?!!!'

'Maybe that is the point!' I sketch on my board...

'What - that he is getting lazy?' Sophia snaps back...

'No,' I rejoin in chalk, 'he is subverting the dictionary!'

Aire laughs at our bizarre, incipient conversation - he, slaps me on the back, 'At least someone fucking understands what I am doing --- too bad you can't tell anyone how fucking brilliant I am!'

Sophia laughs amidst this bizarre turns of events, but dives onto, upon us in rapture.

We roll around over each other laughing realising how dysfunctional and utterly pointless our lives are -- though we are all happy enough, as far as that may be one of the goals of life... and, each of us has a tenuous sense of the meaning of death...

('TV Party' by Black Flag)

Our significant, though utterly tangential conversation seems a million miles from these myriad events shattering our eyes - each a step in the intricate dance of chaotic fate - all leading to the shattering storms that birth new dispensations - for good - or for ill.... but, even our riots have become about better TVs... perhaps, we are lost .... no one seems to care since existence has become merely a simulacrum of ghosts -- nothing seems sufficiently real to matter - indeed, our scientists themselves have refuted 'matter'.... but they had no power to direct funding away from orgiastic wars... let's kill that peace dividend son! Yes, papa, to the stone age & beyond!

News sources looking at news sources looking at news sources looking at news.....

We forget CocaCola death squads in Columbia in our distraction - misdirected through the house of mirrors as thousands die --- It's the real thing!

'It is all bullshit, you know - total bullshit - we should learn to blame the right people,' shouts a deranged Sophia, who could only, at this point, speak of ghosts - specters of this - our life here now upon the planet - 'As each abides in the Nothing,' she would often say - 'Only architecture holds us to the ground!'

Greece was the first to go, as it was the first to arrive.... Spain & Italy - the entire Eurozone --- Amercia is now owned by Blue China Inc., barely limping after its own persistent - though officially denied debt, social, & environmental crises ---- Kim Jung Un - if you can remember that far back replaced Kim Jung Il - threatens the south with nuclear annihilation - Most may not comprehend the impending attacks upon South Korea, but, you can always buy a Team America doll which sings, 'I'm so wonely...' - Thank God for Capitalism... seriously - thank God! Mark that...

'Shite, we are circling the drain, our descent into the maelstrom...' Sophia screams at the sky, frightening these ecstatic ten year olds who continue to plan & build, who knows for what - 'to know how - it is only a question if they know that -', she slips off into her own private incomprehensibility.

Aah, who remembers the balanced budget in America after the Clinton presidency, when the fucking worst thing was a little cum on a blue dress?,' Aire sighs, 'Bush was surely the Beast, surely - someone surely should check his head for the sure sign...... 911 - I mean 666... - you know what the fuck we could have done with all that fucking money? He broke the back of history!'

Italy was the second major event in Europe - (although Spain has done its best on the PR front so as not damage its tourist trade - elected their own brand of Tories with the collateral damage of increasing protests --- flies swarm the dead in the streets -) --
The joyous whore monger of Italy should have fled his shitty country when he had the chance, sickened ---- though it is hard to be against an 84 year old man who is so incredibly lively in his erotic life........ he is a great man - despite or even because of his alleged immorality & corruption - we will miss him - I envy him.... he falls in disgrace - hopefully he got immunity..... Or, perhaps, he will win the next election...

Aire, fallen now deeper into his usual night time drunken delirium, whispers words back at the newscaster, a beautiful blonde, who he is convinced is looking straight into his soul & into the soul of the world...

This Dionysian desire is already always here ----

a spark, a prairie fire..... that is all that is needed....
to set it off...... it is already raging in the winds -- upon the streets...

Poseidon shakes the earth - the earth shatters
& awakens the terrifying goddess Tsunami....

It begins as a revolution of the middle world --- of the Mediterranean -

The event will come with the end of this world... (Aire passes out, his head crashing onto an exposed slat of the futon, but he nevertheless smiles...)
Blue usually resists most contact, but having just slipped in the door, becomes unexpectantly ecstatic, as Aire's Dionysian Dithyramb still echoes in her head - 'Shit, Hugo - do you feel the streets -- it is finally here, it is now --- talk is talk --- an orgasm in the space, our place, this open.... it has finally happened - the event .... (taken off her guard, she dances in a circle singing, 'Free at last, free at last, we bruthas, sistas, are free at last!')

Blue screeches like a giggly scream queen as she falls twirling onto the futon.... I cradle her head in my hand, and let her rest upon my chest...

Aire bathes himself, like a cat - with others near by, who admire his shiny coat - he wanders in utter utopian dreamscapes after all - at first he traverses a sublime desert - but phases into a soulless labyrinth of exterminating rules - magically embodied as a mere 'system of needs' - enslaved Life - he would rather die than be a tool, a slave - that is the difference.... he whispers in his sleep, 'For we all must die - there is no escape - but - must life then be squandered, turned into a wretched misery - -- must there also be a time for catastrophic negligence and narcissistic genocide?'

Blue kisses him on his passed out cheek, whispering, 'Some day, all this seemingly pathetic jabber - will be extremely significant... indeed - you are a fucking prophet!"

*****

We all live off & on in the Trafalgar encampment - crop rotation, shifts, like camping for a squatter - someday it will be a true market again - for the people - this had now become the Occupy protest after the last court ordered eviction from St. Paul's Cathedral - the point of which, of course, was that it was near the Stock Exchange.... but, the police, these sublime operators, made sure it became a haven, magnet for crime....

Trafalgar Square will always be the most profound - the best choice - any way, there can be no doubt... symbolically, historically charged.... it pertains to the Nation.... the people - though its main symbol was always a dissimulation, a fraud....

Jesse was there too for awhile --- until the tragic event ---- it was vastly different from anything before --- this - a community of the people -- at its very radix, root ---

It had all the grace, solemnity of the Lady Di funeral - (canned laughter) - but this time as an event of deeper significance - but ultimately of uncertainty, risk....

'... we can have lots of fun at least, & go shopping.....' one of the less ideologically driven protesters whispers... she merely repeats in her own biotic existence the inexorably violent reproduction of capital -
The streets themselves come alive with this dance of rebellion ... dance

of life.... this profound opening, departure, one that cannot be ignored....

Albion awakens - though not all of this is beautiful..... nor sublime.... a Shamanic troubadour walks through the vast crowds, giving bits of poetry to many ears as he snakes by, through & away.... he is a psychedelic town crier, reminds us of the ambiguous transfiguration of our existence ---

'From my perspective - although I will never be one of you,' poetises this romantic stranger, with a shell upon his head - he is sopping wet & covered in seaweed -- 'this is not a land of freedom or liberty...... this is not a people of creativity, singularity.......

I have just come onto ground from the sea... but, I will become your pale narrator ---

This place is a fractured, broken mirror of sterile pictures & tones - despite the allegedly unimpeachable practices thereof -

Cold philosophy - homogeneity, mere power, has been shattered... impeached as a mask of anarchy... its mechanisms grind forward in the effervescence of the same....

The masks of church, military, civil society & the 'state' have been torn....

heterogeneous forces disseminate their rage across the topology of existence.......

though some of them are children of impotent revolt..... overthrowing mere idols....

We are never honest with others or ourselves......perhaps, we never get that far.....

But - that is true everywhere - so many fake revolutions - aspirations taken up as puppet strings for other overriding agendas ---

The street will. can never be surrendered..... this is the near truth - that is why there are shops, after all - capitalism wants to get close to you, just like religion, your mum...

It is better to be free upon the streets - even if one has no explicit political voice - than to have a piece of paper that says I have technical, formalistic representationism - & it be a lie -

(Advertisement -

OCCUPY FASHIONS™

When I am not free upon the streets --- free to be - beyond the repetitive stratagems of bureaucracy & police control - then, I am not free..... Kill me - at least I will die looking this good!)

The new law & maxim for the 'West' - only those who can endure radical boredom - & utterly master this radical boredom - can.... & will rule....

Sorry - that has already happened..... everyone else who exists can either submit or go involuntarily to the madhouse & then be put into community care.... then, the final destination - privatised prison, soylent green.....

The most boring people will rule - the most boring people are the 'power elite' - philistines of merely satanic power - with their masks of moral rectitude - bad actors who operationalise the fix of their own petty addictions - their surrogate power means nothing - at the end of the day....

Jesse, by that time & space had already become a celebrity --- at least, on the most wanted list... 'I do not even care about this Orwellin 'world, ' he would smile...

(But that was before the accident, his event....)

Jesse spins around, drinking in the crowd ---- amidst the effervescence of the street.... the tent city holds itself as hundreds of activists handcuff themselves together, pink fuzzy handcuffs they got in a sweet deal with Soho sex shops - they are all utterly interlinked around Nelson's column --- - the square itself is organised --- but still surrounded by thousands of riot police with horses, water cannons, and weapons - the encampment ascends all the way up the stairs of the National Gallery ---- not to mention, the obligatory black helicopters - can you imagine it ---- a circle of blind, brutal force around those who simply wish to have their freedom & dignity ---- fairness in this mortal life… even you will die…. no matter what…

They had been awakened from their dogmatic slumber, learned the lessons - & the skills - from the Mediterranean..... who themselves had ironically learned these skills from us in an earlier time, though we had forgotten... and we have learned from them in a still more previous instance - these courageous souls are still learning new lessons amid old explosions... everyone has fallen into the maelstrom - we will all learn, together, we need to work together - in this moment...

'When will we learn to go for the juggler in one sublime instant?' Luce whispers...

Aire taunts the police officers (who are themselves not at all happy to be there at all anyway, & who - given that their own budgets are always upon the chopping blocks - would happily switch sides - but, who would have the courage? Or - yet ... as everyone has seen, the police have more cards up their sleeves than mere protest actions or strikes) -

> they run in the streets
> this is their only freedom
> these feral dogs & cats
> freedom is e(il)lusive....
> away from the parents
> not to mention the bureaucrat-politicians
> & this utterly banal routine of 'culture'
> have a cup of tea, have a cup of tea!!!
> (various noises indicating a clearing of the throat)

They surround the space, the place .... Jesse now taunts them ... this imperfect circle...

'Perhaps --- we could say that the 'west' has never been tested.... existed .... not since, at least ---- may 68 or at it alleged 'origin'.... it holds its sanctum of lore... but it is no more of anything than anything that is anything - seriously.....' Jesse sneers, 'The truth is the Ottomans, the Monguls - that which shows our lie, our impertinence.

When they had swooped in to occupy Trafalgar square, the Gangster & Lapdog Coalition said predictably that everyone was a criminal - feral animals to be either neutered or put-down - just like the lawlessness of the looters - & they should all go home immediately as the protesters are threatening stability ---- & the fragile economy in an already difficult period... blah, yada, yada, blah....

The first night, the police stood by as neo-fascist thugs attacked the tent city --- these were the first deaths since the seven workers were killed a month earlier at the Westminster protest..... The BNP, Combat 18, EDL.... & others.... did not need to be paid to kill protesters ---- their lust for blood is only enlivened by their insanity as they - the tools that they all are - spout that there is clear evidence that these protests are merely echoes of the rebellion of the slaves - the Arabs & the Africans ---- but, once the British Empire is restored, these silly ones say, all would be set right....

Thatcher's fanny gets all wavy as the ghost of Enoch Powell eats voraciously at her rancid trough... there is much urgency in this question upon a lonely island...

*****

At least ten protesters were killed tonight, dozens wounded with pepper spray, broken glass & beatings ---- but, we - unlike the last attempt late last year - held the square ---- with no small help from Jesse & his droogs - they hated fascists anyway, 'Give me a reason,' Jesse taunts the fascist thugs as they begin to push the protesters locking arms in a circle around the square.......

Just as the first bottle shatters across a young protesters face, a blonde girl, Hypatia - 'Ok, then - you have given me a reason, you sons of whores!!!' Mayhem erupts, the fascists etc... attack the democratic protesters who move with wisdom now to hold their ground, to resist the onslaught of sadistic economics..... Jesse et co race to the tents storing their gear....

The canny police dissolve away as the streets run amok with ultra-violence.... the protesters outnumber the fascist thugs anyway, but being by temperament peaceful, it took at least five protesters to subdue a single fascist..... Many were brutalised even before this could happen - a pagan girl, praying to the goddesses and gods for aid was be-headed, her head rolling and bouncing like a frenetic pin ball ....

Jesse & his mates return from their tents with their weapons ('For is not self-defence a natural right?' he whispers solemnly to his droogs) - only pseudo-American baseball bats - and dive like banshees into the utter chaos ---- but, on any other day, such actions would be counted as GBH --- but not today, as the ultimately ugly underbelly of existence rears its insurrectionist head in old Trafalgar Square, beneath Nelson's column.....

(In the style of a Japanese anime cartoon, Ichi the Killer)

Jesse transcends time & space into pure action, as he swings his bat into one fascist thug face after another.... he & his mates feel suspended in heaven, in a dreamland --- the rest of the protesters become - for an instant - inexplicably frozen as each face gazes upon the carnage being inflicted upon their enemies --- the false mask of terror evaporates away as even the fragility of a fascist is exposed (as Chaplin exposed & unmasqued Hitler) - amidst this collective revelation, the protesters take heart & continue to fight, understanding that in this world, one who cannot master himself will himself be mastered...

Jesse & his comrades were surrounded with an aura after that first night .... they had protected & defended the incipient community, the embryo of a new democracy... on any other night, they would have been criminals - last night, they were heroes - the police had stood aside, letting the fascists in to attack ---- but when the thugs lay on the ground bleeding, they ran in, attacked, attempting to dislodge the crowd --- the communion of protesters instinctively re-configured their circle ---- the very next day, the community deployed the pink fuzzy handcuffs, secured as a donation by the Union of Sex Workers... who themselves gave freebees to Jesse et co...

The police & their informers had noticed Jesse & his droogs - though the freedom fighters were now protected by the energised mass of faces, bodies & spirits... they knew that they were on the same side.... but, the police were relaxed since Jesse had chilled with them, had given them coffee - & had comically - asked them to join the protests, to rebel - he repeatedly tried to persuade them of a higher mission - that their rebellion also was in his heart ---- protect & serve - 'What better way to protect & serve than to fight against insipid, ignoble tyranny?!!!' - most of the coppers just hid behind the clear masques of their riot helmets, looking in a line over the heads of the protesters, expressionless - maybe because so many were from Bristol -- or wanted one of those gigs at the palace...

The entire square & the streets adjoining are now filled with masses of people - there are two rings of police, those around the central tent city, ten officers thick with about forty horses - & thousands of riot police buffering the crowds in the streets - three helicopters circle over the site of the event..... something is in the air - a potential, everyone feels it --

Maybe we need to call Ian - CJ - since he has a bazooka .... etc....

It is so many days now - everyone has stayed for the first time - they live in their tents - they are finally serious, dirty - their demands are simple - an honest, authentic democracy - the slogans, signs say it all - 'Stop the Cuts!' -- 'Reclaim the Streets!' - 'The Stock Market is Genocidal!' - 'Make the Bankers Pay!' - 'End the Wars!' - 'People before Profits!' - '99%', and a plethora of expressions, infinite as leaves of grass....

These slogans - statements - will only appear extreme to those who do not know the truth ----- barely complicit in any conscious sense, they wander sleep walking, but ceasely rubbing the exteriority of their purse - though ignorance has never been a very good excuse..... and greed is never an excuse -

*****

Aire shares his tent with Jesse, but quickly departs each morning towards the myriad poets who assemble by the water.... they live in different worlds, de facto..... de existentialia... after all, though he fought back against the thugs like the rest of them, he would always prefer the sublimity of voice, song and words....

('If I close the door' by Mo' Tucker)

A poet named Sasha Forte had the square in her moment --- she spoke with an American accent - they said she was from the East Village in Manhattan, a radical anarchist that has been around to receive many black eyes..... a veteran of all the Tompkins Square Riots - in Britain she now dances, acts out her words, conjuring the ferocity of the irretrievable voluptuousness & ironic perversity of women.....

> LOCK UP YOUR DAUGHTERS 'CAUSE YOU NEVER
> KNOW WHAT THEY'RE GONNA DO NEXT
> LOCK UP YOUR GO-GO DANCING DAUGHTERS
> YOUR SKINHEAD DAUGHTERS YOUR SEX-LOVING
> DRUGTAKING HELLRAISING DAUGHTERS!
> LOCK UP YOUR DYED-HAIRED PIERCED DAUGHTERS
> YOUR MINI-SKIRT DAUGHTERS YOUR LAUGHING
> TEETHBARED IN THE NIGHT DAUGHTERS!
> LOCK UP YOUR LONGAGO DAUGHTERS IN
> CHASTITY BELTS SO THEY WON'T
> FUCK BEHIND YOUR BACK
> LOCK UP YOUR DAUGHTERS TODAY WHEN THEY
> THROW MOLOTOV COCKTAILS
> IN YOUR EYES AT YOUR LIES
> AT YOUR STUPID POWER GAMES
> DENYING THE WISDOM THAT PRECEDES THE
> MILLENIA OF THE FATHER & THE SON
> LOCK UP YOUR DAUGHTERS

Of the Feral Children

YOUR CRAVEN GYPSY DAUGHTERS
YOUR CASTRATING VAMPIRE DAUGHTERS
YOUR UNWRITTEN DAUGHTERS ALREADY
DOOMING FAIRY TALES TO DUST
LOCK UP YOUR IMAGINARY DAUGHTERS
YOUR LOST DAUGHTERS
YOUR STOLEN DAUGHTERS
& YOUR DEAD DAUGHTERS
LOCK UP YOUR BOOKLOVING DAUGHTERS
YOUR ROCK'N'ROLL RAVIN' DAUGHTERS
& THE ONES WHO DO NOTHING
ALL DAY LONG
IF YOU LET YOUR DAUGHTERS LOOSE
THEY WILL CHANGE YOUR WORLD
IF YOU LET YOUR DAUGHTERS LOOSE
THEY WILL NOT COME BACK
IF YOU LET YOUR DAUGHTERS LOOSE
THEY WILL DO WHAT THEY WANT
& THEY WON'T ASK YOU WHAT YOU
THINK OR WHETHER YOU LIKE IT
SO LOCK UP YOUR DAUGHTERS
YOUR ANIMAL DAUGHTERS
YOUR MUSHROOM GODDESS DAUGHTERS
YOUR TOO FAST TO LIVE
TOO YOUNG TO DIE DAUGHTERS
YOUR REBEL DAUGHTERS
YOUR FIST-CLENCHED DAUGHTERS
LOCK'EM UP BEFORE IT'S TOO LATE
LOCK UP YOUR LAZING
IN THE SUN DAUGHTERS
LOCK UP THE DAUGHTERS OF STRANGERS
THE DAUGHTERS OF TOMORROW
LOCK UP YOUR BOLD BAWDY DAUGHTERS
YOUR LOUD RASH DAUGHTERS
YOUR MUSICAL MOUTHED
EERIE EYED DAUGHTERS
YOUR PAINT SPLASHING
IDOL SMASHING DAUGHTERS
YOUR FINGER SUCKING PALM READING
HERETIC DAUGHTERS - YEAH! LOCK'EM UP
LOCK'EM ALL FUCKING UP
BEFORE IT'S TOO LATE

Aire acts as the impromptu master of ceremonies - of the poetic revolt, rebellion.... a Renaissance dancing with the audacious spirits of the Beats in San Francisco @1955 - as an aspect - a thread - of this total state of eruption ----

He stands upon the fountain, taking out his papers from his pocket..... he obsessively rustles his papers to the point of utter confusion..... those who were gathered began to become agitated, the rite of spring would erupt into riots --- but, then - suddenly, he regains his composure, speaks to these assembled, calmly, in a measured tone - 'This is a poem about our present & future.... it is surely not as entertaining as the last great poem --- but - nevertheless - it is about our life & what it could be.... it is called, 'The democracy to come...'

(the sounds of a British train, chance operations style)

She bends over
grasps crisps &
sardines from
her bag
Reveals supple
breasts wrapped
in her jumper
Political Crime
Thought Crime
unspoken
She eats sardines &
tomato sauce
on a cracker
with her legs
spread in jeans &
cowboy boots
She drinks from
a water jug &
licks her lips
another cracker
& sardine
as she talks &
chews wiping
her mouth with
her hand
She stares into space,
leaning over to an

invisible other
to whom she gives
a portion of her meal
The smell of sardines
penetrates the cabin
dead sardines
pressed into a can
to be eaten with tomato
sauce & crackers
She has spilled
tomato sauce
on her jumper
as she smiles at other women
laughing (who are
talking about sex
with blushing faces)
Cardiff Central
She moves to an
abandoned table
revealing her lovely
son & daughter
They sit together
around the table
eating crackers
& sardines
She speaks on her phone
about knibbling
sensible food & snacks
asks her love what
he? wants to do for dinner
The boy shouts, "Chips!"
They will see each other again
in an hour & a half
The sun sails across
blue dome toward
twilight beckons
Welsh hills shine
in the last moments
of golden radiance -
in tattered letters
on the daughter's
hoody reads
the word

"Republic"

The listeners who gather applaud his elliptical expression, noting his thin political mask for a sentiment, a feeling that had become wed to the actual..... to the everyday life of the people..... but still was peripheral as the occupation was not yet, & does not intend to be about a political revolution in a constitutional sense -- it is still more like feral animals outside your house, smelling your food - & who perhaps will attack you & eat you if you do not feed them...though we are peaceful, winter taught us other, unexpected lessons, Leningrad, cannibalism - (canned laughter)

('Laudanum' by Velvet Cacoon)

'Here is another voice to weave into the tapestry, dear Penelope,' Aire steps aside as she roves around amid the faces & bodies & speaks directly into people's eyes -

'I am haunted by the fact
that we are here at all -
We rarely talk about this ----
Fear is our God! Yet, that just
makes us look only at the past -
at the graves & monuments -
like Nelson's column there.....
Who in the fuck is he anyway?.......
A big penis, a phallic symbol.... a fetish.....
We are oriented to fear - we seek escape.....
We do not realise that after fear ....
with true anxiety - in that moment -
the truth of mortality opens for us ....
But this truth is our radical freedom,
& the fruitlessness of our malignant
attempts to flee in the face of our destinies,
to merely escape.... to merely get through this -
survive - without ever rocking any boats,
destroying pestilent & meaningless
monuments, or shouting in anger.....'

The crowd, swelling now, shouts in ecstasy & anger, as Penelope smiles, blushing -

I write a few lines about this situation..... although, I am never quite sure what I am - declining the name - I am in the nameless, but the silence of poetry sings amid this nameless existence -- although, for obvious reasons, I did not read my lines, but sit instead upon the edge of the pool, watching the reflections of slowly rolling clouds oozing against the sublime blue sky -

> impossible turning away from the body,
> as the text resembles,
> a sign amidst the visible,
> a mark upon many surfaces ,
> just another body,
> the breath of speech is also of the body,
> writing, a writer, a pad, a pen, a text,
> inscribes amidst a situation
> detaches from the real,
> reflecting, recounting, reconstructing -
> positing an ideal real –
> but, detached from the text
> is the writer, as the fabrication,
> the marks of inscription,
> this labyrinth, is only a 'model'
> deployed in our instruction
> into the divine mysteries.

(although, to be truthful, I did make this insane contribution:

O katalominai rhinozerossola
hopsamen laulitalomini hoooo
gadjama bimbala oo beri gadjama
gaga di gadjama affalo pinx

gaga di bumbalo bumbalo gadjamen

gadjama rhinozerossola hopsamen
bluku terullala blaulala loooo

Even activists have their limits though, & not many were that interested in either my curse or my peculiar bewitchment by my namesake, Hugo Ball. Although, the revelation of my feral incomprehensibility did open some vague door as a strange German theology professor approached me, saying in good English that my intervention was entirely appropriate.... that Hugo Ball is a singular icon of radical rebellion..... but, seeing that I am mute, the professor hands me his card, inviting me to enter into written correspondence with him... I give him my poem - He smiles, nods his head & wanders quickly away, scalding the page with his pensive stare....

After he composes himself before his own special performance, Jesse pounces upon the ecstatic Aire, rolling with him across the ground..... Jesse stares into his eyes as his sweat drips... 'You need to come with us now! There is no escape!!!!'

*****

Jesse shakes Aire - 'There are no other divine mysteries than you getting your arse out of here & getting down to business - ya hear? You know what we are going to do??? It was your idea, after all, muthafucka!!!'

'Yes ---- you are right - it is high time!', Aire acquiesces to his utter fate..... he scans around, looking for Sophia, at least - of course, no one could not expect Ian to ever leave his cyberworld or Blue to leave her utterly masochistic humiliation --- but, he thought that Sophia should be here, especially tonight -- for many reasons -

'Are you coming, oh silent one?' - he looks deep into my eyes...... 'You are like Thoth, the wondrous Egyptian scribe' - (as he laughs & puts his arm around me)

I hold up my board, 'Yes! - to both..."

The idea is simple ---

Pull Nelson's Column down........ that oppressive Corinthian phallus, recalling our own lack of imagination in the wake of Napoleon's challenge to Europe.... it is not to climb so as to enjoy cakes & a cup of tea at the apex - nor to stand upon the pillar in symbolic protest - not to merely explode it as with Dublin in 1966 --- but to have the full weight of the people pull it down & everything for which it stands -

The feminist reasons for doing so would be alibi enough, but the current situation now erupts like a volcano.... the killings of the union members at Parliament Square would have been enough --- the Coalition is no different than any dictatorial regime, Syria on the Atlantic - it is just an Eaton dictatorship veiled, masked in the cynically nihilistic production, reproduction, & dissemination of spectacles -- false, forced choices -- ten different brands of soap, but hands still covered in blood - and not an inkling of genuine democracy --- whatever that is -

demonocracy ---

The state sanctioned murders of the workers is always only exacerbated by the recent scandals over the re-emergence of BSE in the food supply & the swift boycott by the European Union ---- which itself is utterly meaningless in its pale disintegration - the food situation as a whole, the tampered lack of quality or flavour - they have even begun to add more sawdust to the bread, cloaked under the Nutritious Trees Act of 2012.... right after their declarations, 'Water does not aid hydration' & 'Food does not prevent hunger' - what a distance from the joy of the beginning which was about freedom of movement, etc.....

'Fuck Europe!' Luce screams from her corner by the phallus - 'It is a pseudo-state of betrayal --- if only it could be a true situation of freedom.... that is what my parents hoped at the beginning as they hummed Beethoven's *Ode to Joy* while they did the washing up - there was a reason, there finally is a reason.'

('Laudanum' by Burbank International)

Not to mention anything else - the burning images of the Panorama investigations of the meat industry still shatters my mind & soul ---- reminds me of my days at the abattoir during my gap year.... a year that seems never to have ended.....

Where did we go wrong when the quality of food, ground beef - simple mince - when was quality determined by the amount of fat added to the weight? Or, the sheep content of the food fed to other animals, etc.... a truly monstrous site -

Not that not being able to even trust the questionable quality of the food we eat - there is everything else, the collateral damage of the wonderful varieties of cynical, savage - bad faith politics - like a bunch of bulls in a pen smashing their heads together - when all around upon the ground are Moses baskets plump with babies - the babies are families, lives - faces - smashed into a bloody mud mass of hoof marks, bruises & broken bones, skulls -

Hacking scandal, the corruption of the police, expenses scandals, several pointless opportunistic wars - (not to mention all the entire socio-political-economic-cultural etc etc so-called 'system', a question neglected year in & year out - decade upon decade... the crisis that comes as the reaping of this utter whirlwind - the abyss of uncertainty that engulfs everything up until now) - can I even bare the task of listing all of the symptoms of the same thing - the same monstrous site - the same players amidst a perverse power racist gangster matrix --- ?

The Royal prostitution scandal should take special pride of place though - as it pertains to the execution of the spoils of conquered peoples - the monarchy as an integrated agent & force in contemporary sex-trafficking -- that would be, after all, the sadistic allure of power & the only explanation why anyone would want to be a royal - fringe benefits - one is beyond good & evil, free, very free to dance amidst the sensual economy & erotic game of disposable bodies - a glimmer at first, but then erupting into sheer fire - it was that more than anything that excited the 'animal spirits' of the economy, this society of spectacle & ghosts ---

gestalt run amok - Subversia ascends from the earth amidst a deafening eruption...

die Zeitgeist brews a perfect storm, the tensions, the bow & arrow...

I follow Aire, whisper in my own heart, as we run to his tent --- he grabs a black sack & tells me to grab the crossbow that lay upon his sleeping bag...

I follow as he runs through the myriad people, faces & bodies - Aire comes to a halt near a bin & unzips the bag, snaking out a string of rope ----

'We were, are, will be together, stone soup & dead souls.....' Aire sings to himself...

'This protest is like stone soup, each brings what they can..... at first not knowing that they can....,' Aire chants as he organises his gear, equipment....

'from each according to ability, to each according to need.....

this movement of hope

it is quite clear

it is

all is flux'

[N.B. from the typist: there is no music on & I am wondering WTF...... so - I am going off to pee & get more ice ......]

('Laudanum' by Ursula Minor)

Aire hands the gear to Jesse as he streams midst a narcotic dream toward the target ... he had studied a documentary of a guy who climbs a huge tree just to get honey for his family - - he could do the same - though it is Jesse who is climbing........

> this sweetness is ecstasy, joy -
> perhaps, this only joy that would
> ever be open to us - we get excited
> about the human planet - however --
> we are tragically disintegrated ---
> kept from thoughtful action
> via a lame 'fuckaround'....
> our 'leaders' sick enough
> to be totally confident'....

Jesse & Aire are not exactly confident - but, each is open to his own anxiety - & they begin to laugh at the facelessness of it all - remembering all those around them in this moment - the smell of sweat, the still edible moldy bread, ganja, drink, music & fucking --- & each & all of myriad Fate is twined in this instant -

Moment -

All prudence be damned ---

('Not to touch the earth' by the Doors)

Everyone's eyes meet in one last glance of the eye - The pink fuzzies, as they were now called, began the diversion, the distraction, as the sex workers began, almost thrity in number, to dance lasciviously in front of the riot police, who were only too happy to have such sweet entertainment.... as the girls begin to whip themselves up into a Bacchic frenzy, Jesse runs toward Nelson's Penis in Trafalgar Square --- he snakes the rope around, & though wider than a tree with honey -- grasps these handles .... climbs, scrapes up, a bdsm homoerotic protest, rebellion....

(Liszt Sonata in B Minor)

The police begin to stir - the black helicopters locate & target Jesse with lasers.

The tarantella of power has begun - this pathetic dance even Nietzsche loathes...

('Icarus' by Enter the Haggis)

Jesse climbs up, pushes his gear incessantly around the pole ----- the ropes have been distributed - it is pure performance, act --- up the pole --- some of the more sensual femdoms in the crowd touch themselves to see a man on da pole - but they could not applaud him as they were touching themselves.

'Howl,' the mass crowd surges as it, amid an explosive scintillating shock wave - becomes aware of the happening - THIS - each plunges into his or her fate amidst this moment of destiny---- but each, just as soon, locks arms with his, her fellows - the great push surges..... a war of attrition unfolds, bits of territory given and gained...

Jesse climbs Nelson's Column as do the indigenous tribal men seeking honey ----

The crowd - the mob - is no longer a crowd --- but a network - de facto organised - spontaneously & - as it is alive - not in need of bureaucratic rule structures based upon outdated mathematical, quality-control assumptions about body management - Eichmann should have been enough to convince ourselves of this 'fact' -

Jesse pulls himself up Nelson's Column with his African harness - he ascends up & up --- he feels the cold marble as he ascends the great mass..... - he regards the stiff hard-on he has achieved in his ascent as an omen of fertility from Dionysus himself -

Aire holds the rope as he witnesses the ascension of Jesse up & up the column ---

The fire brigade - or at least the scabs that have remained - assault their rockets of water upon Jesse - water cannons upon his fragile body - he swings around like a tether-ball as the crowd below lets out a collective gasp of alarm - Aire - though grabs a few of the crew who set upon the firemen with liberated pepper spray - the hoses quickly cease their function as the noble firemen stagger in pain & blindness.

Jesse has harnessed himself in - he is tied to the column --- the water refreshes him - the lovely water, but punches & burns him --- 'Fuck you! -

water, water, water!!!', Jesse gasps as he climbs further up Nelson's column -

Aire distributes the ropes to many hands throughout the crowd, each person amidst this event of contestation - strife 'in' this world --- a grand gesture - one of the utmost seriousness gestures.... everyone places his/her pink fuzzy handcuffs upon a pile near a Jesus candle, purchased from our local Voodoo Emporium...

A crazy, American Jewish woman wanders through the faces, laughing, chants with a broken, New York voice, 'Jesus is magic!' (laughs hysterically under the column -- she shouts with a sound system on her back - she is in her element...)

Simultaneous to the rubber bullets, water cannons & sonic weapons, the two lines of police begin to push against the people, batons cracking into happy faces .... they start getting the plan, but do not know the full extent -- - they had only read the tales of the past, but they have learned creativity the hard way......

Despite the police assault on Jesse with an array of rubber bullets, gases, & water tortures - he, though injured, does not fall from Nelson's rather ostentatious penis....

Jesse climbs to the best point of Nelson - he wraps the hook around the marble....

I could just imagine that the sculptor was Nelson's secret gay lover who wanted to express the old English adage that it is not the size but how you use it - the column is thus big since Nelson had a big heart & tried real hard, even though, as a man, he was deficient - you dost protest too much, my good sir!

'Well that explains his homosexuality,' comments a passerby who just passes by...
The faces in the crowd - with the ropes - begin to pull - all on one side –

('Rise Above' by Black Flag)

At first nothing happens - & many almost quit in their hearts - but Aire screams with such intensity - 'Pull, my brothers & sisters - this is our greatest act!'

Riot police descend in a final push, rubber, steal bullets, repository of violence -

Each pulls with all his, her strength...... as the united people around them enact a wall of defence, their arms lock in civil disobedience, resistance ---- so that we all can do what they need to do -'fuck you! - water, water, water!!!' to do ------

I am dazzled for a moment by the vision of a beautiful, sublime struggle.......

Sweat & blood begins to flow from these myriad massed bodies & sublime faces, intensity overwhelms as more join in - pulling, scraping their hands - Aire urges them on like Odysseus through the Scylla and Charabdis - the united force of the people pulls harder, more ferociously --- All at once -

A vicious silence swallows the space, when all birds go quiet, there is no breath, all sounds have evaporated --- perspective expands to reveal only a kaleidoscopic panorama of this -

The Column quivers, shakes, & begins to crack at its base.... the deep groan of a thousand lies - masses of bodies, faces thrust away, seeking refuge from the fall...

The outer crowd loses its integrity of a moment ago, scattering in the other direction to the fall - the police themselves disintegrate as it is every man for himself - horses bolt, rear on their hind legs, trampling dozens of riot police seeking only safety from the disaster... in the vast congestion, the police become tea-kettled in their own escape...

Nothing matters any longer as the Column is coming down, just in this instant beyond decision (although each had signed a consent form), the big cock is groaning toward the ground --- it is coming down, it is coming at us -everyone lets go of the ropes & scatters away to the designated safety locations.

Jesse mounts the apex of this phallus - as it all comes down --- petite mort.... He rides Nelson's column like a nuclear rodeo where only Dr. Strangelove can laugh...

Nelson's Column comes down like an earthquake, smashing a McDonalds with the building that housed it, etc., but not at all damaging the protester's haunts - Walden Pond in Trafalgar Square -

[A small wooden plaque at the site - 'The People pulled down Nelson's Column on Trafalgar Square - 2012']

'The water from the pregnant fountain rushes across the surface of flesh........ ', she whispers to me from afar, contagious magic, her beautiful phasing chaos -

Jesse rides Nelson's Column all the way to the back wall of the McDonalds etc......
He is mangled.... damaged.... but he lies there with a sublime smile, as there is a Big Mac in his mouth.... the rent-o-cops, minimum wage mercenaries beat him senseless as he whispers, 'Two all beef patties, special sauce, lettuce, cheese, pickles on a sesame seed bun - (say it in 7 seconds or less & you get one for free!),' although he is rectally impaled on Ronald McDonald's throbbing penis...

The deceased clown, it should be said, was excited by viral destruction, utter rampid childhood obesity, & I am only speaking of the clown.

Jesse is in a coma --- &, he is still in handcuffs as he lies in the ICU.... Each night there is a vigil on the streets below his room....

9 NOTES FROM THE UNDERGROUND II

('Lumpy Gravy' by Frank Zappa)

'I will tell you why I strip....' Blue rolls over upon her bed, giggling, 'I wanted to be my mother...' she laughs out loud.... 'I wanted to feel what she felt - or, at least how I thought she felt --- it was the way they all looked at her when she walked onto the stage or through the room.... she was a golden goddess.....'

There were sounds of conversation & laughter outside, amid the commons, free space - this clearing of openness, play across myriad perspectives of mortality...

I did not wish to write upon my board, as I was content to just lie with her on her bed, listening to her obsessive, though endearing narcissism.... I lay sideways, resting my head upon her supple belly - she gently strokes my hair as I gaze upon the ligature marks on her neck, wrists & ankles....

'Actually - that is not really true .... though I may imagine it to be that way -

'I cannot simply blame all of this upon my dearly departed mother... it was only the moon-sheen that shown -- through a little girl's eyes -

'I saw the vagina - the cunt - pussy - only as a positive force - never as a lack - though - my own feelings of dire Electra were projected upon all of the many shapes of men who frolicked around my own senseless joy... I wanted them to notice me too - to look, gaze upon me as they did my mother, this princess of the smoke filled room ---

'They put me to work as a cigarette girl - in the old fashion style - I walked from table to table --- the pathetic men were sweet to me --- I began to feel that someday I would become a goddess as well ------- beyond my own explosion in the mirror -

'I passed through each & all of the psycho-sexual stages of human development in the strip club - I have to admit - (though I have my own fixations & neuroses) .... I was captivated by an image, by the mirror - the image emerges, crassly alienated from my own feeling of my fragmented body ---- though this... too is me...

'The audience is my mirror, my confrontation with the audience is my only cure,' Blue explains, 'the impetus that compels me to face my desires & the overriding fear that always sticks in the back of my throat..... We can say whatever We like ---- this will not conquer this strife of existence in our depths ----'

'Neither science nor religion is the answer - nor, a combination of the two - as the most important thinkers have expressed..... there is a deeper thought prior to each -

'Neither is certainly the truth....

'Neither is certainly the truth....

'I am not talking about the truth of logic & facts - I am not talking about catechisms and moral laws - but of the tragic self - forever snared in this double bind...

'The unconscious seals our fate ---' I scratch upon my board....

Blue kisses me, squeezes my face & laughs ----

'Or, maybe it is just our bodies that hold us here, where we are open to the sublime truths of existence... in each & all of its surreal, impossible aspects....' Blue articulates, whirling around in the abyss of her irrelevant thoughts....

I roll over upon her, utterly seduced by her speculations upon psychoanalysis & sexuality -- Eros fashions me into an arrow - she was my target - she was the *topos* - this place of joy...

('Cinnamon Girl' by Neil Young)

I kiss her lips gently -- she at first giggles, then shyly smiles into my eyes --- for the second time she blushes as I bathe helplessly in the light, abyss of her eyes - that she would ever bother to look at me - but look she did, neither did she turn nor did she seek to escape with a joke - our eyes simply froze together as we experienced the eternity of this moment -

[Private Content]

Some accounts have it, although this is disputed in some quarters, that I licked her pussy like a tornado - with no expectation of reciprocity.... just as Jesus had once counselled - for God is Love ... 'But, what is love?', asks Pilate...

'Aaaaaaaahhhhhhhhh!', she groans, moans, clawing like an utter animal ....

She scares me.... I tremble..... This pointed position, that fold of lovely petals.... She was, is already always beautiful, ugly - beyond even pseudo-revolutions of the slaves... my joy shatters my recent self-composure as I explode with the ecstatic annihilation of all visible objects. Opens - Open --- concealment...... Truth..... she is poetry - THIS..... We dance through the dark horrors of THAT....

I go with her this time - I will protect her, at least in my imagination - words... she intends to quit the fucking place but needs to pick up the money she is owed....

Blue scatters amid this street, twirls around - gazes at the rare star filled sky -

'Look at it all,' Blue gasps, 'This abyss of night - we are radically thrown in our mere mirror projections of perspective - these - this howl of the winds --- this breath of my mouth...'

We joyously travel to the Munchkinland of Soho - , jump the train, switch, jump off - coaxing the acid lights & the sublime bodies with voices who ask us questions as they blur by...... Blue, always the most cautious girl, wants to hook up another gig before she quits... & Soho is simply a better place to work, though it is a fair journey compared to Streatham Hill...

'I know that it is wrong - or should be wrong.... ' Blue whispers as she dances in the streets, 'But --- there is an urge inside me that ---- ', she stopped in her tracks, & she kneels in front of a neon signed whore house in Soho, her sacred temple ---

'This is a place of freedom - here - I can do whatever I want - if only I could be such a proper whore - ', Blue threw her wine glass at the neon sign shattering the symbol, clandestinely advertising dancers - Blue tells me to stay outside as she enters this finely lit establishment ---

I stand, light a smoke ... witnessing the surging life of the streets at night, the beauty of a girl or a boy in the prime virility of hopeful impossibility..... before I could finish my thought or my smoke, Blue returns, upbeat, she smiles, 'They said I could start whenever I want, Hugo! I am finally free of that horrid dungeon of misery.'

Of course, that was the precise place toward which we now wander in the night, jump the tube, jump off, wandering some more in our return to Streatham Hill.... but, just as quickly, we fall from despair to despair...

I went with her to protect her - she was already far away, in her heart, from this space - but she needed the money ------ lest we forget - these sadists are in charge everywhere, across the monopoly board -

There is no true nobility any more - just a bad theatre company.... with guns pointed at the audience ---
All white trash masquerading as higher men - thank [God] for them..... Obviously - the epoche, the event is Jesus - or, is it Mohammed - or something else besides...

They have always got what they want through sheer force - their world as this place, situation of domination, torture, abuse - she was the meat....

'If only I could be such a whore... if only .....' - the myriad pieces glisten upon the sidewalk....

'How can you say that this is freedom?'- I write on my board....

'We are travelling to a place of domination...' I whisper inaudibly to her as she dances upon abandoned cars....

'I like it!' (Blue places her lips close to Hugo's ear) 'I do not know why, but I - like it - the impulse comes from deep within me, it is primordial.... like an electric shock -'
Blue twirls amidst the street - this anarchic space for a generation of unconscious subversives..... She laughs as it lightly begins to rain, drops

glisten upon her face.....

'I like to be dominated,' Blue laughs, slapping Hugo, 'Tied, slapped - spit on - with a red ball gag in my mouth ---' Blue slips into the performing voice, 'Cum like a volcano, bad boy ---- I like to be used - please take from me my burden of freedom!!!,' she laughs louder now, 'Just don't make me bleed ....', Blue spins around in ecstasy as contemplates her masters in their own absurdist & tragic irony... 'unless you want to cut me.... - but, I also like to give,' she whispers with a wink...

'Wot? Does not this not offend all dignity?' I scratch feverishly...

Blue swirls around under the stars, laughing - 'OMG - another bloody theory - again another fucking paradigm, or post-paradigm .... I am so tired of it all --- I grew up in a stripper household - feminists would run from the likes of us, if they would ever have had the chance to come into our midst - even though my mother was a stripper & a whore --- she was post-feminist even before Paglia was sucking her first cock.... She was Annie Sprinkle before Annie ever sprinkled -'

'Hell - it is not like all this shit has not been happening for all time! ---- the key is the attitude, and the politics among the girls --- my mother kept control --- then, it was a different ethos --- hell, things change when entire peoples are enslaved.... - shit, most of the girls do not even speak English & are from all sorts of different, exotic places, like Lithuania, Nigeria, Mexico, you name it! Try all 33 flavours!"

I was on the verge of running out of chalk, but managed the most scratchy reply...

'What the fuck are you talking about?'
'What the fuck are you talking about?!!!

'Well --- you see it named - there are so many - subjugations --- the media does not report the most - sorry - it does not even know or have any inkling of the horror ---

Blue laughs as she downs some chilled Stolichnaya - the last third of her sublime bottle.... as we come closer to the Underground... 'Right now though, I was referring to Eastern Europe & the big brothel that it has become...'

'Things bleed into things...', I wrote to her....

'But, that is the problem, after all - it is not about things but that ground of things - for this is an abyss - there is no ground - only primal depths - maelstrom.... chaos......

'It is this situation - this era - but, now, it seems different.... possibility swells, erupts -

'We are all revolutionaries now!' I write upon my board with spit.... 'Even amidst the utter blandness & malaise or perhaps because of this big sham!!!', Blue finishes my thought...

We were nearly on the doorstop of the Underground - this sickening pig porn trough of bankers, brokers, & pseudo-aristocrats - trust fund assholes, addicted to coke & whores - & increasingly of late, to murder, fat rendering & cannibalism...

We walk under the sublime moon - intimate with the river of the sewers, still alive, barely...

The stars seem to call out to us, if only we could hear their message...

I put my arm around her sweet waist as we traverse the labyrinth of chain linked fences, ornamented with barbed wire, jagged broken bottle affixed with adhesive...

I hold her hand as we enter the club through the dark, stanky corridor --

'Do not worry, Hugo ---- this has all been done before --- just let me go ---- it is my fate, which I love....'

The coat check girl, attired in bondage gear, looks at me funny - says I should go talk to her........ that this is not a good idea.....

I grasp Blue one last time - I gaze into her - I kiss her upon her sweet lips, tears fall from her eyes - all around various women are being consumed, used as brands...

Blue walks amidst the men - like prey - they grab, claw at her - she is a mere target - a whore - she was always the most submissive of all of the dancers - set radical new standards like Sasha Grey - but they had taken it all too far -- they would kill her & fuck her dead body at a whim.... always have an exit strategy....

The suits tore at her & did what they liked ---- they formed an amorphous, kinetic circle around her, taking turns slapping her in the face, her tits, ass & pussy - one gentle soul smacks her feet with his marble & diamond encrusted cane - taking short sharp vigorous shots at her petite bottom after each exhalation of his cigar....

I stand, frozen in utter amazement..... breathless -

'Hey, there, Blue --- you lovely whore - slut - remember your grandpappy?!!!', the Controller talked to his 'lovely girl'....

I quiver impotently at the door - I taste, smell the utter savagery of these so-called well-heeled freaks - a volcano of rage wells deep within my being....

'I would walk a mile for that vertical smile.....', an old man sings as he pathetically fucks Blue's pussy with his cane - 'Head to head, head to head!!!'

('Ted, just admit it' by Jane's Addiction)

A young buck stockbroker slams the old man aside - the doddering fool twirls once & falls fortunately upon a cashmere couch next to an 18 year old prostitute, petite, supple - golden hair......... 'Are those sublime locks natural?', the old man queries as a waitress hands him a Pim's on the rocks...... 'Aren't we lucky! Aren't we lucky! Seats in the very front row!!!' The blonde whore unzips the old man's fly... strokes his supposed petrified organ, which responds nicely & spontaneously -

The circle closes tight onto Blue as the slaps'n'spits accelerate - they tie her hands behind her back, with handcuffs for good measure & insert a spider ring gag into her mouth - they tie her tits until they are purple, snaking the rope around her body in the usual manner - she sways & slides upon the slimy, wet floor as they push her to & fro -- she bobs about in her humiliated helplessness ----

A skinny, freckled former prime salesman can no longer endure this monstrous dance & grabs Blue's head... [censored content]

With this spark, the prairie fire of throbbing gristle, donkey punches, spit, chokes, slaps & various other penetrations coalesce as a frenzy of orgiastic usury...

('Unadulterated Brutality' by Impetigo)

'Take it bitch --- all the way to the balls, cunt.... '

All the time - a skanky slapper x-factor wannabe dancer twirls around a pole upon the stage.... oblivious to the carnage upon the floor...

The pillars of the community all at once - in response to these usual signals - begin to collectively piss in Blue's face, although each insists that it is a voluntary, individual, & above all consensual act between consenting adults...... (consent forms signed all around as the film crew descends from RapeParty.xxx - 'Can I use your back noble sir, it seems that my table is covered with a whore!' he laughs at his own joke, as everyone around him clucks, 'Good show! Good show!')

'An utter electro-magnetic urge scintillates within...... pulsating from the Nothing to the surface - ', she shouts out, 'I do not know why, but it feels like the very Will of the world itself, expressing its primal irrationality through me!'

I lust to kill them all right here... right now!!! The deed is all!!!

As a tiger, I lunge at them.... I see her eyes look into my own ---

shocking light - a sudden flash of pain ----

the fist dislocates my skull

they grab me too

others grab me....

'What, who are you - Don Quixote?'

'You want some of this, you little boy bitch?!!!! What? No response? Hell, that's as a good as a yes from where I am from....'

An endless train of bankers & stockbrokers slap their cocks in my face... & spit all over me, pissing to boot from many streams, others taking turns fucking my ass, just as they had with Blue.... The only difference between me & Blue in this regard was that while they fucked her pussy, they tied up my cock & balls & stepped upon them...... although neither of my balls ever did pop.

'Any friend of Blue's is a friend of mine', the sadistic camera man Quentin whispers... 'Just don't forget to sign the release form....', he laughs in his concealment, spitting in my face..... you can still find us on RapeParty.xxx.

I gaze upon my love as five stockbroker/bankers fuck me up the ass in a train...

The stockbroker shouts in ecstasy, 'Take this you little worm, slave, citizen.... I am a Sorcerer & an Exorcist! I have stolen your soul!'

They fuck us for what seems hours amidst our utter public disgrace.... We were just part of the show - the clientele, men & women, approach me & Blue & slap our faces, spit upon us, & insert rolled five pound notes up our arses....

'Here's your back pay, you dirty little piece of shit whore!' A cock in her every hole & a Guinness record four in my mouth.... at once, can you imagine!!!

Once we were sufficiently consumed & beaten, they vomited us back out - as the bulimic ideal of all slaughtered vomit dolls - threw us into the skip in the alley at the back of the club....

We were bloody - wet - bruised.... slices in our skin...... 'bleeding from all holes,' I think is the customary turn of phrase....

Instinctively, we franticlly climbed out of the dumpster, falling to the glass decorated asphalt... the rain came at that instant as per usual - but, this time it was savage, fierce - lighting lighted the sky with repeated explosions of thunder -----

Winds dance chaotic blowing curtains, papers, & the chain linked fence scratches, screams its song, crashing boards, lose upon windows.......

She - Blue crawls over to me - she faints upon my belly as she sees the blood pour from my face & ass.... streaming down across myriad possibilities.......

We lay there - in the wind and the glow - gathering our senses & the five pound notes that they shoved up our arses.......

'Mutherfuckers!!!!' - Blue shouts as she gets to her feet....
Outrageous!!!', I write on my pathetic board with my own blood....
Blue stands upon the road, shouting to no one - 'The only martyrs are

those who are burned at the stake - fire cleanses the heart, the priests dominate - ...'

'Wot you talkin' 'bout Blue?', I ask in a differing voice...

'Sorry if I am a bit cryptic - but I want to take this muthafuka down -----

They need payback, as the masses say.... an utterly deranged revenge scenario!!!

I shout at the gods of winds & storm --- & lightning ------

I am attacked with wind & lightening only, all becomes dry, I can hardly stand in the face of this sudden surreal glow, hot, swirling with caresses of wind....

I have a vision of Blue, myself immersed in each other's flesh, fucking, kissing in front of an immense fire, engulfing the world......

It was at that moment that we shared a hallucination of our divinely inspired task.

*****

Blue & I gather the five pound notes that were deposited in our arses.... quite a bit of bob...... to say the very least.... we had bling, muthafuka...

'We need to do the right thing.... ' Blue attempts a whisper in my ear......

Then shouts like a Queen Elisabeth the Second, when she is smokin' cigars... bettin' on the horses on her Iphone, 'We should burn these monsters alive'..... she dresses in her Chav track suit... 'We should burn these monsters alive.....

We run under the starry sky with the wind toward the 24/7 petrol station - thank the Lord for America... at least in matters that require mass killing & extermination.....

We fill up our brand new gas cans hastily, hungrily, eager in our joyous frenzy of monstrous revenge..... We nearly skip like Dorothy, Toto & friends back to the Underground, holding hands & whistling the tune, 'Follow the yellow brick road' - the Wizard of Oz, he turns out to be the Owner, a stone cold *pimp*..... When we arrive we scurry about out of breath, chattering as to our plan - Blue twirls around with the gas can that sails at the limits of her reach, deciding -- 'We need to set fire to the doors - but pour the petrol under the doors at the same time - bricks do not burn, unfortunately .....'

Immediately, as if I were under her spell - & finally, thankfully so - I ran down the alleyway to the courtyard behind the Underground.... I notice the blood all over the skiff, otherwise filled with rotten food & rubbish from the club - rats scurry in all directions with my intervention - I feel pulled invisibly toward the door, as if by some occult magnetism ---

I begin to splash the door with the petrol --- then I let voracious gravity guide the can to the lip at the bottom of the door - I pour the stream of accelerant underneath into the Underground - into the club....... when the can is empty I slide away from the door, throw it into the skiff as I slip around the corner & back down the alleyway....

When I return to the street, I witness the brilliance of a dancing orange flame upon the front door of the Underground - 'Did you light it, Hugo? -- They must not have any chance of escape!!!' I look at her sheepishly, shaking my head... 'Well, get back there & light the fucking thing..... what in the hell do you think we are doing!!!.....'

Blue threw me a lighter & I ran anxiously down the alley & over to the door.... It took three strikes but the old silver lighter finally set ablaze - I held the flame close to the pool of petrol & the courtyard was suddenly alight with the tremendous flame that now engulfs the door - the entire rear end of the Underground ... in a panic, I run feverishly back to Blue - the flame in the front is now nearing the first floor, the crackle & explosions of this unrelenting power of pure nature --- matter....

We begin to hear the outright terror inside the club - shouts & screams from the lechers & whores who wallow within - but at that moment, Blue clutches at my hand with her own, gently resting her cheek upon my shoulder ---- she turns & embraces me - ' It is finally over -- the foul horror of my life is now a thing of the past!' With this sublime realisation, Blue suddenly breaks out into an uncontrollable laughter, as she dances around in a chaotic figure eight, singing as if she were still a small girl,

> Ring-a-ring-a-roses,
> A pocket full of posies;
> Hush! hush! hush! hush!
> We're all tumbled down.

Blue quickly turns about & begins her figure in the contrary direction, flailing her arms as if she were a magnificent bird.....

> Ring a ring a Rosie,
> A bottle full of posie,
> All the girls in our town
> Ring for little - Hugo.

At this point, she spins around in a circle until she falls into my arms from sublime dizziness... she clasps hold of me tightly, pulling me away into her dancing vortex - we spin around & around, in eternal recurrence, her singing loudly, laughing

> A ring, a ring o' roses,
> A pocket full o'posies-
> A tissue a tissue we all fall down.

Just as she sings out the last verse, she pushes us both over & we tumble down upon the sidewalk by the deserted, though now well-lit street ---- she lies on top of me & looks deep into my eyes --- feeling the pleasing warmth of the fire, Blue whispers, 'I love you, Hugo - who else would stand by me this way -'

With that admission, she begins to kiss me, at first gently, but she soon dances with the same tempo as the cascading fire she has awoken - she tears at my shirt & belt with an effortless gesture --- she opens my trousers, tearing off her own knickers with another simple gesture - Blue pounces upon me ... taking my bloody, beaten & bruised, though unavoidably aroused, phallus deep inside her - she dances upon me with the fire as she rips off her last threads in the awesome heat & noise of eternity....

Blue rides me like a rodeo cowgirl as she touches herself... Like an oldskool porn film --- I hungrily caresss her breasts, thrust my cock with the same tempo - I clutch at her neck with my hand, gently strangling her - Blue erupts with accelerating excitement as she slaps my face, grinding me hard in the glow of the volcanic eruption of the Underground ---- she moans louder & louder - her cries become bestial as she chokes me with her knickers ---- she grasps hold of my shoulders & climbs upon me like a tree, pushing herself up, as she squats upon my face - she clutches my head between her hands & pushes my face deep into her bloody flower - she grinds my face, becoming ever more ecstatic in our act of sublime intimacy.

'The spirits are all around us!,' Blue shouts into the night sky, 'They are the spirits of all the dead girls killed in this club! They have come to celebrate us!' Blue gyrates more ferociously upon my face as her moans begin to resemble the howls of a wolf - she dances faster, faster, moaning now in a deafening intensity - all at once an orgasmic invisible shockwave sails through her body - she convulses with an erotic existential event, the power which was unique for her.... she falls over - shakes, quivering like an epileptic.... She had never ever felt a better orgasm....

We lay next to each other, catch our breath as we feel the warm caresses of the fire - I reach over to her with my embrace but she pushes me back -- - 'No, not yet.... it is still surging through my body .... '

Little drops of rain begin to spit upon us, the proliferation of the intense pinches of unexpected coldness stands in shocking contrast to the fire.... I shout at the clouds in a language perhaps only they & their lord Zeus would understand......

jolifanto bambla o falli bambla
higo bloiko russula huju
hollaka hollala

blago bung
blago bung
bosso fataka
ü üü ü
schampa wulla wussa olobo
hej tatta gorem
ba - umf

My invocation does no good however as the rain comes now in torrents, washing us clean - but the rain had no effect upon the inferno which at this point was far too hot to douse - the steel is melting, the water, annihilated...

Blue is not bothered as she suddenly hops up, exhilarated by the streaming caresses of tiny fingers all across the supple topography of her body - she again begins to dance - skipping naked & laughing in circles under black clouds - the effervescent light from the raging fire mocks the impotence of the rain as it lights upon the voluptuous nymph who frolics in the glow of peace, painting the streets with her blood.....

In the distance we begin to hear the sirens approaching the fireball - The sirens come ever closer - we begin to see the flashing lights of the police &

fire brigade through the stained glass windows - 'We should go,' Blue whispers as she skips toward me, clasping her hand in mine... she pulls me as we run away through the streets in the opposite direction to the sirens.... & flashing lights...

10 THE LADY MACBETH COMPLEX

('Unconscious' by Sepultura)

It is a strange fate that explosives & soap are derived from the same alchemical process - as with Coke™ & coke - explosives of violence, of blood & carnage - washed away by the detergents of innocence - it is also no great surprise that the most violent militarist nations are those which consume the most soap -

a proportional relationship - the mathematics of blood & soap ... fire & ice...

We could perhaps explore a psychological basis for this behaviour - the impossible reality of murder washes away from the symbolic realm, from our words, this horror of freedom in its stark ambiguity... in our cowardice, we give leave to this depraved master murderer to return to the imagined innocence of his mother's womb - proper murderers murder again & again... the 'again' is only possible if he forgets again & again -- he is not held captive by this horrifying image since it is never spoken - he merely interprets the manifestation of his own horror in a different way...

But there is no Book of God, no ultimate conversation - no 'talking cure' - only evasion, postponement - even the horror when realised will not be washed away - there is no rational state of normality - every impossible erupts, buried deep within - it is only architecture, as Sophia ironically reminds us - that at once incites and limits our dire existential propensity to rip, tear - slash - each other to shreds..... gotta control the castle - for this is the only basis of memory, the sword of the narratives.... for mortals...

Lady Macbeth sleepwalks through the darkness of life - at first whispering, rubbing her hands - even as these themselves never touch blood - she never mentions - out of polite respect - her menstrual blood, flowing with the Moon & Ocean...

It was desire that pushes him toward - into the ghastly acts - the most sublime & satisfying acts amidst this brief moment - before the insatiable even returns with its ever voracious hunger - the bloody bloody bloody, purchased with biases, bad faith promises & boring lives - were not my concern - but it was She -

('Deep space 9mm' by EL-P)

Murder made sublime by the ecstasies of love - it was not only me who feels the dim fangs of guilt - our murder is not murder - it is a joyous gift for her, amid the drama of redemption - her redemption -

Her kisses, caresses are not of love - upon the surface, it is play - scintillates this fragmented reflection - smashing the rages of revenge - neglected powers - there is an irreconcilable conflict in her - she seeks any resolution .... the easiest target - the stray dog.... Upon both sides of rumour, she dances - her own feral desire & play demands it - as the damsel in distress - she plays her part well, but who can blame her - hiding the darkness of revenge, cruelty, ambivalent desire - yet upon, inside the glass, in all cases, she invisibly frolics amid the diverse trajectories of her masochism - her utter lack - loss of control - She relishes her humiliation, adrift at sea...

('Five nails through the neck' by Cannibal Corpse)

But, it was only her nocturnal wanderings, that it was clear there was something she would never remember - but in the darkness of sleep, she at once acknowledges the horror of her in-capability - sprawled in the shower, water beaming down, steam shrouds her naked figure setting upon the tiles, her hands, breasts, face covered with blood, as she smears herself with her menstrual blooding which snakes in myriad threads through the streaming water, around & down into the blessed drain...

'I am of the flow of all things, each face will be grinded into dust...' she chants as her head rocks back & forth to an inaudible drum, her eyes closed, but open to a different world...

I exhale as I hide in the wardrobe across from the shower... I poke my head out & try to speak, but only manage 'yadayadayadan lol omg lmao sts ktq' - She still cannot understand me, not even in her subconscious - But, outside, they think I am feral since I speak like that.... they do not comprehend.... &, they always call me crazy, insane - they want to round us all up, we chalkboarders, subject us to experiments, surveillance & training regimes toward docility - But, I escaped from the 'insane' asylum years ago & they - none of them - have caught me yet...

After a time, Blue opens her eyes to the blood, still unconscious gasps in panic, she frenzies to wash away her ultra-violence with the detergent suave & ubiquitous water - a sudden narcissism that would not bear the pedestal of her elevation in her own eyes... she seems incapable of honesty, except in light of an even deeper somnolence, in spirit possessions of forgotten epochs - 'History is propaganda!' she whispers coyly.... with a wink...

In her sporadic moments, these surreal visions of excess, she drives him toward ever greater powers, transgressions, with the hope of his-her utter abasement, subjection --- but, also of utter abjection - this rejection of torture, not merely a trope -

('Killa Klan' by Juice J)

But - that was impossible with her own increasing psychopathic delirium, he - acting - murdering - their parts - dancing through the eyes of the lover - forever raises her higher into the vertiginous heights - the perseverance of the subterranean - although there are other readings of the original scrawls, cries...

She wishes, lusts to be brought low --- but finds herself flying - she caresses the waters of the sea & this placeless centre.... recoils in her utter astral sublimity... she is not her - a nightmare slashes within without her in the dark - she suddenly wants marriage - conversion, & co-dependent certainty - abyss of the end.... When she finally wakes up the next day, she is refreshed & ready to kill again....

'Simultaneous - Successive - both at once - neither - nor - the centre is everywhere?' Blue gurgles out over her breakfast, 'Damn, why did I say that?'

I am always beat - tired from the splatter of the night before -- humble, shaking upon my bent knee - violent discord of her seductive treacherous desire, dizzying death - health of wicked narcissism - it tears her apart upon the radical bed sheets, the place of psychotic de-singularisation - She is fated, cursed (Subliminal underlay - 'Cuffed'] to wander the cold stone halls seeking to expiate her guilt ----

The unexpected climax amidst the flames at the Underground - it was too much for Blue...it was not enough - she hungers for a repeat performance - she is insatiable for an orgasm that had rendered her quirky, shivery - wack - until this very moment - 'I will destroy each - every one of those fuckers......'

I fall down next to Blue, snatch a piece of chalk -

'Tonight?!!! -- I ask...

'Tonight,' Blue suddenly interrupts, 'is the first day of the rest of my life!'

"What will we do?' I touch her hand...

'Last night was pure ecstasy - the best orgasm of my life -, ' Blue shouts, 'Not even to mention the utter satisfaction of revenge... '

'But, what of the other strippers?' I scratch upon my board....

'What of them?,' Blue waves her hand, 'those who simply watched or looked away as I was tied, tortured & raped - night after night?!!! Fuck them!'

'They were afraid just as you - ' I inscribe....
'I can't think about that right now - & why the fuck should I - they kept me down on the floor while they were Ladies of the Pole...' Blue cries out, 'Tonight is mine, ours -- Tonight is the beginning of something sublime!'
'Beginning?' I jot on the board....

'Yes, dear one,' Blue erupts, 'This is only the beginning - not only are these rabid cellars of torture & humiliation all around - proliferating underground amidst 24 hour licensing & the wholesale buying & selling of flesh - these places need to be burned to the ground so as to protect the innocents from the abuses of power --- but - & perhaps more selfishly, it gets me fucking off - my best fucking orgasm ever as the Underground exploded into its own vertiginous fireball!!!'

She lies back in her sublime beauty, seductively caressing herself - 'We must return to the prowl,' she whispers, 'We must do it again, & again,' she smiles, relishes her joy, & as I, her devotee, am captivated by her voluptuous brilliance....

'I think we should go to church Hugo,' Blue smiles, 'We must consecrate our feral union, our divine mission, amidst a sacred space...'

I smile & immediately walk to the kitchen to assemble a picnic basket.... we walk hand in hand through the dark streets, in the open air under a dark, turbulent sky - approaching the abandoned church, we enter the courtyard - the spirits wink at us in the corner of our eyes.... I open the old wooden door with my trusty crowbar & we enter the sacred chamber, gazing at the elegance of the statuary & interior design -

Blue grabs the basket & sets up table upon the altar, I pull out the bundle of wood & light the fire near the altar....

The fire warms Blue - as she is naked in church, we drink, lying upon our blanket --Saturday at midnight - as I lie feverish, dismembered - transfixed to her trembling moaning beauty..... she hops up like a pixie & twirls around, around, birthing my obvious lascivious gaze...

('Satan gave me a Taco' by Beck)

My witness - the light of my eyes only made existence more ecstatic - she gazes at me with a singular purpose..... clasps my head with her left hand - her fingers tear my face, seemingly at my hair... clutches at my belt with her right h&, she kisses me voraciously....

She tears off the button of my trousers, rips my metal zipper open claws my jeans down below my knees - the brass buckle of my belt rings upon the pavement - Her mouth & tongue slide hungrily across my face, down across my neck, chest with a licking sublime fever... her hair drapes sweetly across my flesh....

All goes black, & then a commercial break for adult lifestyle nappies - an elegant man playing golf, 'Hell, when you're on the 14th hole, you don't want to have to try & find a loo! Thank God for my Lifestyles...' He relieves himself with a smile - & grabs his next club, approaches the ball & swings.... 'Nice shot, gov,' the caddy shouts...

'Lifestyle Adult Nappies --- It is not just for the incontinent anymore!'

Coming to a Cinema near you - 'Meaningless 2 - trailer monologue: in a(n) x where y (function) r, s, t etc., Z (function) y, r, s,t (function), x (function), y (function), where p=-p...

From the creators of Tuna Fish Trees™ & Meat Corn™

NEW!!!

Brainiacs cereal!!!!

Stem cells, enzymes & nucleo-viral agents in every box!!!

'Science is Yummy!!!' a horde of small children shout...

Make your kid a Brainiac!!!

[Subjects may exhibit myriad symptoms of illness for an unspecified time after ingestion, but - to be extremely clear - this is merely a virulent agent that efficiently transforms the DNA of the test subjects so as to make them Brainiacs!!!!])

Now, back to our Feature Presentation

('I wanna love you' by Bob Marley)

Blue falls to her knees & breathes me in like sweet air - she touches herself fingering frenetically as her head gyrates around & around in delight... She grasps my wrists - forces my hands around her neck, 'Fuck me in every hole, Hugo - fuck me hard!' I fuck her just as she requests - in every hole, I claw at her hair thrusting faster & harder deep inside her as she moans between erotic chokes, gasps for breath - as we make love we are surrounded by the spirits of dead strippers who effervesce with ethereal frenzy - My cock enters faster, in one hold or another as she squeals, grunts & moans louder, louder like an animal or a Latvian sex slave on the Royal Estate...

The sexualised spirits come much too close..... lick our faces.... a phenomenon which only intensifies Blue's ecstasy... I thrust & slither between her lips feeling the horizon of impending scintillating orgasm - the impending explosion becomes apparent to Blue as I implode, moan, gasping for air...

"Cum on my tits, Hugo, my sweet mute man,' Blue laughs as she moans theatrically, lying back onto the altar - she becomes sheer electricities of necromancy - I pull my cock out of her sweet bum, stroking myself as she fucks her pussy with her fingers, black nail polish into the void...

I gasp with a deep groan as I explode my white force upon her supple face & yellow hair... I caress her neck as she kisses the tip of my now retreating phallus.... in its own little death - but, at this very instant, Blue lunges up grasping my head, pulling my face into her pussy as she lies back again upon the altar -- almost instantaneously she climaxes with a jolt that we both still feel to this day -

In an impossible blur that neither of us can remember, we return home to the squat, crashing through the door - Blue falls upon the futon on top of Aire who was already passed out - Jesse sits still in his wheel chair, drooling & making a few inarticulate sounds, gurgles - Rolling off Aire onto her back, Blue clutches the bottle of Jameson's sticking out of his mouth --- he smacks his lips, sticks out his tongue, asleep, he rolls over onto his side, plunges his face between Sophia's legs... Blue slides her way up off of Aire & takes in a deep draught of the Irish potion - the bottle comes to rest betwixt her tits as she sits in a trance, communing with the spirits of the candle....

Blue is lost in the flickering light, hissing out of her mouth - 'We must return to the prowl --- Hugo, we must do it again, & again,' she droans as in a trance

'What the fuck are you talking about?' Sophia suddenly flashes into the light - Blue still caresses her thighs & the power between her legs, but gently rolls over to gaze into Sophia's dark eyes.... My eyes eat Blue, this supple creature writhing - though with one eye I look over toward Sophia who is as perplexed as ever... she scans my face questioningly but I can only place my finger to my lips to remind her ... she smacks the chalkboard with he claw-like nails, 'Tell me, Hugo! What you are up to?

'Whatever you got....' I laugh with my chalk....

'It is an act of sublime sacrifice & ecstasy - the great night of dark seduction!' Blue shrieks, laughing hysterically as she rolls like a clown back & forth across the futon --- over all the others who lie there.....

'We cannot tell you, Sophia - it is for your own good,' I write upon my board -

'Whatever - you sad muthafukas - you smell like smoke & semen - I have had all I can possibly stand at the moment,' Sophia hops to her feet -

scatters off toward her & Ian's bedroom, slamming the door behind her...

'Turn off that boring ass game & come over here & fuck me you worthless piece of shit!' we could hear Sophia call to her lover from behind the door - (although to be honest, we hooked up a web cam & are watching them now on the flatscreen) 'Fuck me! that has to be better than GTA, any day of the week! Fuck me hard, you piece of hacker shit! Fuck me like you fucked the News of the Wound & DJ Rup M....'

Blue rolls onto her back & rests my head upon her belly.... we gaze at the candle as we listen to the symphony of the night, the many snores of Aire & the ten year olds - amidst the usual drunken screaming out on the streets - Jesse's sputtering mouth & the violent ecstasies of Sophia & Ian, 'Fuck me, fuck me, you little bitch!!!'

A joyous night of a symphony of chance!

***

We begin to undertake our conspiracy of desire... lust & revenge upon the local under-culture of Brixton's Streatham Hill - they import girls to order - the cleaners throw the refuse into the 'sewer system' - filled as it is with all the blood of funeral homes mixing with nameless chemicals & other sundries - someday it will melt us all away, if we are not poisoned first by some other man-made plague -

We were on a crusade, a holy war, a jihad - each night we went out to cast our demonic spells & to undertake our ecstatic rituals --- the best orgasms & flaming prisons & torture chambers, the Honey Pot, Blue Velvet Lounge, King Arthur's Sword & Sheath, Flower Motel, House of a Thousand Whores.... the authentic perverts do not want the nice clean escorts from the ads - far too many rules, not to mention the extortionate prices, the more rules, the higher the cost - & the run of the mill strip club is just a tease fest --- the over-stimulated knaves run onto the streets to fuck any street whore with herpes or AIDS sores painting her face - not to mention the pimps who will kill you if you go too far - unless you pay them enough...

The underground clubs offer everything for one flat fee, in a secret lair in which the foxes guard the chickens - & sometimes eat them - within these walls, do as thou wilt --- invitation only - no one need apply - there is an online site with Live Chat & the most popular item, the Request Room - it is from this site, otherwise quite respectable, that the clubs groom & lure their clientele...

Blue & I explode for days on end, moving from site to site wipe out the vice squad through radical violence, topped off with the most sublime orgasms -

This is especially the case with Blue who, for the first time in her life, no longer tries to be pretty, 'Fuck you, Andy Warhol, I do not need to be pretty! You merely ironic decadent pseudo-catholic fascist!!! Though, to be fair, Catholicism is intentionally founded upon an abyss.... Just another net for the eternal fisherman...'

'What else is new?' I scratch across my board....

We chatter on & on, pontificating own new wild wisdom, but yet, it is changing from day to day, night to night... the unsaid, concealment, nothing & laughter... our task becomes a ridiculous performance, as we crave the extravagance of danger, risk - Each night we burn, but with each day, the event is not reported, the police never come - but that is not yet the whole story by any means - yes, each night we bust out to purify another underground 'establishment' (you would not even know where they were if you did not already know) --- but as we grow more confident, we no longer just set the place afire from the outside - we of course prepare all the 'exits' with puddles of ether, with a 30 minute timer we rig together with a pack of matches & a cigarette ---

But - we also enter - make a fucking big entrance - I pretend to be Blue's agent/pimp, as she seduces the man at the door to let her dance - 'We don't have many dancers in here,' the man grasps Blue's arm, 'But I think you have a pretty mouth... sure - go ahead, don't be surprised if it is not money that they throw at you --' he laughs diabolically, his eyes twitch as he grabs his junk through his cum brushed jeans....

> So you can see
> We're friends in need
> & friends in need
> Are friends indeed
> We'll keep you safe
> In the jungle forevermore
> That's what friends are for!

Blue ascends the stage with a large bag, wearing a blaring yellow fireman's coat - she bathes the bag down, whispers to the enraptured dogs of an audience who were merely her toys --- girls are already tied to all four walls on bondage crosses, whipped & abused by the tuxedo clad patrons -- several other girls are being led around on their hands & knees on dog leashes - in the back, in the so-called quiet rooms, screams amidst punches & slaps were the order of the day --

... this is only the common room, the public face of Black Snake Moan - there is still the dungeon underneath, which requires an additional £500, a bargain for sure, but profitable nevertheless due to the quick turnover & group rates -- & there is always another girl to consume, in the Dining Room - but, that is more pricy, £5000 an hour just to chat (as it came with expensive wines & liquors) - not to mention the individual interview rooms upstairs that can be hired in 15 minute slots - can you imagine a better or more enjoyable evening, dinner & entertainment for less than a thousand quid - ?

It would certainly not cost that much to have several of these honey's for the whole night... everyone laughs as they slide into the taxi....

*****

Blue requests her song, 'Burning down the House' by the Talking Heads - as the music beckons, she begins her routine - it is clear that she loves to dance, to strip amid the warm glow as a thousand angels descend upon her radiant face - she slowly, seductively unties the belt of her fireman's coat, spinning it like a whip as she twirls, permits us a glimpse of her undergarments -- a black leather corset, a tiny silken tutu & a pink fuzzy thong -- she is breath-taking as she suddenly spins like a hummingbird around the pole, the coat fills with wind like a great sail, angelic winds flow from this sublime creature into the audience....

That aristocratic mob instantaneously enamors of her beauty & energy - even the sadists stop whipping their slaves amidst this sublime explosion of utter erotic transcendence - the dogs come to heal & the waitresses set their trays down - Blue leaps off the pole in an inverted summersault with a half twist & immediately begins to spin around in a vast whorl where the coat literally rises from her arms as it floats upwards into the lights overhead..... she makes strange hand gestures across her face as she walks rather coquettishly over to her bag of toys.....

By this point the audience was in such a state of arousal & excitement that there were politicians, judges & celebrities dancing upon the tables in rapture.... she made a coy look at the audience & places her hand over her mouth - feigning a blush - she opens the bag - shaking her ass & tits, lest the spell be broken.... she removes a toy fireman's hat from the bag & puts it up to her mouth - she licks it if it were a big cock, & in her dance, proceeds to make love to the fireman's hat rolling around with it, humping it as she flails her arms joyously throughout the smoky air... suddenly she begins to spin around on the tip of the hat, around & around in a vortex, but just as suddenly she stretches out her legs & ascends as she brings her legs together - elegantly flipping the hat onto her head with her labia as she spins around again, six times round, on the pole before she returns to her little bag of toys ---

'What a woman!' an old man sighs....

I was so exhilarated by Blue's outstanding success that I fell into a frenzy of panic when she took from her bag of toys the petrol can.....

The panic consisted in the oil & water of strife & love -- these people loved her - I began to doubt -- to doubt our conspiracy - what is the problem with a bit of fun - we all say that everything should be 'consensual' - surely - but, that seems to be the ethos of, at least this room, of Black Snake Moan - this room loves Blue -

As Blue is dancing a ballet in which the spout of the petrol can was a cock fucking her, slapping her face, choking her - she seems to be replaying, dramatising with modern dance, her own utter humiliation by the brutality of the underground mafia..... 'Your entire existence as a female - designated because of the sly slit between your legs to simply fuck - & your mouth looks so much like a pussy & your head cannot get pregnant,' the banker barks laughing at the politician....

There I say it, the terrible twins branching out into ever greater revenue streams --- all the same product, but not even just them, not even close - they are just not that important, mere handlers of produce at the clubs with a mere taste of the real action --- one day, they hope, to take over the whole racket --- we need poor people after all to fulfill the dreadful desires of the sado-masochistic power matrix --

For, as they always say, rich people must not ever really 'experience' anguish, but instead must cause it.... they must be able to whip the flesh of the whore - to take revenge on death, our dear Hades aka Cum Hau, Ah Pukuh, the protector of Persephone, by making him so busy that he has no time to take them.... they will drown Hades in souls through war, pestilence & genocide.... & they will laugh hysterically at their accomplishments ---

they will live forever.... in the ceaseless moment of their own narcissism.....
&, they will get away with it ....

Blue dances upon the stage as a sublime bird, as if she had been born upon the stage of a strip club - (lol lmao.... etc....) - she was home - for this brief instant - but, she had a greater purpose, & - as she spun round & round on the pole with the gas can - as she pretended to be a fireman stripper -a fire stripper - she opens the cap & begins to spill the bloody liquid upon the stage as she spins in a blurring wheel of lust - she becomes a vapour amid the space of stripping frenzy - petrol is everywhere as she dances more & more devilishly - suddenly - as Blue dances ever more frantically, sexually & pointlessly, she walks off the stage - crowds of people scream for her to return - she walks back out - she spins again, again with the gas can ---- everyone is covered, drunk with petrol - it remains only the match - the spark ----

'If any of you are still clean - innocent - then you had better run - as we are coming for you!' Blue laughed hysterically as she lights the sweet silver lighter -

I wanted her to stop, but I had no voice, no power...... nothing.... nothingness.......

I scurry around to the slaves with the simple sign, 'Get out now! Fire!' I untie the girls strapped to the S/M crosses...those that have been eaten are out of luck...

Blue throws the lighter into the crowd & all explodes into flames --- Blue does a triple summersault toward the door, with a quadruple twist - as she pulls out with a power landing ---- she grasps me, pulling me by the hand out the door into the street outside - we pass by the lucky slaves who listened as she pushes me against the brick wall - we fuck amid the horrific situation... but that will not be all of it --

there will be further nights of terror .....

*****

('Before I Forget' by Slip Knot)

Blue is possessed by ghosts, exploding into frenzied anguish --- she smashes our door open, throwing things down in her wake, running through the squat - She always ends up in the shower, crying, as she rubbed an old flannel across her body ---

Each night ---- the water flows ice cold as she whimpers, 'Out mutherfucking spot - wash the blood away,' as she rocks hysterically --- 'Over & over - sex, flesh & death,' she awakens each night, screaming - each night she squirms in the shower moaning her guilt - her lamentation, 'The spirits of the dead surround, suffocate me....' I would hold her as she screeches, clawing at my arms in panic, drawing blood which mixed delicately, disappearing with the water down the drain..... But, with each morning, just as with the water, her memory of the night before is cast into oblivion, as she would wake up, refreshed, energetic - always wondering why I was so beat..... 'Who are we going to attack tonight!'

I am so tired of it all - the repetition of nightly setbacks - not to mention all else - takes away any respite of joy.... it was not as if we were even being pursued - it seems to be the common assumption in police circles - as if they even cared anyway - that this was a gangland situation & would eventually wear itself out when a new mafia power structure is established - stability is good business, after all ... I just did not like all the killing of the slaves & the way it made me feel about Blue....

As she lay upon the bed, amusing herself with her multi-coloured painted fingers, I lay down beside her, looking at her in the mirror - it was her room after all in which we settled - mine became a sort or strange library, art gallery & museum - some in the house are even talking about moving in somebody new, to share the costs, etc... there is even talk of putting Jesse in there, 'He can't stay in the front room for ever....'

Blue smiles as she notices me next to her in the mirror, slowly walking with her fingers across my thigh to my crotch - I suddenly hold up my board over our heads so that all we see is the board against the obverse background of reality - I had simply written: 'Can we take the night off - 8 days - & the police?'.....

'Fuck the police! What have they ever done for me?,' Blue screams, clutches hard at my balls - I screech & gasp convulsively - 'No - I do not care about any of that - there is only our mission' - I grasp my board & begin to write as she continues her rant, never stopping touching herself, '& - wat the fuck if they catch us - we would become instant celebrities! Talk shows! Books! Memoirs! Movie Deals! & before we know it we could nestle into Never Mind the Buzzcocks -- or some other place where celebrities go to die....' Blue laughs diabolically, as she slaps me across the face....

I hold up the board again, pleading with my chalk - '&, you forget - PRISON!!! Haven't we done enough?'

'Did any of the greats of history ever stop? Sure - they may have had doubts or fears - but they did not become great --- no, I am all messed up - they only became great in that they went all the way to the end... (I began writing again as she becomes inspired with the spirits of the earth) think of it, Gilgamesh, Thoth, Dionysus -- hell, Jesus the Nazarene, even - (she says with a sigh) - you must understand my resolve to act, my dear Hugo!' Seeing my obviously starstruck gaze, Blue intones insistently, 'Should I name the rest of the greats? Will that change your simple mind? --- Do you not wish to become great!!!?

As it seems the most splendidly appropriate moment, I hold up my board, which reads simply, as usual, as I am simple.... 'Greatness for burning stripclubs? They will throw us away where we will be raped ever more than in the Underground...' - there was quite a pause, a deathly silence, as Blue read the unusually small letters - then, with a great sigh, she, who had sat up to read my message, collapses back onto the bed.... unconscious & slightly drooling....

I pull the cover over us & lay upon my side, hugging her tightly, lest I fall off the earth.....

11 THE AWAKENING OF THE SPIRITS

('Rite of Spring' by Stravinsky)

It was a hazy time since Jesse had pulled down Nelson's Column - he is now lost in the Void - suspended between worlds... The only glimpses of him have been - still - these surreal wanderings of Sophia's chaotic dreams - some of which, she contends, took place while she was awake, as a sort of instantaneous glance of the eye.

Aire is tireless in his care of Jesse - the poet wheels the fragmented anarchist down Coldharbour Lane & through the hectic market - they make their usual stops - as if it were a religious pilgrimage - the bookstores, Bookmongers, where the ever faithful dog, Tony Benn, licks Jesse's hand --- Index Books, one of the last resistance bookshops, packed full of hardcore socialists & of course the various Voodoo shops, complete with authentic zombies from Haiti -

Aire would buy his usual supply of incense, Jesus candles & the latest books on witchcraft, shamanism, & magic....

Jesse's eyes were open but he was obliviously elsewhere -

Aire even ventured to take Jesse to a couple of massive protests - each just another of the myriad revolts, rebellions &/or criminal explosions that are now raging across the globe - perhaps the most glorious nobilities, sinister tragedies of humanity merely go unnoticed amidst the noise of all of our clever spectacles - displacing the resistance movement surging across the plant --- no one hears much about the ongoing momentum of these movements, though the resistance is everyday making it more & more impossible to be ignored, erased - the 'Arabs' (well, at least those who have 'oil') have been placed front & centre by the media in the most hypnotising of ways - mis-direction - more of the discourse of the other - criteria of a hypocritical so-called civil society - downtrodden slaves whose only aspiration is to emulate our own perfect lives ...... how wondrous we are to watch it all LIVE.

Jesse is greeted as a hero by the smiling faces, this supple network of sublime bodies with faces, even though he would merely sit with his usual blank stare as ever energetic Aire performed his poetry - He even wrote a poem about Jesse's tragic exploits, 'Icarus of Trafalgar Square' - he performs the poem for those assembled, enchanted as Jesse sits motionless -

> The sublime sun beckons
> burning out the eyes
> of those who
> dare to gaze
> into its depths
> The abyss of light -
> You were already
> blind to the light
> of Terra, of Earth,
> You long stare into
> this luminous event
> the mere distance
> of the gaze is
> no longer enough
> for your joy -
> You seek to fly - seduced
> by the sun of your
> voluptuous desires
> You fly higher & higher -
> climb the column of the sun -
> You throw down the motes of light
> the ropes that tie even the sun -
> You fly toward the scalding apex -
> calling those below to grasp
> hold of the motes of light -
> to pull it all down - back to the earth -
> the hordes upon the surface

respond to the call, harvesting
the motes that cling to the sun itself -
the ties that bind - the masses pull
with the kinetic exertion of panic -
Prometheus smiles at the grand
effort of his children toward
the implosion of a world -
of light recurring upon the earth -
All at once -
shattering cracks, explosion -
the moaning phallus of marble
lusts for the embrace of the earth -
the depth of the abyss -
Icarus, already burns -
descends riding the phallus to the earth -
Crash, exaltation - into the shadows of sleep -
wandering upon the banks of the Thames -
waiting for the return of the sun -
a different sun, one of joy,
upon the earth of a different world

Things fall apart - an old African saying - things are now falling apart - all around - it was not just the scales of political masks that are falling - indeed, one could rightly say that all politics is already always a falling - disparate striving worlds claw their way into the light - only to implode into the darkness of the earth....

Something slightly more profound - surreal - is occurring at this present moment - primordial - a radical shift that perhaps only the Mayans & other Archaic cultures could understand - & still warn us, however, obliquely in their wealth of stories - the so-called myths which earn the sneering abuse of our intellectual pride, as we were originally reminded by Khomeini --- the words which survive the maelstrom, are those which anticipate the fall & do not resist it --- indeed, not by vain attempts at escape through technological power, force & hypnotic meta- propaganda, but in learning to float & fly across the turbulent waters of time...

As the edifice cracks under the power of the primordial - as things fall apart, as Strife seeks her recurrence - so the confidence of the cult of science - the arrogant destroyer of worlds - lies prostrate upon the wet concrete basement floor, humiliated, displaced as it only offered us a sigh of learned despair... pervasive mundane nihilism teeters upon the precipice of annihilation --- after all, our constructions - never homes - fall & fail ---

what will be left of us? -- as we are deleted, erased, forgotten - what stories did we tell - perhaps, rap, incorporating jazz, blues, punk, grunge, dub..... things you can do at home.... will be the only arts that will survive our destruction –

It is as if we never existed, whispers the spectral stranger from the past...it would have been well for us to have heeded the wisdom & the warning - myths of fertility, hubris, nemesis & death - our heedlessness would be the fault no doubt of the secret incestuous liaison between 'Religion' & 'Science'.... these higher men & their otherworldly hopes -

We are all Bela Legosi now.... & we are all seeking our Misty Mundae.... 'We are all Roman Catholic now.... lapsed, satanic -'

The roots of the fatal pattern strike deep, always prior to manifestations of clarity, in the truth event of Japan, for instance - indeed, the manifestations of a failure of our modern techno-industrial commercial militarist mercenary etc. etc. pseudo-system, this shallow mask of the bad anarchy --- proliferate across hundreds, thousands of time units -- even out of time - are we afflicted & complicit in the transgression of our father & creator, Prometheus, the light bringer? --- Is this perhaps a better way to understand our situation upon the topography of myth as opposed to the pseudo-truths of 'logical' and 'moral' reason, as any reason will do in the ever shifting whirlwind of collective paranoia -- we run to each new event, true schizophrenics incapable of symbolic intercourse, lost in the crazed flight from death into objects, images - distraction - any deviation will do....

'We' seek the destruction of memory - who even remembers the Tsunami in the Pacific Rim any more.... it is so passé.... (not to mention the indescribable echo of the scream that is the royal agony of history....) - the destruction spreads, leaps, spits to another unsuspecting, soft target -

Woland does not discriminate in his irony.... neither do his cat nor assassin...

The plates of the earth are moving toward a new configuration.

Even now we fail to listen to the faint whispers of the horrific terrorizing superstition that 'grounds' our entire 'system' of mortal existence - the threads of remembrance, primal orientation - this makeshift thread to which we cling as we already feel the breezes & gusts of the gaping abyss over which we hang - suspend -

It hungers beneath....

The philosopher whispers
into the ear of the King
who would make himself a god
'Remember, thou too art Mortal...'

Do we hear these whispers - or, will pride be our suicide?

('Critical Beatdown' by the Ultra Magnetic MC's)

It is Poseidon who is behind this disaster -
his co-conspirator, Nemesis comes after -

It was he who destroys Argos for Zeus....
His golden shower upon Danae, the ruse....

Poseidon is - as everyone knows - the god of the dark wine sea, but he is also the earth-shaker - for they are all one & the same - Terra quakes - the volcano (Vulcan, Hephaistos, the son of Poseidon) erupts as the blood of Poseidon infiltrates the crevices & recesses of the mountains & land .... Earth, moaning with her opposite - quakes & rocks - splits open giving birth to the violence of her inexorable jealously, concealed darkness –

She also releases the spirits, souls from her womb as it is death for a soul to become wet - the dancing catastrophe of the shaking Mother reverberates & ungulates surrounding waters which then ascend as is the art of Poseidon into a tidal wave, tsunami - the waters cleanse the earth of the blood which drenches her skin ----

Perhaps it is an old story, an old remembrance, sheltered in mythopoetic echoes, that will illuminate a more profound perspective upon the destructive earthquakes, tidalwaves, of Japan & each of the other destroyed cities across the planet - the emblems of the earthquake & the great wave - the hubris of man (the secret weapon of the Titans) - given fire by his creator Prometheus - for is nuclear fission not just another form of fire? Fossil fuels?

One would have thought that the tears of Hiroshima & Nagasaki would have been warning enough for most - after all, there must be better ways to heat water - perhaps, a simple life in the sun receiving the awesome power of this August god - it was the lights spied from heaven that provoked the serial nemesis - the lights - electricity - symbols & symptoms of the hubris of man in his ever greater building projects, wars, timid attempts to spread our virus to other celestial orbs - as we have already done in princeps -

alchemy of incipient life - 'I cannot remember that well at all, but something about some weird life form linked with some woman - experimentally created, but now everywhere - prions, cryons, something like that?', Aire said once during one of our more paranoid exchanges...

Or, should we listen to the Preachers, Clerics, who assert that the disaster is divine punishment for the severe perversion of the radiation scorched culture, just as AIDS is a plague upon homosexuals, etc.? --- perversion smited by the True God - for the Preacher sees the signs of the times, he watches the extreme animation, tentacle porn, a never-ending vomitorium of films like *White Rose Campus... then everybody gets raped* - for instance - especially the used tampon masturbation scene; used knickers in vending machines, vomit porn, tumultuous bukkake - he names it... he watches it, and he condemns it -- 'It is such depravity that has called down God's wrath! He shall cleanse the wicked from the face of the earth!'

Perhaps, to play devil's advocate, the divine spirits take pleasure in such excesses.... or do not care at all... or are only names for the powers of nature, which are forever indifferent - but the devastation comes as a necessary re-adjustment of the relation of whole and part, with no moral significance at all -- only cosmic significance....

Poseidon commands Odysseus - 'Without Gods, Man is Nothing!' The rape of the earth, land, water, air - the only true gods, goddesses amidst a living divine cosmos, the devastation of forests, peoples, animals --- the ever rising temperatures - rising levels of the sea, this home of Poseidon --- fighting the fires that men now possess - the disaster is a direct consequence of our action, our way of life as it aspires upon the spiral of escape, of a denial of tragic existence, to a false God --- Yet, we witness, live the collateral damage of this will to escape, in its various contradictory trajectories - in its denial of the primal truth that we mortals cannot release ourselves from this ultimate double bind as we are incapable of achieving such cowardly aspirations --- it is our peculiar tragedy that we defy our limits.

The incestuous twins seek to either storm heaven or solve the riddle of the universe - they pretend to have in their possession the answer of answers, one claiming possession of the keys to the kingdom, while the other declares that 'heaven' does not exist -- everything is possible, everything is at our fingertips ---- yet - always just out of reach as 'our' malevolent, malignant *polis* orients us to fragmentation & despair... exploitation, lies & ultra-violence, a state of decadence & corruption - from such ugliness, who would not wish to escape? Both wish that we deny this earth, lust to escape this primordial cosmic situation, the sublimity of which eclipses the twins, noisy though ultimately insignificant in their recent arrivals.

Truly, neither has ever seriously contemplated or even fathomed the question.

Rising waters penetrate the cracks & crevices of the land, of the mountains - giving rise to eruptions, earthquakes & the cleansing tidal wave - this is the lesson of the mere story, the myth of Poseidon....We write a new chapter for this story - we who, like Oedipus, have an eye too many - but not enough to hear the wisdom & the warning - our destruction will again vindicate the gods & their noble restraints laid down to cajole us to the Open - to meekness - to the mortal wisdom of the aboriginal peoples whose meekness will give them the inheritance of the earth -

One must have patience...

One great city after another destroyed - through capitalist looting & preternatural disasters - the children of the incestuous marriage of 'science' & 'religion' (amidst their mock combat) whirl around falling to their knees in the face of the destructive power of the earth & sky - pressed to hide away with their flock, still mesmerised by the false idol of intellectual & moral progress - but never listening --- for it is in silence that the divine speaks - of course.... although Panic! has reared her ugly head across the surface of the earth, it was always assumed that some were merely better than others - that some races had the 'moral luck' to obviate the worst disasters that this life could bestow --- as all ideology harbours at its heart an expression of hope - & all ideology always already excludes, erases any, all bad press from its myriad orders of encounter.... in its ultimately vulnerable echo chamber....

Even New York City got its own earthquake just before the beginning of Occupy Wall Street, the volcanic eruption of anarchy & food riots.... the shadow is everywhere....

*****

Aire & Jesse sit upon a bench at the Brixton Oval, betwixt the library & the Ritzy Cinema.

It is a lovely, bright sunny day, surreally still just upon the Oval, with majestic cumulus clouds arced toward the plenum of the Sky - everyone else all around busies about agitated by the frenetic pulse of everyday existence --- shopping, drinking, working & fucking.... sleeping & dreaming -

Jesse stares blankly forward as was his usual custom - his head made slight movements, a pale response to the breezes whispering around the square.

Aire pulls out a bagette from his Aztec bag & the strawed-container which houses Jesse's usual milk/nutrient shake. He plugs the jug into the holder - places the straw gently into Jesse's mouth, upon which the feral dog begins to suck - his eyes are open but whirl around chaotically with no light or insight....

As he took a bite from his bagette, crumbs fall to the asphalt ground - in a frenzy, the pigeons begin to scurry, fly over - with the movement of these first few, many others begin to surge in their fight for the crumbs. One lands upon Jesse's shoulder, though he is oblivious to his visitor. Another shit upon his bowler hat which set like an anti-crown upon his hoody - 'It's good luck!', some crazy hippy bag lady Bridget says every time it happens... that is, a bird shits on anyone... she wanders the streets, making her living collecting bottles - she is also an astrologer & an artist...

Aire takes pity upon these mad hungry birds - pinches off small pieces of bread - scatters them around - all at once, there is a near orgy of frenetic pigeons scratching, pecking for each morsel - until it is all gone - an ancient lady with blue hair sitting close by sneers at Aire, shakes her head (he immediately has an instant fantasy of Hitchcock's *The Birds* in which all of the pigeons finally decide, after much careful deliberation, to eat the old lady once & for all - 'She has been vicious to us for decades,' one bird shouts [flashbacks]) - more pigeons land flutter upon Jesse, one upon his lap - he sucks at his straw, seemingly oblivious -

Aire notices one pigeon in particular with a missing foot & a diseased leg which attempts to get at the bread, each instant unsuccessfully - he aims carefully, pitching a piece of bread toward the lame bird - but the others still beat her to the meagre feast - Aire throws one piece after the other, but the poor bird remains unsatisfied.

He dubs the tragic bird Oedipus, due to his club foot, but, adds the surname Byron - Frustrated by the utter cruelty of a selfish nature, he claps his hands repetitively scaring away the orgy of birds - but Oedipus Byron, unable to flee or fly, sets alone, receiving a morsel from Aire's attentive hand. Soon the swarm returns, but Aire now turns away to eat the baguette himself. The pigeons, still surging, deposit droppings upon Jesse's hoody &

his shoulders.

Aire puts the straw back into Jesse's mouth, knocked out by a fight between rival pigeons. They still scurry at Aire's feet, obsessively scanning the ground for the least little crumbs... Aire jumps up onto the bench shouting nonsense, spinning around - pigeons begin to scurry haphazardly around - they are out of control..... as the best things are - the old lady scoots down the bench away from the madman.

He jumps off the bench, running chaotically to & fro as the pigeons begin to scurry haphazardly around the square - a blistering frenzy of feathers - some flying off - but quickly returning as Aire returns to the bench & his pint of Guinness. As he is chugging down the lucky black nectar, he hears the rushing flutter of hundreds of wings.... he looks around to see what has scared them away - he notices nothing - but, indeed a strange silence descends upon the space - a weird darkness haunts this space - all at once -

The blue haired lady's hair stands up on end.'I ain't gonna work for Maggie's farm no more' ---- (Rage Against the Machine) is the only sound in the distance, coming from an open window....

Suddenly - the square convulses as an invisible wave shoots through every fabric of instantaneous space - everything curves, twists, shifts across massively undulating contours as buildings all around are torn apart disintegrate in the struggle between countervailing forces of explosion & implosion ... the statue dedicated to WWI veterans cripples to its knees falling upon & shattering the head of the blue haired lady near Aire & Jesse....

The ground lurches, shakes as those gathered in the square struggle to their feet amidst the inexorable & continuous eruption of power - each staggers, falling down as the earth quakes with relentless force... the old dead Lady still holds her small white dog in her arms - it is still alive - Aire grasps hold of it & sets it upon Jesse's lap whereupon it climbs into the folds of Jesse's bomber jacket... Time dilates as an invisible train seethes through every visible object -

Aire fights against the shock waves lunging at Jesse's wheel chair - it begins to roll toward a vast chasm that had opened up in the middle of the square & all the way down Brixton Road - the chair does a frenetic jig as Jesse's body lurches from side to side - Aire dives at the careening chair grasping desperately at the wheels - Aire skins his arms & his fingers crack, snapping as he is pulled across the asphalt.

Aire moans, 'Jesse', as he flies out of the chair, smashing to the ground, cracks his head near the chasm... the small white dog sails into the abyss -

It would seem that Poseidon himself is unleashing his onslaught upon the earth as Aire claws his way toward Jesse - his body palpitates with the rhythm of the shaking ground... Aire forces out of his lips, 'Jesse!... Jesse!!!...'

(Amidst the Void)

> Still suspended in the void,
> Jesse could hear the diffused
> voice calling out to him
> but, in this instant, he could
> see light through a crack in
> the upper regions of the abyss.
>
> Other spirits begin to gather
> near Jesse, smelling the flowing
> blood upon the streets
> through the crack.
> Jesse, swept up
> in the surge of spirits
> this carnival of souls
> thirsting for the blood
> surges toward the light
> outside into the Open

As the earth rocks & waxes, Aire finally scratches his way to Jesse, who ecstatically gesticulates upon the ground, as if in a seizure... Aire turns Jesse over - holds him in the nest of his arms, whispering, 'It is alright, Jesse, it is alright.'

> Jesse thrust out his arms & legs
> feeling the gesticulations of his body.

Jesse opens his eyes, gasping & grasping at Aire -

'What the fuck?' Jesse screams.... 'Fuck you! - water, water, water!!!'

Aire held Jesse's head between his clutching fingers, 'You are awake, you coma mutherfucker! You're finally awake, Jesse!'

The Earth itself dances as fires spread amidst the network of chasms that now crevice the entire domain of London - live power lines flail about whipping abandoned & stalled cars with their luminescent sparks -

'What is happening?' Jesse whispers in his surreal fatigue - he feels the quaking ground, 'Where are we?'

'Don't worry, Jesse - it is an earthquake - in Brixton, the whole of London, probably -

'Fucking earthquake,' Jesse struggles to his knees, 'in Brixton?'

'Yeah - we gotta get the fuck outta here,' Aire cautions, as he pulls Jesse to his feet.

Jesse wobbles, his legs atrophied, but he hangs onto Aire's shoulder. They limp down Coldharbour Lane home toward the squat -

'How in the fuck did we get here, ' Jesse rasps in a perplexed voice, 'The last thing I remember - well, I don't - voices, ephemeral faces & hands --- ' He falls silent as he searches within himself for memory -

'What about Nelson's Column,' Jesse shrieks as he recalls the last thing, 'the Column---'

'Jesse, Jesse,' Aire interrupts, 'That was a long time ago ---- I will fill you in once we are safe.'

'The Column - what about the fucking Column?' Jesse shouts, as Aire keeps him from falling into a live wire….

'It came down,' Aire discloses, '& you road it down Kubrick-style - Slim Pickins - it was totally awesome, except for your injuries…' Aire pulls Jesse into the archway of the squat, 'It came down - it is still down - they cannot even ever pick up the pieces of humpty dumpty's cock - they cannot even do that right.'

Jesse slides down the wall sitting in the archway, 'It came down, it came down,' he whispers to himself in his dream, as from eyes gently closed….

12 THE DAY THE WORLD STOOD STILL

('Humming' by Portishead)

Jesse & Aire lay back upon the futon in the glow of the earthquake - not thinking at this moment of the death of the oceans, the quagmire in Iran-Afghanistan, the spectacular collapse of the Eurozone or even the farcical return of mainstream fascism - (not to mention the depressive maelstrom of the global economy & WWIII) - watching the Ravens swarm in their sublime tribute to the setting sun - but eventually these messengers come to nestle in the great Oak tree of Zeus overhead.

Birds - these dark celestial creatures caw, cackle, squawk, each, together in their own sublime language. Better even than our own 'revelations', which are dubious at best - at worst, distractions from the truth of our existence - no more comprehensible than ravens in the evening - even less so - it has been hidden from us for nearly two thousand years....times of change.... after all, epochal economies are not that self-enclosed --- hermetic.... all, each is open

They had slept in the archway through the night - with the first morning light, Aire grasped hold of Jesse & carried him up the staircase toward the squat.

The house, home lies quite broken, shaken, each step is perilous, all the doors a jar - a ten year old straggler named Bill giggles, stoned in the corner, 'The door is a jar - think about that for a while,' he runs out the door & down the stairs, out into the streets... The squat was quite something at the beginning - even more when I was blind drunk - there was no limit that we did not seek to transgress...

It was quiet inside - but picturesquely bright - as they gaze at the All - the stars - the abyss of light - the roof has been shaken off by the earthquake. It came to rest in the trashy back garden... Nothing is that out of order - the squat still stands, stuff in its usual places, it was already quite a tip... except of course the sudden opening to the heavens, not to mention the chasms in the ground... The death of electricity - the snake from the adjacent house is meaningless now, as are all the electrical gadgets, tools, etc... - the water trickles, but is brown -- Majestic London is a different place now - the silence beyond the surging winds & ravens - no one else seems to be there in the surreal darkness - they have perhaps been assassinated....

Aire grasps a bottle of Jameson's, with two short glasses, ice, & his stash from his room - he plunges toward the futon, but lands, face first upon a statue of Guy Fawkes, he rolls over shouting, 'Where in the fuck did this come from?' He spills his stash, twisting to his knees sweeping it up with his hands... he springs to his feet, 'must've come from the attic,' then dives under the statue's arm onto the futon which cracks as Aire spirals upon his back with arms outstretched to the sky --

Jesse lies quietly upon the futon trying to remember his place in the world - indeed, his 'world' - but in the context of a world which had begun to disintegrate. He had awoken, ascended to the eclipse, this absurd rebirth of his nothingness...the many nothings of which we speak, of transition, of failure, of the silence between the notes - Jesse rolls over to Aire - looks deep at him, into his eyes, 'You need to tell me what in the fuck happened, you need to fucking tell me now.... & what the fuck... what the fuck ---- where is everyone? What in the hell is going on???'

'Only the devil would know, 'Aire responds, 'where everyone is - but first things first - sit down here with me & let's drink a toast to your return - & smoke a nice kind spliff - hell, it has been nine months to the day -' he gasps as the world around him falls to pieces, 'a fucking, goddamned strange year!'

'Nine months?! What the fuck? I guess I was born again!!,' Jesse spits in exasperation, '... all these obscure memories - visions ---' 'Wait ---,' Aire interrupts, 'The warning sirens have stopped, the generators must have gone --' He waits, listens to the silence...

'Finally!,' Aire rejoices at the nothing of silence, 'Yes, nearly a year, Jesse - & a lot has happened (just a few things) - but perhaps not as much as yesterday,' he remarks reflectively, 'although there are far worse things than our own tragedies.'

'What in the fuck happened to me - what was I doing?' Jesse falls onto his back, upon the futon, gazing into the sun at its apex amid the noontide festival of life...

Aire sits up to pour the drinks & to roll the spiff - 'as you ascended Nelson's Column the police starting shooting at you with rubber bullets & tear gas canisters - you slipped around to the front of the column - but as you had set up your apparatus - & as the masses upon the ground were protected by their guard - they started shooting live rounds - into the crowd as well --- but there were too many of us as the police were surrounded by the external ring of a massive support protest which proceeded to kettle the layer of riot police -'

'Nice,' smiles Jesse, 'We live & learn - 'Shit,' Aire punches Jesse on the arm, 'You were almost crushed when Nelson's big cock met his little death - it looked as if you released the harness - then you catapulted through the glass window of McDonald's - the building was completely shattered...'

'Well that is something at least,'Jesse breaks out laughing holding up his hand for a hive five, which is immediately & hysterically reciprocated....

'They were not quite sure what was wrong with you,' Aire blows out a huge cloud of sublime sativa, 'one side of your mutt soul going one way or the other another, as they say... - a sorta coma & paralysis, but at least you could eat, suck - & still an awareness of some sort - your eyes would open, but roll around wildly - but at least you would eat --- & shit , & slash - had a special wheel chair made with a built in loo - a tray & everything - simple as an American, as they say....'

'Eat? How did I eat?' Jesse pleads, ironically... (he convulses into laughter)

'Through a straw, my friend - a fucking goddamned straw - & out through your arse-' - Aire chokes from laughter - but flails his arms, &

exhales, 'You been nothing but a retarded baby for almost a year - shitting into a glorified nappy & farting uncontrollably --- & the whole nine yards....

('Oh, Me' by the Meat Puppets)

'A nappie?' - Jesse agitates - in his abject humiliation --- (his laughter is a 'diversion' - one, that however, invokes even more laughter -)

'Well, that is when I could not get you on the bog on time,' Aire laughs, 'Don't worry brother, it is what friends are for - at least true friends - those that stay, stick around, when the times are rough....'

Aire hands Jesse his glass of Jamesons' & ceremoniously makes a toast... 'To your resurrection, my friend - You are back from the dead!' We fill our glasses & empty them of their absurd certainty!'

Aire fills them again & passes another virgin spliff for Jesse to deflower, 'You do the honours, most gracious Sir - it has been awhile.' Jesse puts the spliff between his lips & closes his eyes. He burns a red hot cheery on the end & breathes deeply - this sacred fragrant smoke - he imbibes this snake, opening his eyes as he exhales.

Jesse breathes a sigh of relief, taking another draught from his glass.

Jesse & Aire lay back upon the futon, gazing again at the blue abyss above.... They pass the spliff between them in a sublime silence, feeling the world turn around them in an effervescent simultaneity....

The rain begins to fall, but they do not stir...

*****

Sophie & Ian crash through the door, their arms loaded down with bin bags & a couple of boxes - they were wet from the rain & scurry toward the kitchen... they stop in the front room as they gaze upon Jesse & Aire sleeping upon the futon in the rain - 'Retards, Jesus!,' Sophie shouts, 'It is fucking raining - at least open an umbrella or two -' Unimpressed, Ian carries his cargo, loot, into the kitchen.

Sophia walks toward Aire & lays one of her bags onto his face. 'Feel that Aire - I bet you can't breathe!' After about a minute, Aire begins to struggle & squirm, finally pushing the bag off of his face, though turning over, still asleep....

Sophia pulls the bag to the side, 'It is raining, douchebags - you got to get Jesse into his chair, Aire,' she kicks Aire, who bleeds back into waking life - 'What da - wow, I was dreaming that I floated upon the ocean,' Aire mumbles as he pushes himself to a sitting position - the empty bottle of Jameson's rolls off of his lap & rings as it falls upon the concrete floor...

'Shit - Jesse!', Aire shakes Jesse, remembering that he is now awake, 'Jesse!'

'What the fuck, Aire!,' Sophia hisses, 'You know how he is - hello?!!! - in a coma!!!'

'But - he,' Aire seems to fall into a panic of uncertainty, 'He - ' but is interrupted by Ian who returns from the kitchen with armfuls of bottles - wine, vodka, whiskey - & foods - cheese, European sausages, a roast chicken, ham, cans of Guinness....

'Look what we got muthafuckas,' Ian poetises, 'All the fucking spoils you could ever want!'

'With the lights out, it's less dangerous,' Sophia shouts, laughing hysterically...

'We went fucking looting - everyone is out there, taking whatever they can!', Ian breaks in, 'a million times better than the dole! Thank Poseidon!', Ian convulses, laughing in harmony with Sophia --

Aire pokes at Jesse again, 'Jesse,' he whispers quietly, perplexed that his own memories & experiences are merely the creatures of dream....

'The electricity is out in most of the city, the country even - no one knows for sure,' Ian alerts, 'a lot of buildings are still on fire - & now they are even talking about radiation --- martial law is in force - but, even the soldiers have no fuel & only care about their own friends & families - to be fair, what else really matters?'

'We are all Japanese, Turkish, Russian, etc. now!', Sophia blurts out, interrupting, though Ian disintegrates in laughter, 'It is Ichi the Killer as a natural disaster!!!'

'But, at least we got some treats out of it,' Ian reminds her, laughing...

'Yeah, you have finally mastered all those GTA skills in da real life chaos mode! It was all worth it!,' Sophia laughs even more hysterically.

'Sure was muthafucka!' Ian throws the rest of the loot onto the futon, a sausage hitting & coming to rest upon Jesse's face.

'Well, when you are already so lowdown & feral - ' Sophia laughs, 'major disasters make little difference - they are like a lottery for slaves without hope,' she again descends into hysterical frivolity.

'The meek shall inherit the earth!' Ian sings like a Southern preacher with a Jerry Lee Lewis soul.

'What the fuck is on my face?!!!' Jesse suddenly gesticulates, screaming, throwing the sausage against the wall.... He comes to a sitting position upon the futon...

Sophia & Ian are slammed with a shockwave - She screams, running around in circles with her hands in an Eduard Munch pose, Ian staggers backwards, tripping over pieces of rubble which trip him down on his back....

'What the fuck are you screaming about?', Jesse rampages -

'Jesse!!!! Jessie!!!!!,' Sophia screeches, 'What happened?!!!! You - are -'

'Awake,' Aire interrupts in his excitement - 'Yeah, it was the fucking earthquake - it woke him the fuck up!'

Ian struggles to his feet, looking in awe upon Jesse. He had known him before he was in the coma, but did not take much notice as they moved in different circles.... he only knew that Jesse & Sophia were friends, would hang out....

'Yes, I am awake - don't know what the fuck is going on, but I am fucking awake!'

Sophia, as if by an invisible force, seems pulled toward Jesse & falls toward him with a divine smile of relief, joy & delight.... hesitantly at first, but in an instant - she falls to her knees grasping him around his waist with her tattooed arms...

Sophia puts her hand upon Jesse's shoulder, & gently strokes his cheek,

'Jesse - ', Sophia gulps deep in her heart - 'Jesse -' She gently places her hands upon his face - she bends downward & blesses him - her eyes close as she rubs her cheeks against his face - feeling only an indifferent coldness, she grasps his face - 'Jesse! - do you not remember? ... not remember me?!'

Jesse turns his eyes to her slowly, he grasps her forehead, looking deep into her eyes, 'Sophia - Sophia - it is really you - & not -'

Jesse falls silent , welling deep within his soul, to the heart of his memory -

'Of course it is me.....' Sophia gushes with tears in her eyes....

'But, I saw you -,' Jesse whispers, 'I do not know where - some place... I was looking for you in my extreme destruction.... I could only hear your voice - there was total darkness, strange caresses - '

Aire falls back, resting his head upon a large block of blue cheese.

Ian, by this point, had become noticeably restless - Sophia had been his girlfren for a few years, even before she met Jesse - yet, it must be said in all honesty that everyone knew that Sophia was fucking Jesse, but in light of the circumstances, no one ever mentioned it - no one thought he would ever come back & around....

'I was so lost, Sophia,' Jesse exhales with tears, as he quivers in his flesh...

'But, you are back now, my sweet!....' Sophia cooes like a dove -

'I can finally see, touch, hear, smell - taste - you again,' Jesse whispers...

Suddenly - Ian explodes - 'What da fuck muthafuckas???!!! What is up?!!!!!!!!! Sophia nestles Jesse amidst an intimate embrace, but turns her head to Ian - 'He is awake, finally awake - don't you see?'

Sophia turns her head back to Jesse, her cheek caressing his as the rain drops glisten upon & under their skin...

Ian stands frozen in traumatised silence.... after about five minutes, he screams in exasperation, crashes out the door, returning to the streets....

******

All of them sit in a Karen Carpenter circle - before the second show - upon the futon - with their sad guitars - a single candle between them - this tiny campfire -

Sophia had found some plastic sheets from the builders & built a makeshift shelter for each & all of us -

I was not there at the moment, but I soon made use of this sublime improvisation…

'Outside is like Armageddon - inside as well, muthafukas,' Ian trails off, now utterly forgetful of his jealously - better than GTA - '

'Then, why aren't you out there? ' Sophia torments - 'You are just a coward!'

'I was & am 'out there' - we got what we need - one cannot deny that,' Ian retorts, turning his head toward the candle in the centre….

'There is big difference between a simulation of violence & the real thing,' Sophia quips, basking in her own assertion of will. … but she is beautiful -

('Heroin' by the Velvet Underground)

'Surely enough, but - ' Aire interrupts , 'the key is clear - look around - the world has withdrawn - it falls apart - look around -' as he conjures forth an impromptu rant upon the poetics of electification….

'Electrification - the life force of the homogenous regime of state POWER - amidst a corporate context of significance….

'Electrification - is gaze - glare - it does not have to be this way….

'The fire of Prometheus has been removed from transgression -

Aire stands up, spins around amidst of all the faces of the calendar…'Dionysus is the destroyer of the household - but, it is Poseidon who is our liberator!

'Illustrious, Madam---' Aire screams out, as he crashes face first into the flatscreen, which falls on top his battered body….

Sophia interrupts his ridiculous illumination…. 'Jesus! What in the fuck are you on? We need to fucking work on surviving - the government has gone on holiday!!! Fuck man - isn't this what the fuck you wanted all along?!!!'

'That is what I am saying - what I have always been saying,' Aire lunges back to his feet in exasperation, 'This fatal regime - behind most of the destruction - Hades, Cum Hau, Ah Pukuh, himself is suffocating with all the souls, not only needlessly produced, but senselessly destroyed -- the all-too-superfluous…'

'You were saying what? Come back to earth - just for a moment,' Sophia seethes in her venom, as she sips from her blue absinthe.

'I am of this Earth,' Aire contests, 'I am singing the song of the earth & of life - not of the restricted economy of the fatal regime - you of anyone, with all of your little Shinto shrines, should understand this -'

'But, that is all gone now,' Jesse whispers, feeling the fatigue of his ascension, 'Now, there is only the tiger!' 'Grrrowwwllll', Sophia purrs winking at Jesse…

'There are dead bodies all over the place,' Ian screeches, 'No one even picks them up, except the rats…. the fire of electricity has been extinguished - & all that implies - the system is broken - all returns to the streets -

'But as I have said before, even with the worst holocaust,' Sophia interjects, 'it is the buildings, the architecture - the city plan - that remains in its traces - the Tsunami, the dread earthquake of being merely wipes out the names & kinships - which recede & return…'

'But, there must be some hidden connection - even if in plain, all-too-obvious sight - between the ancient city plan & the street,' Jesse responds, picking up Aire's long lost purple translucent bong in the rubble of the front room - 'For most of its history, London did quite well without electricity…'

Suddenly - ominously - a group of five of the ten year olds stood before us - each having blonde hair & blue eyes, 'Yes, there is a hidden connection - that pertains to what we feral children have all been working on all this time --- You too will see the truth in the sublime moment to come!'

Just as suddenly, the children, with their glowing eyes, return to their toil.... making, incidentally, castes of the Mayan Calendar stone, with cement & wet sand -- they already had the original stone --- they sold each for 20 upon the high street - 2012: Merchandising the Apocalypse - brain storm everyone ---

'Shit - look at these kids --- yet - as if what is & what should never be - 'Wake up! (Aire slaps himself) - the fires of Prometheus torch our city- that is what is outside, what in the fucking hell are you (toward the children who ignore him) going to do about that...' Aire drunkenly shouts, glancing at Jesse through the corner of his eye... it was obvious it was time for his evening run... in the streets like a wild animal...

Sophia, feeling stakes of jealousy in her heart, lunges to her knees upon the futon in Aire's face, 'We all know - we have all seen it hundreds of times - it will only get worse - intensify...'

'That is why this is a time of revolution!' Aire exclaims, laughing hysterically....

'What do you mean by 'revolution'?' Sophia sneers, 'There is only chaos!'

'If you do not have chaos in your heart, you will never give birth to a dancing star!', Aire echoes, laughing.... 'Chaos gives birth to all - well, at least we still have that!!!'

'It is not revolution, not now - these are only the preconditions for revolution - ' Jesse rasps, 'It is indigenous organisation - defence committees - that is what we need now - & this will happen & is happening spontaneously - to protect us from the more uncouth aspects of chaos - the night shelters all....'

'But, we are all on the same level now,' Aire amplifies, 'despite the guns - there is an emergent spontaneous order - '

'I say we all go outside together, into the night,' Sophia dares.... anticipating Aire's own attempts to run off alone with her Jesse...

'I am up for that,' Jesse snaps at the chance, 'Been cooped up for far too long...'

Blue & I fall through our bedroom door, into the common room & just as quickly onto the futon, plunging upon Sophia, Jesse, & Aire.... Dazed, we merge into this space - intrude, penetrate - oblivious seemingly to something entirely important....

'Hello, all - so what's up - anything new?,' I scratch upon my board....

'Fucking A,' Blue notices Jesse gazing into her eyes, 'You are awake!!!"

'God, we slept a long time!', I wrote upon my board.

'Strange weather we been having....' Blue pulls out her tampon, gives it a whif...

'Hey, who in the hell knocked over the fucking flatscreen -- there must be something to fucking eat around here ---'

Something wyrd is going on, though the truth has not yet been revealed to us.

13 THE REVENGE OF HADES

('I Dreamed I Dream' by Sonic Youth)

Sophia gently caresses Jesse's hair & tickles his forehead.... he rests upon her supple thighs - dreams of amorphous space -- of myriad spirits, each seeks the Open.... though, he himself feels hunger, thirst... but ignores these voices of hunger, their teeth marks he still displays....

'You are sublime, dearest Sophia', Jesse whispers, opening his eyes, 'from the flesh torn rings all over your face to your ever effervescent eyes --- your ecstatic body -- you are a catastrophe of loveliness ---'

Jesse laughs as Sophia kisses him so violently that he bleeds from his mouth....

'You were gone so long!', Sophia licks Jesse's whole face… his finger tips…..

Jesse is not quite the 'person' he was a year ago - none of us are, but even as he is awake, a sublime supernatural aura always scintillates around him - he is not quite ever in the 'now' - somewhere else, it seems - listens to voices which no one else hears .... He is a reincarnated Henry Miller, warts & all - & especially the nightmares.....

Aire had already passed out feeling an ecstasy of alienation & liberation - perhaps the best kind of feeling.... he said that later he is going to an 'End of the World' party on the South Bank at Occupy the Tate - there is talk of taking the Palace with the dawn of Christmas Eve..... the end of the world becomes yet another fucking excuse for a party --- thank the "Germans" for British consistency.....

'Yes - I was gone - not gone - I heard you each time you slept, night, day, sometimes all day long & into the night - calling out to me in your dreams,' Jesse replies, 'Yet --- your words were drowned out by the overwhelming throng of -- of --- spirits...... there - I have said it --- that is all it could have been - beyond even a dream ---- (he becomes happily excited) the fucking goddamned underworld motherfucker...

'I know that it is the truth,' Sophia gasps, ' I have also been engulfed by this reality - there are spirits actually living in my Shinto houses --- better than any Doll House -'

('Freedom Time' by Lauryn Hill)

'But - there were too many spirits --- population density - carrying capacity - Cum Hau, Hades himself is angry,' Jesse begins, '& - as far as I felt while I was in his dimension, I think he is seeking his just revenge - too many spirits, too many killed, victims of Empire - victims of profiteering wars, collateral damage - genocide, civilian casualties, poverty, disease, privatised murder --- murder, rape of wives, strippers, & prostitutes...

'I am glad you have said this -, 'Sophia whispers, 'I was beginning to think that there was no justice in the world.... that I am somehow crazy - even fucking insane!!!'

'Yes - good - yeah, from my own bizarre experience, I too feel that Hades is angry...

I can understand that - ' Luce adds from her corner, 'He probably has never gotten over his displacement by Satan ----' (she pauses, laughing) 'These Christians etc do not know how hard Hades works --- indeed - all the souls go to him, after all .... '

'Indeed, where are they before the resur-reaction?' the lead --- though persistently nameless --- ten year old shouts over, not missing a beat from his work…

'Hades himself suffocates under the vast quantity of souls - ' Sophia screeches, 'War, pestilence, genocide -- He contemplates his revenge….. in this way he is Shiva!!! –

'The Death of Electricity!!! - I can already feel the spirits ascending from the cracks in the earth -- they are no longer afraid as the light has gone -- ' Jesse whispers, 'The powers that be will yet soon seek to restore the light --- to chase away the spirits who inflame the chaos in the streets…'

('The revolution will not be televised' by Spearhead)

'The apocalypse will not be digitised ---, ' Sophia laughs, 'If, that is, we can speed things along before it is too late…. '

Jesse begins to shake with foam frothing at his mouth, as if in a trance, 'Restless dead --- troubadouric wanderers - Thames as Styx - Charon sits still smoking on the shore - Hades, Cum Hau suffocates on the plethora of tragic corpses'…..

With this strange poesy, Aire awakens, shouts at Jesse, 'He is a rabid wild dog' – 'A feral animal must be put down' - So say the vicious & ignorant readers of the Daily Wash, Polygraph, & all the other regurgitating rags - well where in the fuck are they now?'

With this last gesticulation, Aire departs for the End of the World Party on the South Bank, perhaps never to be seen again….

'See you later, my main droog,' Jesse smiles as Aire explodes out onto the streets…

*****

('Bathory Aria' by Cradle of Filth)

Blue & I ascend from the abyss of our incipient, depraved room - the bowl of milk for the pussy has become stale & curdled - with the most rancid smell - like sex after incessant days of flesh - or an abattoir …

It was last night that the dreams - nightmares - just stopped - but, who knows what will happen tonight - the earthquake has been good for her --- perhaps, her dreams were merely premonitions of the event...

We swan into the living space & as Blue passes Sophia, she kisses her gently upon her quivering lips....

In this instant, Sophia envisages the dark caresses of Jesse, in her dreams of year.... She rests her head upon his chest, listening to his erratic heartbeat.... Ian came in suddenly, his arms saddle black trash bags of 'Loads of shit!!!', he says, just to tell us of the chaos in the streets... 'Pedestrian Riot!!!, muthafuckas!!!!', Ian spills himself as a vortex in the middle of the sublime futon -

Blue & I continue around the icon, like an amputated human centipede, taking the offerings of Ian as we crawl toward the kitchen with its already vast & practically profane supplies of looted food, alcohol, tobacco ---

('European Son' by the Velvet Underground)

Blue obtains the aspect of a young, fair maiden, as she grasps an old picnic basket from the corner of the hearth.... She shouts out, with an old television in her hand, 'They shall never control us -- they shall never have a say about what we will ever do again, muthafucka....'

She threw it out the window - tv - the 'system' - to the ground....in a surreal, comedic rage of sublime releasement - 'Thank the gods & goddesses.... spirits .... memories - remembrance - ghosts --- ' Blue whispers to herself out of the depths of her primal superstitious nature...

Ian gazes at Sophia, who whispers into Jesse's navel, 'Are you still in there? Can you hear me? '--- Ian leaves the flat in despair, never to return --- 'Nobody fucking loves the man of action anymore!!!', but, as in every pedestrian riot, there is always some reckless asshole with a rocket launcher or bazooka who shoots your face off - Ian, for his part, was killed when a fire extinguisher mashed his head from the roof above...

'We shall have a picnic tonight! We will find a nice spot --- I am sure that they will be there for our picking ---- we can then build a luscious fire,' Blue laughs out loud as she fills the basket with bottles of red wine & an assortment of cheeses, meats & pastries ---- together with six glass milk bottle Molotov cocktails... 'I hope that will be enough,' she whispers with a look of shy concern....

Blue pinches my ear, hands me the basket, & forcibly pulls me across toward the ruinous space of our lovenest - which, strangely, has remained un-effected by the catastrophe.... Hell, we didn't even know that it had happened..... until, I dunno, the next day? the day after that... who knows how many days we were in the dark of our lair.... we had an extremely good time amid a sublime smear - we live our lives as shit in shit.... as we mythically suspect of the lowest animals...

'I got things I lust to do ----- & --- you are a big part of this, my Hugo Ball!!!', Blue announces, as she throws me down upon the stale, leprous mattress....

'I am not insane ----- please - hear me out - the earthquake changes nothing!!! It is only the beginning!!! We must deepen our exploration of sublime ecstasy!!!!'

As I am mute, I play along, even though I conceive that I am free amidst my own distracted fantasy --- All of the maids of my great castle come up to my room - they will not stay away - with a quiver of my eyes - not one of these sweet girls got what I signal with my tenuous face.... 'Everyone grab their feather dusters! The Palace is dirty, very dirty - & it must be cleansed!!!' I feel like Odysseus, returning to Penelope - killing the ignoble suitors before I can feel her caress....

I have begun to believe that we rarely listen to others when they speak --- that is why we write after all -- but even there.... interpretation, perspective, sweet girls, oblivion.... writing remains a dam amidst & against the snake of crazed desire, birthed in the torment of shadows, of the abyss....

'Most of London is destroyed - on fire, like our own fires - but we survive in the darkness... ' Blue puts her eyes ever so close to my own... 'Yet, we know what is going on - indeed - what has always been going on - but now, even worse than ever ... &, they still serve the masters - who have not been affected at all - they enjoy this, I think.... Sadists!',' she shakes her fist, shouting at the labyrinth of brick all around us at each moment...

With my new piece of chalk, I agree with the simple reply, 'Yes!'

'It is all like before ---- but much more extreme - no one cares any more... - but we will care still - as the grand rhythms of the Kosmos will redeem us our alleged evil'...

('The Spirit in the Black' by Slayer)

We dive into the streets ---- all is fire & chaos --- but we feel our destination --- we sense & we carry on across the streets searching for the places, the right place –

There is torture, suffering on the streets of London, restless dead --- wanderers - Thames as Styx - Charon - Hades, Cum Hau chokes on this exhaust of cut, slashed lives... Since we really did not believe in the end of the world, we decide that there is only one place for us to go - the first of many stops that night - to the burned out Underground... a picnic in the place where our love was consecrated with flames -

We run up Streatham Hill (because the best brothels are always in South London - Soho is an utterly unsatisfying Disneyland, despite Blue's utterly girlish devotion) amidst the destruction, desolation - as we skip & frolic, Blue raps in a merry way,

> We plunge to'rd tha' Underground,
> See if they're still rapin' wif knives,
> We'll nefer-not makes any sound,
> We 'rever burns to dust their lives.....

We skip upon our little yellow brick road - to the Wonderful Wizard (the great & utter controller) - whenever we get there - to the Emerald City -

'We're off to see the fucking wizard, the muthafuckan wizard of Oz!' Blue laughs as she skips with me through the blur of streets like a torrent of golden youth --- before we know it - it is all over as we come near to the place of places...

'Don't even worry about that love - I know you ------ ' a shadow speaks cruelly from the smoky darkness of devastation row...

('Unleashing the Bloodthirsty' by Cannibal Corpse)

He stood there - ethereal - but he seems impossibly alive --- more than alive, perhaps - 'I know you - both of you ---- '

Blue & I become white as ghosts in the shock of our cataclysmic surprise -

'Whore bitch cunt --- We are going to kill you for your crimes & your insolence!!!'

The owner of the Underground spectrally hovers upon the streets - carrying on with his craft, even though he is now long dead - his bizarre networks - 'We know you!, 'the Controller whispers, 'We will kill you - fuck you - eat you - it is blood we crave above all things!'

Blue did not hesitate, but grasps a cocktail - lights it - throws it at the Controller - he dances out of the way of its explosive fire - whispering - 'Now it is my turn...' I run at him, dive, but pass right through him - I have no power over him.....

Two muscled freaks hold me down, pushing my face into the sewer....... once again, they rape my ass hard...... a fetish of theirs, it seems....

'Shit - all bets are off - paradigms crack open ---' the Controller gasps in laughter....

He stands over Blue -'I would have had you as my main dancer - my primal whore --- my daughter - but you resist me - & thus - you are not a true woman....'

'I resist you because you are a piece of sadistic, solipsistic shit!!!,' Blue screams with all her might , lashing out with feet, fists -- "Your daughter?!!! Fuck off, you freak!!!'

The Controller punches Blue in the face, knocking her out of consciousness.... he throws her, as with that other stripper, Eurydice, into a pit of poisonous vipers --- hungrily they snap & tear at her flesh - they enter her, ripping her in half...

('Devourer of Souls' by Broken Hope)

Blue is torn to pieces as hundreds of snakes emerge from her pale skin - in their revenge for her transgression of the law of the father..... she is the lightening rod for all of the misogynist collaterals ---

Although she burned them alive, this was merely a superficial aspect, for even dead, they still had being... the cracks in the underworld are getting wider, more spirits escape with each moment... The Controller screams in erotic ecstasy upon his satisfaction ... at the vista of her destruction - 'For woman is death - there is only one way to destroy death - we must destroy woman!!!'

I scratch across the pavement to her dismembered corpse, but receive a kick in the face -- "With this -- even beyond the grave -- , ' the Controller gloats, 'we destroy the bitches - just as they deserve! Go home boy - your girlfriend is dead! The Controller slaps me across my cuckold face -- punches her in the face to boot ---'Get over it, you fucking idiot!' he stands above Hugo, kicks him in the face –

'Did you hear me boy -- I said scat... go live the life of your unconscious!'

In a flash, the Controller & his minions of spirits disappear with the myriad pieces of Blue's supple corpse...

Every day is Samhain from now on.... we either put the lights back on - or travel the road less taken... or finally - kill ourselves, which is always a mysterious choice -

*****

('Mogwai' fear Satan by Mogwai)

I wander through the streets with the restless dead --- wanderers - the Thames is the holy Styx - Charon waits for each of us - Hades, Cum Hau suffocated by the plethora of souls - wishes them away, but needs help from the outsider - from the one who can open the deepest of dungeons --- the spirit of a dead prostitute kisses me as I pass..... she says she likes to be strangled & beaten, but I sputter on in my utter grief... tell her to go to her rest...

Nearing madness, I scamper down the hill screaming, crying in my soul - - 'Blue - Blue', I screech frantically ---- falling face first into the cracked asphalt road... '... but he is my only hope - he is my only hope... Hades is my only hope - ' I scream inside my heart as I scurry like a rat toward the squat.

I smash through the door of the squat, naked hysterical mad - crying out in debased blindness - 'Blue is dead - Blue is dead --- the mutherfuckas - vicious spirits - killed her - tore her to pieces right in front of my eyes ---- '

Sophia & Jesse, in utter shock jump up from the futon each taking hold of my arms ----- for , all they heard from me was something like,

'gaga di bumbalo bumbalo gadjamen
gaga di bling blong
gaga blung'

But, someone must have heard me, for, at that very moment, all of the ten year olds departed into the night…. they must be feral animals of the Dadaist persuasion….

Exasperated, remembering they could not understand - & having lost my board - I liberate my arms from their paternal embrace & run into Aire's room - rustling through his papers - & then his books, throwing them to the floor -

Sophia runs up behind me, 'What the fuck are you doing - Hugo - you have to stop - calm down --- & tell us what happened?' She grabs a pen & a piece of paper & hands them to me, 'Now - Hugo - tell me what happened….'

I gaze into her eyes, but begin to cry in the intense intimacy - I take the pen, laying the paper upon Aire's table - my hand shakes as I scratch into the paper, 'Blue is dead! - they fucking killed her - they killed her!' Sophia falls backwards in shock –

She is caught by Jesse who reads the note, wincing his head to the left - 'Was it the mutherfukas from the strip club?' Sophia shouts, 'I thought they were dead?!!!'

'There are fucking dead!' I tear across the page…

'Fuck me,' Jesse screams, 'We got to take those fuckers out --'

I scratch again at the paper - 'No - they are vicious spirits - but, there is no time to explain - I must bring her back --- I must open the gate & set her free ---- hopefully Hades, Cum Hau will do the rest….' I spin around slowly with a queer look in my eyes ---- pointing to Sophia & Jesse, who already know everything I know, as I spin past --- shouting , 'bimbalo gl&ridi glassala…' amid the intensity of the event, 'Do not worry Hugo, we already know what you have to do….' - I fall to the floor crying, sighing in despair, grunting tears - I turn over & scrawl upon the paper which tore with the dampness -- 'I must invoke Hades, Cum Hau - share in his revenge - the spirits are arising through the cracks - we must set Blue free!'

'But, will she not only be a spirit, Hugo!' Sophia scratches out of her throat - 'She will not have any flesh --- '

'This cannot be the case - our distinctions are nonsense!' I scratch desperately - I turn the paper over, inscribing, 'They took her - she disappeared - all is not as it seems - shit, I was ass-raped by two spirits just three quarters of an hour ago -- what kind of metaphysics is that?!!! --- 'A bit ambiguous,' Jesse whispers pensively…

'The spirits suffocate,' Jesse intones dreamily, still seemingly half in the surreal world deep on the inside of the labyrinth of surfaces - Cum Hau struggles - the devastation is not enough - the vault still lies secure --- these spirits here are only the ones who slipped through or who have been turned away by Charon - the main gate is closed -

'But, the vault is not impenetrable - there is a crack in everything,' Sophia ecstatically invokes, 'Aire himself almost mistakenly opened the gate to the vault at another time - before he ran away --- Hades needs someone on the outside to open the gate ---- '…. 'Yes - yes, you are right,' Jesse remembers, 'Aire - who did not know what the fuck he was doing at the time at all - ran away just in time, when he realised he would die --- remember that old story he told us about his last mescaline trip, & how he retrieved a lost fragment of his soul?'

'It is all in a little green book about hallucinogenic cacti ---', I write, 'All about fucking San Pedro cactus - St. Peter - the fucking gatekeeper ----' Aire was writing the fateful words, his fucking insane poetry as he closed the vortex ----

Immediately, Sophia joins me in the search for the book, wrecking havoc in Aire's room - himself pleasantly dancing to hundreds of tribal drummers on the South Bank of the Thames - thousands of Chalkboarders (a strange challenge which had developed in the same manner as myself) are expected to perform a percussion piece with chalk - 'Chalk Dog Apocalypse' - the festive air of the end of the world party ---- they had completely trashed Aire's room but had not found the little green book -

('God Save the Queen' by the Sex Pistols)

Jesse begins to hum 'God Save the Queen' (Sex Pistols version) & spins around with a whimsical smile upon his face --- 'What the fuck are you doing, you clowns?' Sophia enjoins, in an even stranger, madder tone, 'Do you not see us here frantically searching - it is not like there is no time limit --- the government is already trying to restore the light & close up the cracks to the other world --- We cannot forget that the capitol of Oceania still has its central power --- '

'This is truly dreary, my sweet blossom,' Jesse laughs, 'but it is also clear that most of the time things are hidden in plain sight ----' his eyes focus down upon Aire's desk, drawing the eyes of the others to the most obvious place --- the little green book was the mouse pad on the desk ---- I lunge toward the book, but Sophia knocks me onto Aire's bed, 'It is surely better if I read ---' she hissed, 'don't you think???'

[Censored Content]

'It sounds positively terrifying ---- but at least we know what to do - &, with the advice from Luce in the corner, that it will probably work ----' Sophia laughs, 'how strange is the world that we do not even see before our eyes - but still do see!!!'

'It must be you who opens the gate, Hugo -' Jesse intones, 'You have the strongest feeling - it is your love after all who has been taken ---- You know what to do to escape the trap that almost consumed Aire ---'

('Crossroad' by Robert Johnson)

'Are we not forgetting something -- more appropriately - someone ---- Hades, mind you? It is surely his justice that matters most?, ' Sophia dances around this space cosmically, waves her hands strangely through the smoke in the air --- 'But, what does he really want? It is surely not merely to alleviate over-congestion --- there will always be more ---- a good doctor never merely treats symptoms only ---

'Yes - you are right! Hades will bring about the end of the world - he will usher in a new world - & in that task, he must strike at the root!,' Jesse burns, with the fire of his earlier days of love & rage.....

'It must be the architecture - the very matrix of primal repetition!!!,' Sophia screams as she hysterically jumps laughing up & down upon Aire's bed - until it collapses, just as she jumps off... over this cliff -

Perhaps, it is better simply not to care - to await the catastrophe, passively, fatally, as do all those lonely people without hope, & who each feels the anguish of defeat...

'Hugo will open the chasm to release the spirits - , ' Jesse, reading from the Green Book, invokes as a necromancer, 'The vortex of spirits will arise with the consent of Hades' - (Jesse staggers with his vision, feeling the surge of pain deep within his skull as he has a primal memory of his triumph at Nelson's Column) --- ' .... to destroy the Palace, Westminster, & the Tower, the diabolical seats of murder, starvation, slavery, genocide --- to destroy anything that cannot stand the onslaught!'

Sophia spins around amid a great circle with Jesse, nearly chanting, 'Oh ye Vengeful spirits, come forth, disintegrate the suffocating prisons of history & architecture - of time itself!!! Come forth! Destroy the arche of terror - Come forth! Come forth!'

'During this rampage of the spirits, he will retrieve Blue from the pit ---', Jesse mystically sputters as if he were the Pythoness of Brixton - breathing his sulphur fumes --- 'Hugo will be Sisyphus - conjuring the spirits - returning to the l& of the dead amid a vast exorcism of the dementia of light - '

'But he must sing, as he will also be Orpheus,' Sophia swoons, 'as with his love Eurydice - & I don't mean that stripper ho - he must sing a magical incantation, a song - & ask Hades, Cum Hau, for the gift of life....'

('Pac Chen' [mayan music] by Alfredo Roel)

They take the cactus (Trichocereus Pachanoi) into their Mayan kitchen --- as time is of the essence they chop the full ten inches into tiny bits - (it should be noted that the shamans always recommended 3-5 inches, but Aire had counselled 10 inches for Europeans) & boil over a fire on the kitchen floor - two hours did it - a green gruel - almost electric in its contagiousness --- after it sufficiently cools, I drink the sublime liquid, this philosopher's stone, with a little ceramic tea cup, as quickly as I can without vomiting - immediately feeling the nauseating dread of death --- that is just 'natural' resistance - but it would not come full on right away - though I have already walked through the door.... & strange is the key unspoken word in every sentence -

The mad max lorry ride toward the river is strange to say the least - everyone seems like aliens from paranoid land - with their putrid, sexual smells, burning my nose & eyes... but the worst was at the end of the ride - when there was only one guy - besides us - who shouts to himself in the most vile tones ---- 'The hungry spirits are already ascending - broken out into the Open - confusing, dissolving the world', he skreeks 'I am gonna kill you fuckers..... no one gets out of here alive...' ----

Jesse sits smiling at him, realising that he is merely a sign of that which was to come ... Sophia races toward the driver & begs him for help --- 'Not my problem dear, sweet honey! That is why I am in an armoured cabin....'

I merely think the threatening man asleep, & he shouts out one last, 'I am going to kill you fuckers!,' & just as quickly lies down in the aisle.

Even as I hallucinate more & more intensely, I remain calm as Sophia (with the oracular Jesse tagging along, as the Pythoness should get much, much more respect) guides me over the sleeping man, out of the lorry to the foot of the Tower of London - the seat of all evil in this world & its lock on this earth...

('Kollaps' by Einstürzende Neubauten)

This is the monument - after all - that was erected upon the very mouth of hell....

'Like I fucking said,' Sophia shouts into the night sky, 'Fucking Architecture!!!'

'Another big phallic symbol, oh joy,' Jesse screams, 'I have been fucking traumatised - beyond belief - by the image of the 'male'!!! Imagination of the 'male' - the sublime artistry - construction of the 'male' - Maybe I should wear a dress!!!- OMG - I already am --- I reserve the right to wear costumes!!!'

Distracted as I am by the event itself which is imminent, I will confirm that Jesse, who has also tasted from the tea cup of St. Peter, thinks he is wearing a very old, white, charity shop wedding dress - but is merely the same as he ever was --- even less so as he strips naked, running to a nearby fountain... these black anarchist garbs he wore - even when he was in a coma - for nine months --- Jesse, who is not a consumer per se, still managed to prevent utterly horrible scabs & such by uniquely developing a hygiene plan that involves a sort of Tai Chi with baby-wipes ---- he wears patchouli & regularly sprays himself with Febreeze - way better than Linx -

'Yes - my darling - your unbelief & rage,' Sophia shouts after him as he dances naked, joyous in the water, 'but, you must understand that it is Hugo - the mute - who must sing the song.....' Sophia retrieves a spare summer dress from her bag & hands it to Jesse, 'You will look nice in this...' 'No!!! I like the one I have on - for I am a bride of Hades!!!', he laughs hysterically as he gazes into the infinity of faces upon the proud wooden statue of

Charlie Chaplin, created by Nancy, a travelling sculptor & perhaps magical being with a chain saw -- she is on her way to the End of the World Party, with her brood, daughter Abbie, grandson Luke & son, Dilwyn....

'Oh, please --- wake the fuck up, you freak!,' Sophia mock scoffs, 'There is no wedding dress! Put on what I have given you!', she pees her knickers with hysterical laughter.... He ascends into the white summer dress & curtseys to the Moon.... 'Now, we are ready to do something less mundane -' she pauses for a moment to laugh, schizophrenically - if only for a change of pace.... life is boring, after all....

*****

('Sympathy for the Devil' by the Rolling Stones)

Sophia guides me to the proper place - the sky is a raging red sea, winds whip me from all sides - each face scintillates with myriad pulsating faces, another in this instant again, again mystically shattering..... a dark vortex of eternal glimpses...

Jesse rides up in his wheelchair, having got used to it, 'Vrooom, Vrooom..,', having become a child amidst the transfiguration of found objects....

'Do you hear my cries, Hugo - ' Blue whispers from unspoken dimensions....

I fall to my knees upon the Mayan stone & beg Hades, Cum Hau, for my love - Blue - I propose the deal, intimating the inexorable bind that welds us together in this moment --- I no longer beg as I feel the winds of his caress -- It is a negotiation - it is this inexorable will that respires -- dies.... Only death is eternal, life is always only a reprieve - Hades does not need to say anything at all - though he sent a searing fire through my entire body just at the moment I whisper, 'Give me back my love!'

'OPEN THE DOOR!', as the words of the Fire seem clear to me... at least what is to be done... Hades, Cum Hau has little friends - perhaps, not many - though, I am here for him.... a snake emerges out of the asphalt - slithers into my hands ---

As far as I am concerned, the deal is done - I will be the outsider - but, as a stranger once again permits to embrace, caress his love....
Earth gives this blood to these hungry spirits - at the right time.

('Shake the Shame Out' by the Feral Children)

It is at this instant that the feral children descend from all sides upon the space - it is Luce who speaks alone to these others - 'To your locations!' at which point this horde of violent uncomprehending animals scurry off to their pre-designated haunts... Luce turns to us, 'We must hurry,' she points to me, 'He seems almost ready to pop! Hugo must sing the mantra!'

'Why are you here?' I manage to rub in spit - upon the stone underfoot....

'We are here to protect you - for, in the moment - when you open the door, you - each, all of us will be exposed to the most awesome power, beyond imagination - '

'How will you protect me - us?', I rub...

'Let us just say we know the ancient plan, we know the streets at their deepest levels,' Luce whispers evasively....

'The ancient plan,' Sophia queries, 'You mean the city plan, at the root of everything - of all architecture? O fuck me, girl!'

'Yes, you understand, Sophia,' Luce whispers, but, at the moment she made a signal with her left hand, she incites the children to map out with their bodies the primal key, in the design of the ancient plan... 'If we look at things in historical terms, the ancient plan in London is quite recent,' Luce speaks more forcefully. 'But - it is far older, & is inextricably linked to this strange instant, this peculiar ending...'

'What are you on girlfriend,' Jesse shouts, skids right up to Luce, 'What is everyone doing..... what is everyone on???'

I begin to feel I am disappearing, a profound syncope...... Luce notices, & whispers to the rest..... whoever comes, comes to help - friends....

I am descending into a maelstrom, the red sky rages, the infinite faces laugh, jabber -

'What do you mean, ancient plan in London?' Sophia dumbfounds as Jesse break dances on his wheelchair...

In the darkness of the vortex, the descent, my only friend is a Virginia opium addict named Poe, who counsels me that the best way not to fall is never to try to ascend... he flies upon the back of a raven, which laughs in my face...

'It is the vast background -- the central hub of power in most recent novae city of London ---- shit, none of you fuckers know anything at all --- you have all been wiped!!!' Luce scoffs away lighting a cigarette, gazing at the Moon...

After considerable silence, apart from Jesse's persistent childhood revolutions, not to mention, my own convulsions upon the utter ground, Sophia approaches Luce with a white rose, & jibbers gently, 'I am terribly sorry --- will you not tell me the truth of the event - what is going on - beyond the fact I do not know anything at all - beyond the fact that we are here now - I feel we are supposed to do, think something...'

'Fine - for fucks sake - will fuck you fuckers for the fuck is fucking going the fuck on -' Luce sends her last encrypted text, as she smiles, 'Everything will be fine!'

She walks over to me --- whispers, 'You will find your voice, Hugo & your love' which seems to ease my rampant convulsions --- for me, of course, I still surf the maelstrom - but enjoy it as all - each - this....

'Shit, girl, can you just spill the beans - serious shit is going down -' Sophia pleads, 'Please, tell me about the architecture - the lock & the key ---

'Of course, of course,' the 'ten year old' Luce faces the music, the Dionysian question, 'I will not tell you that much ... for everyone loves suspense - unless they are already lobotomised - & then the big release, right in your precious face...'

'Well - speaking of the Invasion™ & the Genocide™ - at least as it is understood by these indigenous peoples of the so-called 'Americas'™ .... globalised ultra-World™ -' Jesse jabbers hallucinating upon his axis...

Luce lights a cigarette, thinks in the dark - she sinks down against an old mossy rock... gazes at the utterly milky stars - just like in Death Valley where the goddess Nut nourishes the sublime creatures, plants of the desert...

'It is that,' she drips, 'It was a different time - shit - a very long time ago, a primordial past that cannot be imagined - the only thread that breathes life across this situation -

'The ancient plan of London - it is the fucking Mayan calendar stone --- but it is not just any amulet, but a key for a specific lock - & that lock is right here---- we need to ---' she hesitates, 'to map the Mayan Calendar onto this space right here .....'

'London's ancient plan is Mayan?' Sophia gasps in utter disbelief....

'This topography of existence right here - this part of the city - is built upon the sublime plan of the Mayans - the plan was first stolen by the Spanish, but was taken by the British with the defeat of the Armada - and was immediately sent to the Crown who ordered these great architectural projects that were to be configured according to the plan - and this continued to take place to this very day!'

'Is that all you got, girlfren?' Sophia screams in her face, 'Not interested in anything that fucking crazy....'

I hover in the storm - people, things of various sorts go up & down --- alpaca lips -

Luce steps up with the pressure of the other ten year olds - &, the apocalypse of all things that dances here inappropriately --- she stands firm amidst this eclipse... 'OK - whatever - you do not have to believe me - you will see for yourself that London is not what it seems to be - shit, it was one third the size of the Aztec Mexico City just before the extermination, but afterwards, you had plumbing.... go figure!'

'But, for whatever reason why?' Sophia spits in frustration, I thought we were just getting Blue back, and helping out Hades to boot....

'Exactly,' Luce expounds with relief, 'the power centre of London is built from the stolen plans of the Mayans - to keep hell locked up regardless of the number of killed --- despite the wishes of Cum Hau, Hades... to keep this world in power - to keep Hades busy so he will not take the souls of the 1%.'

With this explanation, she turns toward me, chanting

'The children come to open the door -
they are the key, & it is a lover who
will turn this flesh - light with his song...

this key to these utterly feral children ----'

Luce quakes, falling to her knees --- she rasps with her last breaths, 'Don't you see? We are at the moment of decision -- to maintain the old order which plunges to destruction - or to begin something novel --- the calendar is finished, the Winter Solstice of this night marks the end of the last - the 13th - 144,000-day cycle ending the 5,200 year dispensation since the creation of the world.... Won't you see - it is now or never!

the vague presence of absence - remembrance - a subtle tactic so obvious --- the lords of the night seek their return...

******

Everything is for sale, sail - for the right price - though that is meaningless now -

Voices emerge ---- it is the master of the voices who will sing the utter lullabye ---

but that is bullshit - this is Circe at the last moment ----

they have tried to keep us apart all along --- to destroy our fated love ....

It = all each - is this moment - not this false idol --- mere simulacrum of intimacy ---

******

If iz not coIHNDdhOIHDhdoiH

cleak as thew sweet face, bodies ,,,,

Again & again - utter amateurs with too much to prove ....
it lashes at my throat - a vicious truth......

we are all condemned to die ----- but what does it matter now?

*****

Everything becomes a bit wyrd at this point - I have fallen into an utter singularity - all those around are dispersed into a dissemantic field as nothing is real - I myself am being sucked into an endless subliminal vortex -- nothing nihilates as each moment is swallowed into the mouth of Cum Hau, Hades, but as with his father, he seeks to vomit up the excessive consumption in a bulemic orgy...

There is nothing but the rapturous fall, the plunge into the darkness of nothingness -

I spin spin fall dissolve twirl into the depths - I claw at the least threads to remember that which is most ... most ... fateful - in this instant, her face appears, this abyss of her eyes - it is her, it has always been her, as this outflashing of this ever recurring vortex of the All... ecstatic simultaneity -

I shake into a bare cognizance, lunge, slap my face over & over until I come back a tad into the world --- my face glows as motes of blinding ecstasy explode - I crawl to the place, breathe deeply - I am faced with the impossible abyss of my own lost voice - I am on my knees, I screech - bark, grunt --- meow - oink, & all the other sounds -

'You must sing Hugo!' Sophia shouts ------

I claw at my face, on my knees, as I desperately begin to sing ... for her

*****

Hugo's Song

(emerges out of his own inner terror, tears of frustration, despair.... hope)

laaaaa   laaaaa   laaaaa la la laa laaaaaa   la la laa laaaaaa   (slow, in Minor)

e   c   b   a b c   e   f e d e

laaaaa   laaaaa   laaaaa la la laa laaaaaa   la la laa laaaaaa   (slow, in Minor)

e   c   b   a b c   e   f e d e

    This vortex pulls me down, I am almost nothing, just mere lint -
    but your little lovely face - You are my destiny, commitment, love -

    You are the only one who can save me amidst this disintegration -
    You are my most primordial memory - You are the last thread -

    You are my sublime spark on the dark side of moon
    You are my prairie fire in the deepest abyss

With this second refrain, Zeus, having awakened from his carnal intimacy with the goddess Sleep, sends a cataclysmic thunder bolt as lightening shoots out from the brooding clouds overhead - striking through to the toxic asphalt below the Tower – Earth groans under, shifts her weight, sends out gyrating tremors across the space....

Encouraged & joyous at the re-birth of my voice - at least to the extent that I could direct the melody of my life - sing louder & - let myself go - frenetically ---- dance diabolically dirging in an eternal circle.....

I begin suddenly to speak all sorts of joyous nonsense - for this is the only realm that really matters at the end of the day -

Open up every door - let the spirits arise as a tornado - the old world becomes a funeral pyre.... la la la la llalallalallalallallalallallalll   lllaaa   lal lalaalll   llallall   laalla lalallalalala   e   e   e   c   bcdga ffgggeggaggccggag ggeee ee   cccbbba   baggff   ebaccbbeeggcbae   for old times sake -

'Blue --- (I terrorisingly remembers after a 45 second lapse) - I must save Blue ---'

Amid the event - all remove themselves respectfully, they are kept by the ten year olds away from me, to a safe distance .....

The vagina of the Earth begins to open beneath my dancing feet - the dance - the rise of the spirits who raise even the Thames into their vortex amidst the annihilation of architecture ----

The swallowing of the machinery, these systems of death by Cum Hau (Hades), who melt their billions of stones --- steel & bricks with a breath ---

In revenge against their sending him countless souls of murder, genocide - poverty & disease --- all unnecessary - is it not bad enough we die, but to die needlessly - robbed of the chance to live & to be - malicious, selfish, thoughtless - scum scum, even if you wear the mask of anarchy -

unnecessary suffering - unnecessary deaths - but we are not merely passive as He is our champion - we stream together in our justice - we are the lion - that is good enough for now as we seek to destroy the last vestiges of despair (canned laughter)

They do not even know the cruel lot that Ah Pukuh drew - but at least he is still there - where did the others go? - Did they die, flee --- or did they just change their names & adapt to the 'New New New New New etc... World Order'?

('Pink Stream' by Sonic Youth)

I spin into the vortex with the image of Blue in my soul -- an image - her eternal face - not to protect the mere living, in this instance, but to retrieve a lost one - one who was taken at the wrong time....

Despite my utter terror - it is the face of Blue - in my mind's eye that seduces me to death - to the surreal topography of death -

I lie upon the surface of a sublime world of ecstatic dementia - 'I' stand up - 'I' am self standing - but only for an instant - 'I' wish to descend, to fall --- 'I' am falling. 'I' fall -'I' -

I am the face in the middle with my tongue sticking out - upon it is placed the scroll, the word --- the nectar of the gods --- the circles revolve, the stone comes alive - the bat, dog, owl, turtle ... green storm white storm red storm black storm enclosed by the yellow sun - we succumb to our unlucky days...

The vortex sucks all into it - there is no me as I sink, swirl into nothingness ... I may think - but never imagine.... I am imagination in its transcendence -

I am fractured, with no arbiter.... primal desire surges for her face....
There is a little me - as I finally fall into this most significant abyss -

'Utter suffocating crowds of souls - ,' Cum Hau (Hades) whispers, 'Famine concentration camps - utter murder ---------------- too many, too many souls you throw at me......'

I walk through crowds of faces from my entire life - my mother father sisters others - It is the others who have been the most interesting - & the most devastating -
I turn to one old friend, long dead, still saying the same 'Mere bullshit! Everything is cliché! Everyone knows that....'

I run away from him, jump through another random door ---

'This entire situation could never be more insane,' I whisper to the Moon..... who is incoherent & whose face appears to be covered in shaving cream....

What do you mean by 'entire' - please define that.

- extending our investigation to other matters arising, this philistine stipulation

What do you mean by 'others' - please define that.
What is 'interesting' - please define that.
What is 'devastating' - please define that.

All apologies - you have mistakenly been sent to the Quality Assurance Unit of Hell - though they are comfortable in either sector....

*****

('Helter Skelter' by the Beatles)

I scream out into the Open - 'Blue - my lascivious lover - please come to me.....' I slide through the slippery, wet sector of Hades' realm -

A cabal of treacherous, disturbed voices comment upon our intimacies..... I thought I lay upon a bed - a safe place - or, was it a slab in some nihilistic morgue - subconscious shaman rock spark fire light... but, it is - beyond this nothing but these usual surreal places & situations - '

I desperately descend through the crowd to find her - I lust after her being- yet, lust disagrees with the constant 'I' - is offended - 'It' is not the 'I'.... she says.... it is betwixt - - between heaven, hell, light - darkness - ambiguity is our utter sublime destiny -

After or in between these absurdities, I catch glimpses of Blue - she flashes but is covered over in an instant by the plethora of the spirits who were her own victims, prostitutes, strippers & gangsters.... It is Hell, after all....

I felt that I myself may disappear as the terror of dissolution beckons - I descend into cataclysmic maelstroms of nothingness - all I remember - this last trace of my merely meek insurrection, this abyss of her eyes - Blue's dark eyes ---

'Cum Hua, Hades, please give her back to me,' I scream as the image, simulacrum of Blue in my heart becomes ever stronger as I spin, spin - turning ever faster as if in a delirium of faster & faster - I begin to feel the supple presence, caress of another, of Blue in my arms as I hold her tight, lest I fall off of the earth -

Faster, faster we turn together descending deeper as a tremendous, grumbling ass howls well beneath --- 'I stold an opium coated suppository from my grams ass,' one spirit tells his tale... says his name is William - another ten year old ...

I hold her tighter, tighter as we free fall into the vertigo---- lest I fall from the earth - into the abyss of night - this - cosmic ecstasies, over, again - recurrence -

We swirl, slide, slip this openness - seeking this slither through snake skin intestines, at last belched, vomited out of hell --- surrounded by liberated spirits, vast murders of ravens intimate the heart of winter..... this utter eruption of spirits which balloon, envelop the monuments of power - the key is activated as the vast calendar plan is revealed in hot red light across the entire area - the spirits grasp hold as a cyclonic spider web and pull it all down into Hell - the implosion of the power matrix of London, the disappearance of architecture to Sophia's wonderment ---

All is quiet for a moment - but a great rumbling roars, a vast quaking of the earth - as the excessive hordes of spirits are reborn into the world as spirits of the earth, of trees, rivers, lakes, and all the rest - nature being deprived of sanctity for too long....

At this moment, Bill Hicks appears, fulfilling the Mayan prophecy, with his vital breath, words...

'I've had a vision. & what it is, is although this is a world where good men are murdered in their prime, & mediocre hacks thrive & proliferate, I gotta share this with ya, 'cause I love you & you feel that. You know all the money we spend on nuclear weapons & defense every year? Trillions of dollars? Correct? Trillions. Instead, if we spent that money feeding & clothing the poor of the world, which it would pay for many times over, not one human being excluded, not one, we could, as one race, explore outer space together in peace forever. You've been great. Thank you.'

(three gunshots)

he three vast holes were quickly filled with water, later becoming known as the Cloverleaf Lakes of London, free for the use of the people.

*****

('Porpoise Song' by the Monkees)

Blue grasps my ectoplasm drenched hand, whispers.... 'Lover.... are you there?'

I immerse myself in the abyss of her eyes, her flesh...
'Yes, I am... I have my voice..."I love you!"'

'You are here - ' I explode with joy, utter relief

'I have something to tell you, Hugo...'

'I --' she is possessed again, but in this moment, whispers, as she strokes my hair with her fingers, 'You stayed with me all this time - all the way to the end, dear one --- but I never really saw you until this very moment - before it was different, I was lost - I was incapable of love... only of revenge - I should not have made you kill with me.'

'But, that was a gift for you,' I whisper, 'A gift of your life back...

'Yet - You have given me more than that, Hugo! You have conjured me back from nothingness, have given me a second chance - in Hades I was frozen in a single image of undetectable repetition -'

'You have released me, brought me out into the Open... You have given birth to me.'

Blue kisses me upon my hungry lips, 'I love you.... I fucking love you, muthafuka!....'

'I was only the midwife, the earth is still your mother,' I whisper, as I hold her frail body in my tired arms.

ABOUT THE AUTHOR

James Luchte is a writer and poet, living in the United Kingdom with his family and friends.

Made in the USA
Charleston, SC
01 October 2012